Combatting Fear

Sandy Vaile

Adams Media

New York   London   Toronto   Sydney   New Delhi

CRIMSON

Crimson Romance
An Imprint of Simon & Schuster, Inc.
1230 Avenue of the Americas
New York, NY 10020

ISBN 978-1-5072-0344-6
ISBN 978-1-5072-0345-3 (ebook)

This story is for Paul, who encouraged me to reach for the stars. Thank you for regaling me with entertaining bedtime stories and leading by example.

Chapter 1

A post office box under an alias wasn't much to go on, but no matter how slim the chance of finding his son, Micah had to take it.

The Roman numerals on his Cartier watch read: 9:12 a.m. Crap, he'd wasted time sleeping. Using the front seat for leverage, he pulled himself into a sitting position, and the few clothes he'd had in his overnight bag slid off him—they'd been an inadequate substitute for a blanket. He rubbed a crick in his neck. Regardless of how comfortable the back seat of a Bentley was, a six-foot man did *not* fit horizontally. It wasn't the first time he'd slept in a car though.

Dodging all the wildlife between his new wind farm site in New South Wales to this backwater town in South Australia, had made the journey tenser than playing a game of Frogger. He'd arrived at midnight, exhausted, and the place had been shut up tighter than a preserving jar.

In the morning light, Turners Gully was a charming rural township. There wasn't a lot to it—the obligatory hotel and church aside—but there didn't need to be, so long as ... There it was: a kindergarten sign. The squat stone building was set a long way back from the road, as though surreptitiously nestling against the steep hillside would save it from detection.

A deep creek ran along one side, shaded by vast willow trees, and period cottages flanked the other sides. He pulled into the car park, shoved the car door open, and heaved himself onto the footpath to stretch cramped muscles. A quick pat down of his crumpled clothes wasn't much improvement, but finding a place to freshen up would have to wait. Past experience told him he needed to get onto the trail of his estranged wife right away.

There were a couple of other cars parked out front, and squeals from children playing in the yard. Rowan might be there today. He could see him. Hold him.

As he strode towards the rustic front door, the insidious question that had been burning its way up his esophagus for the past year pricked Micah's psyche. How long did it take a young child to forget an absent father? If he didn't find Rowan soon, it might be too late.

Time and time again during the past year, he'd dropped everything to track his wife, Chelsea, across Australia. It was an unsustainable disruption to his business, and more than enough time with his son had been stolen. It was time to change this game of cat and mouse so the cat got the cream.

. . .

Rowan crouched in the kindergarten sandpit. Neve watched his pink lips vibrate with engine sounds as he pushed a yellow truck over miniature sand hills. Shaggy brown hair fell across his eyes, and she ached to push it back. Her throat closed and her chest heaved with a familiar emptiness.

"Neve! Neve!" Rowan raced towards her, toy truck held high and face distorted with distress. "The tipper won't work. It's busted and *I* didn't do it. It's 'posed to tip."

He was fast dissolving into tears, as he often did when something didn't go his way, and turned moist eyes, the colour of burnt sugar, towards her.

She squatted to get on his level. "Okay, slow down, Ro. Let me take a look. I know how to fix engines, but I don't think that's the problem here."

"Is it busted?"

His bottom lip quivered and her heart wrenched. He leant in for a better view of the repairs, his small, warm body soft against her arm, smelling of Vegemite and the eucalyptus leaves he'd played in earlier. He trusted her to solve his problems, at least while he was in her care. When he went home ... well, that was another story.

A raised voice inside the kindy caught her attention, but she couldn't see what was going on from the yard. Annemarie would handle it. She turned back to the truck and held up a piece of wood for Rowan to inspect.

"Look, there was a twig stuck under the tray," she said. "Now you can tip it up and down."

"Yay! Thanks, Neve." He raced back to the sandpit, engine sounds once again spluttering from upturned lips.

The voice inside got louder. "I demand to see my son right now!"

Adrenaline sprinted through Neve's veins. The children and staff were her responsibility. She dashed across the yard, burst through the back door, and assessed the man looming over her second-in-charge, Annemarie. His hair stood up in erratic spikes, there was a dusting of stubble on his face, and his shirt was crumpled as though he'd just rolled out of bed in it. Fury hung in a cloud around him, vaporising from the angry heat of his skin.

"Annemarie, would you mind taking the children outside to play while I speak to Mr. ...?"

His head snapped in her direction, and her breath caught. Haunted hazel eyes glared at her—eyes so similar to the small ones she'd just been looking into.

She smiled tightly and proffered a hand to shake. Even in the grip of hostility, people usually felt compelled to abide by social graces. Treat them with respect and show sympathy, and even the most aggressive person usually calmed.

"I'm Miss Botticelli, the kindergarten director."

He ignored her hand and turned to watch Annemarie hustle a few children out the back door. Neve ran through the key points of her managing aggressive behaviour training: listen, empathise and problem solve. First she needed to figure out if he was a physical threat. She felt for the phone in her pocket, in case she needed to dial help.

Up close, she could see his dishevelled appearance was only on the surface. He was clean, his Italian loafers were new, the crumpled shirt looked to be silk, and there was a tiny LV embroidered on the pocket of his slacks.

Christ, this guy's wearing Louis Vuitton. Great, a Richie Rich who thinks he can throw his weight around. She clenched her teeth.

His keen eyes were on the children outside, and then his posture relaxed. He scrubbed a large hand back and forth across his face and blew out an exasperated breath. She waited until his gaze returned to her, and this time it looked fatigued.

"Sorry, I didn't mean to frighten the children," he said.

"They're not the only ones. My staff doesn't appreciate being yelled at." She raised herself to full height. It may be difficult to make five foot two look menacing, but if he thought he was going to get the better of her, he was sadly mistaken. She'd spent years cultivating the never say die attitude she admired in her father, and wasn't afraid of height or strength. No one would harm the children in her care.

Chapter 2

Micah saw stubborn determination in the olive-skinned beauty standing before him. She had straightened her spine in a show of dominance, but her clenched fists gave her away. The last thing he wanted to do was frighten women and children. He just wanted to find his son.

Through the wall of glass at the back of the room, he could see the kindergarten staff organising games for the children. Which one was his? Reflexively, he stepped towards them. The pint-sized woman moved with him. Despite the fact he could rest his chin on top of her head, her attitude was gargantuan. She may well hold all the power in this situation, but that didn't mean he was leaving without Rowan.

"Who are you?" she demanded.

"Mr. Kincaid." This time he offered his hand, and she tentatively wrapped her long, thin fingers around it. Her handshake was surprisingly firm, and the soft heat from it sent a strange thrill up his arm.

"What is it you want, Mr. Kincaid?"

"I'm here to see my son, Rowan." He took another step towards the back door, and she moved again, blocking his path.

"I can't permit you to access any of the children without written consent from a parent, and if you continue to disregard my directions, I'll have to ask you to leave."

She was so close he could smell vanilla cupcakes and crayon. Her dark hair was pulled into a no-nonsense braid, with a soft fringe over watchful eyes. He took a deep breath and braced himself for the conversation he'd had many times before.

"I don't have written permission because I'm his father. His mother took him from me, and I have it on good authority that he's in Turners Gully. I'm not leaving without him."

"Do you want me to call the police?" a small voice asked from the doorway.

Micah glared at the blonde, and she recoiled. Bugger, he was being a heel, but desperation was a powerful driving force.

Miss Botticelli smiled reassuringly at her colleague. "I don't think that will be necessary. Will it, Mr. Kincaid?" Her expression remained composed, her voice steady. "I understand you have a grievance and I'm happy to have a calm conversation in my office, but I won't accept abusive language or violent behaviour. Do you understand?" She turned intense eyes on him. Demanding and pleading at the same time.

"Of course," he said.

She nodded for Annemarie to return to the garden, and then beckoned him towards another room. With shoulders set squarely, she strode past a bathroom that looked like it was made to accommodate dwarves, and into a cluttered office.

"Take a seat." She indicated a tubular blue chair beside the desk. "Would you like tea or coffee?"

"No, thank you." The coffee and chocolate bar from a nameless roadhouse in the middle of the night, still sat like lead in his belly.

Miss Botticelli settled in another chair and took a pen and notepad from the desk. It had been stupid of him to lose control. Antagonism never achieved anything. In the business world, he relied on his ability to think on his feet and show restraint. It was this bloody situation with Chelsea that had pushed him past his limits.

"You don't mind if I take notes, do you? Just so I can make sure I understand the situation and work on a solution," she said.

Negotiation technique 101. He smiled. "I don't mind."

"Now, you believe your son is enrolled at this kindy and his name is Rowan."

"That's right. Rowan Kincaid, although he may be enrolled under another surname, like Matten or Smith. Maybe even Sharp."

"You must understand that I can't confirm whether or not a child by any of those names is enrolled here. If there were, you would need proof of legal custody or written permission from the parent who enrolled him, in order to have access. So, you can see that my hands are tied."

"I'm well aware of your requirements."

"Mr. Kincaid, you must understand that my priority is the safety of these children. I can't just hand them over to anyone who wants them. Custody disputes need to be sorted out in court and documentation provided to the kindy."

"What the courts don't take into consideration is how easy it is for mothers to simply move and take their children with them. Father's rights always come second." He was on his feet again, pacing and tugging his hair.

He needed to find a way to make this woman see that involving the authorities wasn't the best course in the long run. It wasn't just about what *he* wanted. It was about keeping his family close. He understood she was just doing her job, and kudos to her for standing up to him, but she didn't have all the facts.

"You don't know what I've been going through. I don't want to involve the courts, but I haven't held my child in nearly a year. How do you think it feels to not be allowed in his life? To have him not know me?"

If he walked out of there without some kind of information to bring him closer to Chelsea, he'd lose another three months of Rowan's life, and that *wasn't* going to happen.

• • •

No way was this man going to tower over her, making his demands, so Neve stood too. A gold wedding band glinted on Mr. Kincaid's finger as he pulled at his brown mop of hair.

"I'm really sorry about your problems, but there is no way I'm going to give you any more information without a court order," she said.

He stilled, jaw clenched, hands stiff by his side. She braced for another outburst and picked up the phone.

The low growl of his voice was even more menacing than his shouting had been. "When Chelsea comes to pick him up and finds out I've been here, she will disappear overnight. I'll be back to square one."

Intense eyes bored into her. She held her breath. Chelsea was Rowan's mother, and although the woman had never specifically warned of an abusive husband, there had to be a good reason why she had left him. Although he struck her more as desperate than violent, after all, once he'd realised he was scaring the children, he'd reined in his temper. But Neve was no expert on domestic violence. It didn't matter if he wore Louis Vuitton or Kmart, for her own safety and that of the children and staff in her care, she would treat him as though he were capable of cruelty until she had proof otherwise. Mr. Kincaid didn't know whom he was up against.

"I'm sure if you go to the police and explain the situation, they'll help you contact her, but in the meantime, I'm going to have to ask you to leave." She held an arm in the direction of the front door.

He snorted and shook his head. She half expected him to paw the ground like a bull ready for battle, but his broad shoulders slumped and he headed for the exit. She followed several paces behind and waved at Annemarie, who was watching nervously from the verandah.

With one hand on the door handle, Mr. Kinkaid turned back, and the desperation in his expression took her breath away.

"Please don't do this," he begged. "I promise I won't cause any trouble or frighten the children. Just let me see him through the window. I *need* to see him."

He grasped her arm, and she stepped back from the contact. Not because she felt threatened, but because the intensity of his anguish made her want to comfort him. At that moment, he looked like a broken man.

"Just one look. *Please.*"

In a gentle tone, she held her ground. "I can't. I'm sorry."

"I *need* to get my son back."

Slowly, she shook her head, and the despair in his eyes turned brittle. The muscles along his jaw flexed, and with shoulders thrust back, he strode through the door. Neve watched him cross the car park to a fancy-looking tan sedan. She made a note of the registration number as he got in, and waited there until the car turned onto the main road.

There was a chance he might hang around the area, and there wasn't much she could do about that, but she wasn't going to let anything happen to Rowan.

Chapter 3

A steady stream of work utes and dusty four-wheel drives passed in both directions. Micah pulled out of the kindergarten car park and cruised up the hill behind a horse trailer. His stomach grumbled. With any luck, he could combine food with discovering more about the post box. It was registered in the name of Chelsea Matten. Not the surname she had taken when she married him, but he was alert to her aliases now. After all, this wasn't the first town he'd followed her to, and he had a strategy. Talk to the locals and search the back roads; sooner or later, he'd turn up something useful.

First he called his personal assistant to clear a couple of days in his schedule. She'd been on his staff for seven years, so he trusted her to hold the corporate wolves at bay in his absence.

The general store was only a few hundred metres up the road. Another old stone building, this time with tan quoins, a galvanised roof, and bull-nosed verandah. He smiled at the pink geraniums swaying in baskets along the porch: his mother's favourites. On the footpath, the scent of warm pastries reached him.

"You look lost."

Micah turned towards a rumbling bass voice. "Pardon?"

A middle-aged bloke wearing a battered felt Akubra, blue work shirt, and stubby shorts eyed him suspiciously. As though sensing his master's mistrust, a liver-coloured kelpie yapped on the tray of a nearby ute.

"Don't get too many Bentley Flying Spurs around here," the man clarified.

Micah relaxed. "You know your cars. Would you like to look inside?"

A smile split the craggy face. "Hell yeah."

Micah opened the passenger door and pointed out the finer features of the interior. Then he popped the hood and they talked cylinders, horsepower and fuel economy. He was comfortable chatting to blue collar workers. Not only did he employ a lot of them, but he'd also been one once: dishwashing in a restaurant from the age of fourteen, and then a fly-in fly-out job at the Bulga Coal Mine.

The Kelpie now wagged its tail and strained against the rope securing it to the ute, and the farmer finally thrust a calloused hand at Micah. "So, what are you doing in Turners Gully? Not much call for suits here."

"I'm visiting a friend. You might know her. Chelsea Matten?" It was safest to stick to her alias for now.

"Yeah, I've heard the name but haven't met her. I don't come into town that often."

Micah smiled at the reference of the one-store, one-pub street as town. "You wouldn't happen to know where she lives, would you?"

"Don't suppose I would." The bloke pushed the rim of his hat back and narrowed his eyes. "You could ask Beth in the store. She knows everyone in town."

"Thanks." Micah nodded and headed up the steps of the general store.

Yes, he'd come a long way since labouring in a mine, and it had only been a chance meeting with the CEO that had opened up opportunities Micah had never dreamed of. Being taken under the wing of someone who had already found success was luck, but it had been his own efforts that had harnessed that opportunity to his advantage.

There was a lot left to chance in life. In fact, he was relying on a lucky break to find Chelsea right now, but he wouldn't sit around waiting for it to happen. He would use every resource available to him to bring his son home.

• • •

Neve scanned every corner of the gravel car park as she crossed to her car, aware for the first time how secluded it was. A narrow park with a deep creek flanked one side, and steep private properties were on two other sides. No sign of Mr. Kincaid. Maybe he wasn't as persistent as she'd assumed.

She got into her car and stopped it at the road verge to check for oncoming traffic. Her heart skipped a beat. The tan car was parked a short distance up the hill. It looked like she'd made the right choice with this plan to secret Rowan away.

With a slow turn of her head, she faced the opposite direction, pulled onto the main road, and went hard left. Her deliberately unhurried pace didn't expose the real panic inside. A hundred metres down the road; she checked her rear-view mirror and snuck down a dirt laneway.

She left the car idling at the end of the lane, where Mrs. Burke waved gardening shears from her front yard.

"Hello, Neve. Is everything all right?"

Should she brush off the busybody or get her onside with a tidbit of information?

"Good afternoon, Mrs. Burke. Everything's fine, but it would be great if you could pretend you didn't see me."

"Oh, reeeally?"

"We're having a custody issue. Nothing to worry about."

"Of course. Mum's the word." Mrs. Burke pressed a withered finger across her bleeding lipstick. "It's all very cloak-and-dagger, isn't it? Just like a Ruth Rendell mystery."

"Umm, sure. Thanks for your discretion."

"You're welcome, dear. Anything to keep the kiddies safe."

Neve peeked over the back fence of the kindy and beckoned to Annemarie and Rowan. She bundled the little boy into the booster seat in the back of her car and waved good-bye to Mrs. Burke.

When she stopped at the intersection, she half expected to see Mr. Kincaid standing in the middle of the road with hands on hips ... but he wasn't.

It was only a five-minute drive up the steep hill, along narrow, winding roads to Chelsea's house. The two-storey McMansion was balanced at the top of Sugarloaf Hill with a panoramic view of Adelaide city and the coast.

Another person with more money than sense. How anyone could justify a house that size for one family was beyond Neve's comprehension. She parked by the portico, ignoring Chelsea, who tapped a sandalled toe in the doorway. Neve unbuckled Rowan. That brown hair, those chubby cheeks and innocent eyes. Rowan's physical likeness to her late brother, Carlos, was uncanny—painfully so. The grief of losing Carlos and her mum had been buried deep, until Rowan had been enrolled at the kindy a couple of months ago.

He grinned up at her as he slipped his hand in hers, and she led him up the stairs.

"Good afternoon, Mrs. Matten."

"I hope you made sure you weren't followed," Chelsea snapped. "I'm terrified of that man, you know."

Neve narrowed her eyes. Chelsea didn't look the least bit afraid. With one hand on the hip of a tailored pantsuit and ruby-red lips pulled into a thin line, she looked ... inconvenienced.

"You know I'd never let anything happen to any of the children. I snuck out the back, like I said I would."

Rowan yawned, and Neve tousled his mop of brown hair. "I think this little mite is tuckered out. He had a big day in the sandpit."

Rowan held up a sheet of paper with a crayoned landscape and stick figures on it. "Look at the picture I made, Mummy."

Chelsea gave it a cursory glance. "That's lovely, Rowan. Now how about you go to your room so I can talk to Miss Botticelli."

Rowan crossed the marbled foyer and climbed the stairs, head bowed, tiny knapsack dragging beside him. If Neve had a child, she'd take every opportunity to let him know how special he was. No doubt Chelsea was too busy getting her nails sculpted and hair dyed to spend time talking about rainbows and butterflies. Right now the woman's plucked eyebrows were arched high.

"Now, I want to know exactly what Micah said."

Interesting that Chelsea was so sure of his first name, because Neve didn't know it and hadn't given her a description of Mr. Kincaid. Chelsea seemed quite convinced that the man was her ex-husband. And that was the other anomaly. Chelsea had called him her ex, but Mr. Kincaid was wearing a wedding ring. So either he was lying about how long he'd been chasing her or he'd remarried. The latter seemed like the most likely scenario, because someone that handsome and wealthy wouldn't remain on the market for long. Not that his financial status personally appealed to Neve.

"He asked to see Rowan Kincaid, Matten, Smith, or Sharp. I told him I couldn't confirm if we had a child enrolled by those names, but he insisted his son was there."

A sly grin spread across Chelsea's face.

Neve continued. "I asked him to leave, but he parked on the street. I assume he was waiting to see you."

"Yes, well, you should be careful of him."

"Honestly, he looked more flustered than dangerous."

"Looks can be deceiving. Don't you even *think* about telling him where I live."

"Of course I won't." A muscle twitched in Neve's cheek. Chelsea always managed to rub her the wrong way. "Perhaps you should call the police if you're so worried about Rowan's safety."

"I am quite capable of managing the situation."

Hang on a minute, Mr. Kincaid had said ... "You're not going to leave Turners Gully, are you?" Neve asked.

"I may have to take Rowan out of kindy until this blows over. I'll let you know." Chelsea stepped back and closed the door in Neve's face.

Chapter 4

Neve needed to work off some of the day's angst before going home to a different kind of tension, so she headed to Jack's Shed. It was a long cry from an upmarket gym, with basic equipment on a cement floor and Jack's house behind it. Simple—just the way she liked it.

Jack was an unofficial social worker in the area. He stopped the local teenagers from spending all of their time driving around and tearing up trouble, by teaching them to box. He encouraged them to finish school and then helped them find work. Jack meant the world to a lot of people in Turners Gully, but he was even more than that to her. He was her tether to a normal life.

She parked at one end of the forecourt and moseyed into the galvanised shed. There was a boxing ring at one end and free weights at the other. No programmable machines beeping complicated readouts, just effort and sweat.

"Evening." Jack Burton looked like your average grandpa in a singlet, with thin white hair slicked back from a deeply lined forehead and sagging jowls, but his arms were defined with decades-old muscle, and he could still go a few rounds with the best of them.

She gave him a high five. "How's business?"

"Nothing since the midday crowd cleared out, so I can spot for you if you want. Make sure you're not slacking off." His sly grin defied his serious tone.

"Just as well you're here to keep an eye on me. Give me a minute to stretch."

There were no lockers, so Neve tossed her gym bag on the open shelving along the back wall and breathed through a few stretches, feeling the tension of the morning leave her body.

Jack cocked his head at the sound of a deep, throaty rumble. Neve listened too. As it got louder, she recognised the unmistakeable thunder of a group of motorcycles. Tremors from the big engines vibrated through the soles of her feet.

Jack scowled. "That's the third time this month the Mutts have been through here."

"What would the outlaw bikie gang be doing in Turners Gully?"

"Nothing good."

"How do you know it's them? It might just be a group of Harley riders."

"I was out the front last week and recognised the insignia. I've seen it on the news before. Anyway, how's your dad?"

"Okay. He wouldn't settle last night."

"Nightmares?"

"Yeah. Sometimes I get tired of all the drama."

Jack rested a hand on her shoulder. "That's only natural, but there's no such thing as a normal family. You know that, right? They come in all shapes and sizes, and sometimes they aren't even related." He grinned, revealing a couple of gaps in his teeth from his boxing days.

She wrapped her arms around his neck and kissed his cheek. "You're better than any real uncle." She hugged him tightly, and when she let go, a rosy tint had crept across Jack's cheeks. "Plus you understand Tony."

The truth was, it was nice to have someone to dilute the intensity of her dad's anxiety issues now and then.

"I know it's been hard since you lost your mum and Carlos, but you've still got your dad and me. It's more than some people have, love."

"I know. Hey, you should come over for dinner on the weekend."

"It's a date, and I'll bring the wine. Now quit gas-bagging and start pumping iron."

• • •

Micah watched the blonde woman, Annemarie, lock the kindergarten door, get in her car, and drive away. Alone.

"God damn it!" He banged his fists on the steering wheel.

He'd hardly moved from his car all morning, other than to use the public toilet up the road. He'd seen Miss Botticelli leave the kindergarten an hour ago, but she definitely didn't have anyone else in the car with her, so he hadn't followed. At eleven thirty, parents had arrived to pick up their children. He'd made sure Rowan hadn't left with any of them either, and he hadn't see Chelsea.

He fingered the binoculars on his lap. How the hell had he missed them? He'd been so sure that Rowan was in there. The tightness in his gut knotted into a solid lump.

Someone had pulled a swifty, and *he'd* be the one to pay the price.

Suddenly he couldn't draw breath. He tried to drag in air, but his chest was trying to collapse in on itself. With one hand over his thumping heart, he shoved the car door open and stumbled onto the footpath.

I'm having a heart attack. Not again!

The doctor had assured him his heart was strong as an ox, but right now Micah felt feeble. With both palms pressed on the cool steel of the car roof, he lowered his head and closed his eyes.

Breathe. It's just a panic attack. All you have to do is breathe.

The street sounds were muffled through the fog of oxygen deprivation, and his body swayed. Chelsea was going to be the death of him.

He hadn't suffered like this since he was a teenager. All this stress was making old fears resurface. It didn't matter how many times he told himself that not being able to find Rowan wasn't the same as abandoning him. It was too similar to the dereliction by his own father.

But Rowan would understand. Wouldn't he?

Finally, Micah managed to suck in enough air to stop the scenery from rolling, but his cheeks felt hot in the cool air. Well, he wasn't giving up. Rowan was close; he could *feel* his own blood pumping through his son's tiny body somewhere nearby.

"Damn her!" He slammed his fist into the car door and was satisfied by the small dent ... for about two seconds. Then pain shot up his forearm and he spun in circles, shaking his hand. "This is all her fault. Shit, that hurt."

He inspected the raw scrape across his knuckles. Stupid move, and he couldn't really blame Chelsea. Someone had to be encouraging her, because *he'd* never done anything to deserve this. And his best guess was the new boyfriend, Dave.

It was the separation from Rowan that Micah couldn't stand. He was usually a reasonable man ... but even reason had its limits.

He knew what it meant not to have a dad to look up to, to rely on, to love you unconditionally. *I will* not *be an absent father!*

It felt like a week since Shannon had called about the post office box, but it was barely eighteen hours. He glared at the vacant kindergarten building. What he needed was to think this through logically. He'd go in the direction he'd seen Neve head earlier.

The Bentley's rear tires threw gravel across the intersection as he hauled the vehicle left. Driving aimlessly along back roads was nothing new. He had done it enough times hoping to spot

Chelsea in other towns. Done it and hated it. The futility stripped his life down to an iced coffee and stale pastry from a service station, when he should be dining on medium-rare filet steak in his favourite restaurant on the wharf at Circular Quay or signing off on a multi-million-dollar wind farm deal. But all the money he'd worked so hard to amass amounted to useless excess if he couldn't keep his family together.

His cursed father had *chosen* to leave his family, but Micah wasn't being given any options. When a man walked away from his wife and children, it left a huge hole of tattered self-doubts and insecurities. When that man was cruel enough to take everything with him—car, house, money—it meant going from a mansion to a caravan, from a full pantry to missed meals. Well, he'd exacted his revenge on his father, and he wasn't going to fail his own family.

The road climbed past hobby farms, wound around gnarled gum trees whose roots had lifted the bitumen, cleared a crest, and then descended again. Micah had no idea where he was until he spotted a familiar sign: Cabernet Bed-and-Breakfast. He'd been this way before. He stomped on the brake. Sleeping in the car again wasn't appealing. He rubbed the persistent ache in his neck. He was a long way from the Hyatt. This would do.

The steep driveway rose through an olive grove, flattened out at the top of the hill, and circled a manicured lawn. Standard roses played ring-a-rosy around a central fountain in front of a white-and-green bungalow with a lichen-stippled roof. He parked at the foot of the steps, climbed to the porch, and pressed a brass button beside a sign that read Office.

A bell chimed inside, and quick footfalls approached.

The door cracked open. "Good evening, may I help you?" A slender woman with long, iron-grey hair framing a softly furrowed face smiled up at him.

"I'd like a room if you have one available."

Her wine-coloured lips thinned as she looked him up and down.

Micah smoothed his shirt. "You'll have to excuse me. I've been travelling."

She opened the door farther. "Oh, I can sympathise with that. I'm Mrs. Travaglia. Won't you come this way?"

He followed her into a small room that was probably a converted lounge, where she slipped behind a reception counter. The office was small, but homely: a wire holder on the wall crammed with tourist brochures, a floral couch, a drink fountain, and jars of homemade jam on the counter. A second woman with long, dark hair sat at a corner desk, staring intently at a computer screen.

"We pride ourselves on personal service and privacy at Cabernet Bed-and-Breakfast. How many nights will you be staying with us, Mr. ...?"

"Kincaid."

The woman at the desk straightened and glanced his way.

"Can I book for two nights and see how I go from there?"

"Of course. Now let me take down a few details, and then I'll show you to your cabin. What was your first name, Mr. Kincaid?"

"Micah."

The woman in the corner now turned all the way around to study him. He pretended not to notice and fiddled with a tourist brochure on the counter.

"Would you prefer hot or cold breakfast provisions? A newspaper?"

"There's no need to bother with any services, thank you. I won't be spending much time in the room."

Mrs. Travaglia finished writing in her book and took key number four from a hook on the wall.

"I'll show Mr. Kincaid to his room." The other woman leapt to her feet, wide smile in place. "Hi, I'm Bronwyn Travaglia." She held an elegant hand out for him to shake. "Don't hesitate to let me know if there's *anything* I can do to make your stay more comfortable."

The older woman sighed and handed the key over.

Micah followed the talkative Bronwyn outside and around to the back of the house, where six wooden cabins nestled against the hill. She had the same long face, elegant movements and bone structure as the older Travaglia woman. In the cabin, she went to great lengths to show him every facility. He dutifully followed and approved of each area, ending back at the front door. He put his laptop on the circular dining table and gazed out the large front window. The cabin had a pleasant view of lush hills dotted with grazing cows and an olive grove. The perfect place to hide away from the business world for a few days.

Bronwyn Travaglia lingered on the threshold. "I'm sure our little old bed-and-breakfast isn't what you're used to, Mr. Kincaid, but if there's anything at all I can get you, don't hesitate to call through to the house. Anytime."

Ah, so she recognised him. So much for anonymity.

"Actually, there is one thing. Could you recommend a gym nearby?"

"Oh, you'll need to travel to Woodcroft for something like that. Let me show you on the map." She pulled a tourist map from a slot on the wall and opened it on the dining table.

"That looks like a long way. Isn't there something closer?" He didn't mean to sound ungrateful, but he really needed to work off some frustration, and think.

Bronwyn frowned. "Well ..."

He nodded encouragement.

"Jack Burton does have some basic gym equipment, but it's just a shed and hasn't even got a pool. I'm sure it wouldn't be suitable."

She didn't add "for someone like you" but he heard it anyway. It didn't matter that he'd scratched his way out of poverty. People calculated his net worth from TV broadcasts and made assumptions.

"That sounds fine, honest."

She marked the Woodcroft gymnasium on the map for good measure and then turned it over and sketched a mud map to Jack's Shed.

Micah thanked Miss Travaglia, showed her to the door, and shut it as she backed away, smiling like a Cheshire cat. He tossed his crumpled suit jacket onto the bed and threw on the only pair of shorts in his suitcase. With a hand on the front door, his phone chirped. A private number.

"Kincaid." There was a long pause. So long that he considered ending the call, but he could hear breathing. Probably one of the paparazzi hoping to record an abusive response or to keep him on the line long enough to trace the call.

As he raised a finger to cut the line, a soft female voice said, "Hello?"

The air in his lungs turned solid. "Chelsea, is that you?"

"Yes. I ..."

"Don't hang up, Chels. Let's just talk for a minute." The feeling of his chest being crushed intensified. It wasn't the first time she'd called since she went on the run, but he'd never managed to keep her on the line long.

"You're here to take Rowan away from me," she accused savagely.

"I've never wanted that. You're his mother, and I care what happens to you. All I want is to be involved in his life too. There has to be a way to figure this out."

"Do you really care about me, after all this time?" Her voice was small and pleading.

"You know I do."

"Even though we're not in love anymore?"

He sighed. "Chels, you'll always be important to me. We shared years and a baby. There's no point in pretending we're in love, but it doesn't stop me from wanting what's best for you. I'll do anything you want *except* stay away from Rowan. We can't go on like this."

"I'm ready to send Rowan home with you," she said, "but I can't come back to Sydney."

"That's okay." His heart took flight. "Rowan can spend a week at a time with each of us, or I'll fly you over every other weekend. Whatever you want to do." He perched on the corner of the large coffee table in the middle of the room.

"I can't handle going through the courts," she said.

"I know. We'll work it out. I'm glad you called."

"Oh, yeah. I ..."

"Is Rowan all right? Are you?" He leant forward in anticipation.

"He's fine. I was just feeling a bit anxious and wanted to hear your voice."

"You know I'm always here for you, Chels. What's bothering you?"

"It's silly, really, but I met some of the guys Dave works with. They made me uncomfortable."

He was suddenly alert to the evasive tone in her voice. "How so?"

"Don't worry about it."

Micah could feel her drifting away. His fingers tightened around the phone. "Trust your instincts. You wouldn't want to put Rowan in any danger now, would you? Let me help you." *Click.* "Chelsea? Hello? Fuck!"

The pressure built in his head. The room swam as his brain was deprived of oxygen. He dropped to his knees and touched his forehead to the carpet.

Breath in. Breathe out. Breathe in. Breath out.

At least if she wanted his help, he had a chance. But he needed to act before she changed her mind again or Dave changed it for her.

Chapter 5

Miss Travaglia hadn't been kidding about Jack's Shed being basic. Micah parked in front of the huge galvanised construction, half expecting to find blocks of wood and rope ladders inside.

In the entrance, he let his eyes adjust to the poor lighting. There was a young guy pummelling a speed bag at one end and an old man supervising a woman doing chin-ups at the other. A long, dark plait bounced along her spine with each movement. Lycra shorts and a crop top exposed the definition of her muscles. He moved closer and then paused to appreciate the slender curve of her thighs, the contraction of her back as she squeezed, and the bulge of lean biceps.

Despite her low body fat, she had a feminine shape that made his blood pressure go through the roof. Her breath rushed out each time she lifted her neck to the bar, and in as she slowly lowered her body. The control was impressive.

She did eight chin-ups and then dropped to the floor. The old man slapped her shoulder and grabbed a medicine ball. They sat facing one another, feet touching, and did sit-ups while playing catch with the heavy leather ball.

Micah couldn't help but stare. The fluid movement of the woman's body frustrated him in a whole different way from the irritation of today. This workout would need to be even more vigorous.

"Would it be okay if I use the equipment here?" he asked as he approached them.

The old man smiled. "I'll be right with you, son."

The woman glanced his way and missed her next catch.

"Ouch." She jumped to her feet and took up the same tense stance she had at the kindergarten. "What are you doing here?"

The old man's casual attitude changed in an instant. He moved in front of her and narrowed his eyes. "You know each other?"

"Did you follow me here?" She pushed past her protector and pointed at Micah.

He crossed his arms. "Well, if it isn't Miss Sneaky." At least she had the good grace to look guilty. "I didn't follow you. I'm here to work out, but I've suddenly lost my enthusiasm."

He strode from the shed and slammed his car door. The engine caught, and he gripped the wheel, ready to take off without even putting the seat belt on. Damn all five feet nothing of Miss Botticelli. If he'd followed her this afternoon, he'd have his son by now. Instead, he'd underestimated her, and now she had the upper hand. Of course she knew where Rowan was, but the chances she'd tell him were remote.

He rested his forehead on the steering wheel as he breathed through the aggravation. There really wasn't anywhere else for him to be right now.

A soft tap on the car window drew his attention to Miss Botticelli's dark eyes.

"Are you all right?" she said.

As though she cared. He shoved the door open before he knew what he was doing, and leapt from the car. Now mere inches apart, the warmth of her body stirred a crisp aroma like eucalyptus trees. He swallowed and took a step back.

"Where the hell did you take my son?" he demanded.

She sighed and stretched her neck from side to side. "Look, I already told you I can't help. I would lose my appointment at the kindy."

"But you helped Chelsea, didn't you?" He spat the words with such venom that she flinched.

"No. I helped Rowan, not his mother."

What an odd thing to say. Almost like she had something against Chelsea. Hell, if Chelsea wasn't taking care of Rowan … All the bloody money he'd thrown at her because he couldn't stand the thought of Rowan going without, and in truth, maybe to remind her what she was missing.

Hey, she just more or less confirmed that she did have Rowan.

Miss Botticelli stood there with hands on hips, her mouth a tight line. There wasn't any point in arguing with this pocket-rocket.

"Rowan is the only person who matters in this twisted little equation," he said quietly.

"Finally one thing we agree on."

"Look … can I call you something other than Miss Botticelli? It makes you seem like a school marm."

Dark eyes considered him with an unnerving criticality, like they would extract every angry word he'd ever flung at Chelsea, to be recounted as vindication of her duplicity. Frosty moments passed, until at last the lines around her mouth relaxed.

"Neve."

An exotic name. "Nice to meet you, Neve. I'm Micah. Do you think we can talk this through sensibly?"

"There really isn't any more to be said. I sympathise with your plight, but there isn't anything I can do to help."

"I know you're worried about your job, but I'm really not a threat. I'm his father, and there isn't a custody issue because both of us have full custody. Unfortunately, Chelsea is a bit confused about that at the moment. Can you imagine what it feels like to be separated indefinitely from someone you love?"

It was supposed to be a rhetorical question, but Neve's response was a pained whisper on the wind.

"Yes, I can."

• • •

Neve made a conscious effort to relax her shoulders. If Micah had found her at Jack's Shed, then maybe he could find Chelsea's house. Maybe Rowan was in more danger than she'd realised.

She looked into his amber eyes and said, "Look, we've been over this before. I'm going home."

The force of his gaze scorched her back as she retreated. As fast as possible, she went into the shed, crammed her gym towel into her bag, and strode back towards her car.

"Neve, wait." Jack put a wrinkled hand on her shoulder. "It's not a good idea to go anywhere with an angry man."

That pulled her up short. Strangely enough, she hadn't thought of being in danger with Micah. Yes, he was frustrated, even desperate, but a threat ... no, she couldn't muster any real fear. "I'm heading home, alone."

They both turned to the sound of scuffed cement. Micah stood in the doorway, tall and leonine, but his expression was contrite.

"Do I need to throw this guy off my property?" Jack mumbled under his breath.

Neve giggled. "As fun as that sounds, I don't think that's necessary. I'd rather he worked out here than follow me anywhere."

She marched out the door without a word. Just when she thought she was safely past Micah, he grabbed her arm. She pivoted, glared at his hand, and it fell away.

"You know, Chelsea called me this afternoon," he said. "I'm worried about her. It sounded like she might be in trouble. I'd really appreciate it if you could tell her to get in touch again. We need to sort this mess out, amicably."

He held out a business card. It couldn't hurt to take it, even if she had no intention of mediating a custody dispute. She nodded at him, pocketed the glossy card, and got into her car.

Her gaze was focused resolutely on the ground as she reversed, but curiosity got the better of her, and at the last moment she glanced at the rear-view mirror. Micah's profile was rigid, and the forlorn look in his eyes reminded her so much of little Rowan.

Chapter 6

A deep breath of country air filled Micah's lungs, and he puffed it out in irritation. Neve Botticelli was never going to help him. It didn't matter, because he'd always solved his problems alone.

He still needed to burn off some energy though, so he braced himself and turned towards the old man in the makeshift gym. "Am I still allowed in?"

The assessment he got was shrewd, and several awkward moments passed.

Then the old man approached and held out a hand. "Jack Burton. This here's my gym, of sorts."

They shook hands, firm grips increasing to uncomfortable.

"There ain't any fancy stuff. You still want in?" Jack said.

"I'm happy with a punching bag and free weights."

"Right you are then."

Jack busied himself with tidying and sorting equipment while Micah threaded two twenty-kilo weight plates onto each end of a bar, locked them into place, and did two sets of twelve repetitions.

"Another twenty?" Jack was already undoing the clamp and threading another disc on one end.

A test maybe? Micah did another set of twelve reps, but held up a hand as Jack reached for another twenty-kilogram plate. "I might head to the exercise mats for a bit."

Jack sat quietly on the edge of a haggard boxing ring while Micah did sit-ups and squats, no doubt waiting for an opportunity to share a piece of his mind. The more sweat that poured from

Micah's body, the less he cared about what Jack might be thinking, and the more attention he paid to the burn in his muscles. The tension of a long day on Chelsea's trail dissolved.

He bent with hands on knees to catch his breath. After only a few hours of broken sleep in the back of the car last night, fatigue was setting in.

Jack finally spoke. "What did you do to upset my girl?"

My girl. Maybe this was her father, although there wasn't much of a resemblance. Then again, the old bloke was so craggy it was difficult to tell what he might have looked like in his heyday.

"It's a misunderstanding, that's all," Micah said.

"Look, you seem like a nice enough bloke, but Neve doesn't need any trouble. She's had enough to last a lifetime."

Micah wiped his face and neck with a towel and stared at Jack. "I'm not trying to cause trouble for her. I'm trying to find my son."

"And you think Neve knows where he is?"

"I know she does, but she can't violate professional confidences. I understand that, but I don't like it."

Jack chewed his bottom lip. "Go easy on her. She's real good with the kiddies but has a lot to deal with at home."

Really? Micah couldn't imagine what kind of troubles Neve might have. An abusive boyfriend maybe, although she struck him as tougher than that. It wasn't his business anyway.

"Thanks, but I don't need any coaching. I doubt I'll see her again. If I don't find what I'm looking for, I'll be on my way soon enough."

"Back to the big smoke." Jack nodded like he had Micah sized up, and escorted him to his car. He whistled appreciatively. "Nice ride. You rich or something?"

Micah shrugged. "Something like that."

Jack laughed. "No wonder she doesn't like you."

"What, is this the tall poppy syndrome or something?"

"It's much more than that."

Micah raised his eyebrows and waited for Jack to elaborate.

"Someone rich took something from her once."

"And that's my fault?" Let her think what she wanted. It didn't matter to him.

"Sorry, son, it's nothing personal. She hates anyone with money."

"That's ridiculous."

"Being right won't make her see the flipside of the coin, mate."

Micah was used to being judged. Some women pawed him to get a piece of his wealth, others were more deceptive, but how dare Neve loathe him. She didn't even know him.

"So what the hell did she lose that was so precious it's prejudiced her for all time?"

Jack dropped his gaze to the floor and shifted his weight awkwardly. "I think you'd better ask her those sorts of questions."

He'd hit a nerve. "What, you can't tell me because of father-daughter privilege?"

"Ha! I'm not her father, sonny."

"Oh. I just thought ... when you called her *your* girl."

"Just a friend of the family." Jack's disposition cooled, and he retreated to the office.

Damn, the last thing Micah wanted was an enigma to stoke his curiosity. What he needed to concentrate on was finding Rowan, not unravelling a brunette mystery, no matter how attractive.

• • •

Five kilometres out of Turners Gully, Neve stopped her station wagon in front of a wire gate. There was a property number but no name. Anonymous, just the way Tony liked it.

She unlatched the gate, drove through, and closed it again. Smoke hung in the air as locals lit their pot-bellied stoves; even in early autumn it got cold at night. A dirt track meandered downhill through dense bush for about a kilometre, overlooking the Onkaparinga Gorge on the left. Several trails branched off to the right.

Where the gum trees thinned, a mud-brick house wrapped around the contours of the land, its corrugated iron roof camouflaged by khaki green and beige paint. A tranquil place where the din of the world was kept at bay. She sighed. This was her sanctuary, although it hadn't always been.

When she first came to live with Tony, the two-room bush shack had had no creature comforts. It had seemed like purgatory to a twelve-year-old, but she had to give him credit because he'd immediately started making mud bricks and added more rooms. One housed a proper bathroom, and then her bedroom and study. Everything was handmade or salvaged. Minimalist.

The moment she cut the car engine, Tony stepped onto the verandah. His dark eyes scanned the bush warily beneath sullen, bushy brows. They alighted on Neve, and laugh lines softened his features. His posture relaxed. Today must have been a good day.

She gave him a tight hug. "Hi, Tony." He'd given up trying to get her to call him dad long ago. "What did you get up to today?"

"Hi, honey. Went fishing and caught us some bream for dinner."

He kissed her forehead, and the barbs of grey stubble scoured her skin. At sixty-five, Tony still had a mop of dark, curly hair, although it had receded to a deep widow's peak. His olive skin and proud stance spoke of his Italian heritage, although he hadn't bothered to continue with the language.

"I know it's not the weekend," Neve said, "but I didn't get to finish my workout at the Shed. There's time for a contest before dinner if you're up for it."

"You're on."

It didn't take her long to disappear into the bush on their two-hundred-acre property. These training sessions had been a part of her life since she came to live with Tony. Nowadays they were an opportunity to release tension, feel the burn in her muscles as sweat trickled across her scalp and along her spine, but for a long time she'd resented her father for preparing her for a disaster that would never eventuate. You couldn't get a quieter town than Turners Gully, and there wasn't any sign of an end-of-world disaster anytime soon.

As she clung to the underside of a fallen tree, wedged between the banks of the Onkaparinga River, shallow water rushed across brutal rocks twenty-feet below. No time to dwell on it though, not when she was exposed like prey.

For a moment, she paused and listened. The river whispered over moss-covered stones, birds twittered in the bushes, bees hummed. No sign of Tony. Of course not; she'd be dead before she saw him, because he'd be moving through the bush barefoot and silent.

With her arms and legs burning with effort, Neve focused on the far bank. A welcome breeze ran cool tendrils across the sticky sheen on her skin. A few deep breaths brought her heart rate under control. She kept moving, hand over hand, boot after boot. Bark scraped the soft, olive skin of her forearms. Each movement sprinkled debris across her face, and the log creaked ominously. With stomach muscles clenched, she slowly lowered her feet to hang in mid-air. Then, kicking back and forth, she got into a swinging rhythm. When there was enough momentum, she arched her back and let go.

The pale cliff face loomed, and then she was falling ...

Her splayed fingers caught the lip of a tiny cave, and her body dropped against the jagged stone with a thud that took her breath away. For an instant, she dangled, and then she mustered one last burst of strength to haul herself into the cool safety of the cavern.

As far from the riverbed as the little hollow was, dried reeds and moss from the last flood clung to the walls. Today, though, it offered respite from the final gasping breaths of summer, which refused to submit to autumn.

Neve couldn't quite stand in the small space, so she knelt on the soft soil to retrieve a Fox combat knife, bow, and quiver from the fissure she'd dug into the soft sandstone wall long ago. With a twitch of one hand, she flicked her long, dark braid over her shoulder, flung the quiver onto her back, and made easy work of the final climb to the top of the riverbank.

After years of practice, it was now habitual for her to seek out straight sticks, sharpen one end to a point, and carve a notch in the other end. Once the quiver on her back was full of homemade arrows, she stepped away carefully. Her leather boots were an impediment as far as sound went but had the advantage of foot protection. She'd sidestepped a brown snake earlier.

With a bow slung across one shoulder and the knife tucked through her belt, Neve crept between a fallen gum and a granite boulder. She stooped to study the ground. Trip wire. Rather than step over it—rookie mistake—she backed away and took another route.

The hillside curved back and forth alongside the Onkaparinga River, but it was a thicket at the top she aimed for. Spiky blackboy grasses tore at her arms as she crawled through the undergrowth, and myrtles added a tacky lemon-scented residue.

In the centre of the thicket, there was just enough room to squat so she could peer at the grey fur about a hundred metres away. The pulse from her sprinting heart thundered in her ears, but she stayed focused. With deliberate slowness, she nocked an arrow into her bow, lifted it to her cheek, and pulled the bowstring taught.

The kangaroo didn't move—of course it didn't, it was just a pelt draped over a bough.

She took aim on an inward breath and held it ...

"You're dead," a deep voice whispered in her ear as a finger was drawn across her throat.

Neve squealed and wrenched her chin from her father's iron grasp.

Antonio Botticelli hung upside down, legs curled around a tree branch, an arrogant grin on his stubbled face, and, yes, his feet were bare.

Neve ruffled his dark curls. "Damn, Tony, I nearly had Skippy that time."

He swung from the tree and landed lightly. "That's because you're too focused on the prize and not your surroundings."

"We can't all be Vietnam vets." In all the years they'd been playing this game, Neve had only bettered him a couple of times. "Okay, time for dinner."

"Hang on. You haven't done drills yet."

"I'm tired, and I've got things to prepare for kindergarten tomorrow, so fun's over." She kissed his cheek and tossed the makeshift arrows on the ground. As much as she enjoyed running about the bush with Tony, working at the kindy offered a welcome reprieve from his alternate universe.

His thick brows mashed together. "It's not fun, honey. Weapons training is just as important as survival skills. One day it might just save your life."

"Yeah, sure, Tony, there's a big call for guerrilla warfare in Turners Gully." They headed back to the house, and Neve pushed the salvaged front door aside and stepped into the warmth of the small living area. Even on warm days, the wood stove was lit in the evening, to keep the chill of the night fog at bay. The ceiling was low, supported by rustic beams and posts, thick walls the colour of yellow ochre had traces of straw showing through, and the back wall was the hillside. Rain was diverted above the house, but there was a fail-safe covered grate along the base of the back wall just in case.

She kicked off her shoes and blanched at the biting cold of the cement floor. The very reason a pair of Ugg boots had pride of place in the shoe line-up by the door.

"Give me a minute to get changed and I'll give you a hand with dinner," she said.

She headed for her bedroom, which was no more than a double bed and a curtain in front of shelves to suffice as a closet. She hung her blouse on a coat hanger and pulled a comfy windcheater from a battered pine tallboy. She unfurled her French braid and ran a comb through the long locks as they kinked up to half their length, forming an obstinate frizz around her face.

Adjoining her room was a study. Tony called it "the library" because two walls were covered from floor to ceiling with bookshelves. The house had solar-powered electricity, but only her rooms had power points, and Tony wasn't happy about her Internet dongle, just in case Big Brother was tracking it.

Tony had butter melting in a cast-iron frying pan on top of the wood stove when Neve joined him. He tore washed lettuce leaves and dropped them into a ceramic bowl.

"Nearly the last of our lettuce," he commented. "Still plenty of tomatoes though."

Bubbling butter sizzled as he dropped the filleted bream into the pan. How had he managed before she came to live with him? He took isolation and self-sufficiency to new levels. If he couldn't harvest it from the land or barter with the neighbours, he didn't use it. No doubt why his clothes hung loosely on his slim frame. At least now, she picked up additional supplies from the supermarket.

She stood beside him at the split trunk of red gum that was their kitchen bench, washing string beans, yellow capsicum, and celery. Neve was suddenly exhausted. Her shoulders rose and fell with an exaggerated sigh, which was loud enough to make Tony stop chopping.

He stared and then tucked a spiral of hair behind her ear. "I would've made the salad, but I thought you'd be home later. Didn't you go to Jack's? Is something wrong?" His brows pulled together.

"Nothing, it was just a trying day."

"Must've been."

She felt an unexpected sting in her eyes before her vision blurred, and she quickly turned her head to the pantry shelves, pretending to look for ... anything. Rowan's chubby cheeks and open smile flashed through her mind, and she sniffed. A warm, gnarled hand rested on her shoulder.

"Honey, what happened?"

She shrugged and swallowed a couple of times before she could speak. It amazed her how Tony could be so attuned to her feelings, yet on a different planet to the rest of civilisation. She left the salad, sat at the four-seater dining suite, and told him all about Micah and Chelsea.

"I'm so confused, Tony. I know I have to protect Rowan, but you should have seen the look in this guy's eyes. It was— was like—" She took a deep breath. "It was like looking into my own soul after Carlos and Mum died."

Tony shuddered. "Is he dangerous?"

"I don't think so. He just really wants to see his kid." There wasn't any evidence to lead her to that conclusion, but deep in her bones, she just knew it was true. Micah didn't strike her as someone who especially wanted to threaten her to get to Rowan. He was desperate, and she knew better than most the compulsion to protect those you loved. It didn't matter though, because she still had to protect Chelsea's privacy.

"You did the right thing. You don't want to lose your job at the kindy. Hopefully this guy will get the hint and leave you alone."

She didn't tell him how Micah found her at Jack's Shed. Tony wasn't entirely balanced when it came to her safety. "Yeah. The only thing that bothers me is that he has the money to hang around and make life difficult for Chelsea."

"A rich bastard?" Tony growled.

"Posh car, expensive clothes, all the trimmings."

"Keep the hell away from him, Neve."

Tony's mood darkened. She shouldn't have said anything. The last thing she needed was to set off his nightmares again.

"Anyway, it's a moot point, because I'm committed to the Department of Education's Code of Conduct and no one can make me compromise Rowan's safety." The heat emanating from the stove and the low ceiling were suddenly too much. The same anger she'd felt while facing off with Micah at Jack's Shed surfaced, and she clenched her fists.

"I'm going to feed Kookapie."

Once on the verandah, she sucked in a cleansing lungful of crisp air. Long shadows stretched across the clearing in front of the house, and it took a few minutes to spot the bird she was looking for. Kookapie rested on a low gum branch, a watchful eye on Neve. She whistled, placed a handful of diced kangaroo on a flat stump, and stepped back. The bird raised its beak to the sky and gave a half-hearted cackle—*Oo-oo-ah-ah-ah-ah*—and then flew down to the stump. It wasn't tame exactly, but it turned up at dinnertime each night.

It was a freak of nature, the shape of a kookaburra but with the colouring of a magpie faded in the wash. Tony had named it.

Kookapie snatched a sliver of bloody meat, smashed it against the stump to make sure it was dead, and tossed his head back to swallow the morsel whole. Life was savage and simple at the same time.

Chapter 7

Micah balanced a takeaway cup of coffee on his knee and watched mums arrive at Turners Gully Kindergarten, with enthusiastic children wearing tiny backpacks. No sign of Chelsea or Rowan.

He was perched atop a picnic table made from slabs of red gum, and the dampness from the wood was seeping through his jeans. He wasn't well prepared for the cold, having left Sydney with no more than an overnight bag. If he stayed much longer, he'd need to buy a few items. By nine o'clock, the traffic ceased. At nine thirty, it was pointless to wait for something he knew wasn't going to happen. Chelsea was probably halfway across the country by now. She hadn't phoned him again, which wasn't a good sign.

He opened the map he'd bought earlier that morning. The only thing left to do was a methodical search of the back roads and chat with the locals. Maybe he'd get lucky and someone would tell him where Chelsea lived. Unlikely, but optimism was all he had right now.

He caught a glimpse of Neve in the kindergarten yard. In jeans and a blouse, her hair in a tight braid, she looked elegant. Last night she'd dominated his thoughts, and not just because he was frustrated with her. She'd smelt so good as they'd faced off in front of Jack's Shed yesterday. The supple and toned body he'd seen didn't detract from her femininity, but complemented her fearless attitude. Quite a woman. But he couldn't forget that if she'd helped him yesterday, Rowan would be with him now, and he wasn't.

A little brown-haired boy ran up and grabbed her hand. Micah's whole body tensed, the way it did every time he saw a four-year-old brown-haired boy. No matter how sure he was he'd recognise Rowan when he saw him again, a part of him was terrified he might not.

A year ago, Rowan had been a toddler with a healthy curiosity, small hands that wrapped around Micah's fingers as they walked side by side, and an infectious giggle. Now he was a kindy kid. A year was an eternity for a child ...

There was a slim possibility that Neve and Chelsea had pulled a swifty again and snuck Rowan into the kindy. He picked up the binoculars from the table and scrutinised the child, but it was impossible to see clearly with them on the move.

He'd lost faith in his ability to tell when a woman was lying to him. It's not like he'd thought his relationship with Chelsea was perfect, but he'd committed to forever and assumed the same of her, right up until she had done a runner with Rowan. The family he'd always craved had dissipated with her.

The only way to be sure his son was in the kindergarten building was to see for himself, but his reception was unlikely to be warm. Besides, he didn't want to frighten the children. But phoning couldn't hurt ...

He dialled the number in his notebook, and a female answered. Not Neve, because he could still see her in the yard, crouching to speak to the child on his own level. She looked over her shoulder and nodded. The blonde staff member he'd yelled at yesterday, Annemarie, took the little boy's hand. Neve went inside.

"Hello, this is Miss Botticelli, the director. How can I help you?"

So polite. Micah felt the pilot light of his annoyance flicker to life at the sound of her voice, but he took a calming breath.

"Neve, it's Micah Kincaid. We spoke yesterday," he added awkwardly. It wasn't likely she would have forgotten.

"I see. I'm working Mr. Kincaid, and have nothing further to tell you."

"Wait! Hello?" For a moment, he thought she'd hung up, but a faint exasperated sigh made him smile. So, he was Mr. Kincaid again. No matter, he was going to keep it friendly. A tactic he should have employed yesterday. You caught more flies with honey than vinegar.

"I'm here," Neve said.

He hurried to speak before she changed her mind. "Neve, I promise I'm not going to come in and make trouble and I won't ask you to tell me where Rowan is. All I want to know is if Chelsea has contacted you. Maybe to cancel Rowan's kindergarten registration."

There was a long pause. He set the binoculars down and leant towards the building, willing her response.

"It would be unprofessional to compromise Rowan in any way or give out personal information, but"—she cut off his argument—"I can tell you Rowan isn't here and Chelsea hasn't contacted me."

"Shit!"

"I'm sorry. Really, I am."

"It's not your fault. Look, can you call me if she shows up or phones? I only want to make contact with her. Try to sort this out."

"I don't know ..."

"Please. It can't be good for Rowan to be without a father. All I'm asking for is a heads-up."

"If you promise *not* to come onto the kindy property, I'll ask Chelsea to contact you. I don't want this centre involved in a custody dispute or whatever this mess is."

"Thank you, Neve."

He gave her his number again—she had probably thrown out his business card at the first opportunity yesterday—and thanked her yet again. Whether she made good on her assurance remained to be seen.

• • •

Neve cursed Micah Kincaid and his fancy car and Louis Vuitton clothes. Why did rich people always think they could get whatever they wanted? Still, it wasn't his fault she'd agreed to talk to Chelsea. She blamed it on a sleepless night spent worrying about Rowan.

The nightmare had woken her last night, for the first time in ages.

Neve sat with her eyes closed, crisp country air whipping in the open car window, and Carlos sniggering beside her at something on his iPad.

"Would you shut that window? It's making a drumming sound," Mum complained.

Neve sighed and reached for the button, but the car lurched sideways. There was a squeal of tires, a careening of metal, and glass crunched. Then they were spinning, spinning, across the road, through a fence, into a paddock.

Neve stared right into the eyes of the woman in the other car, which was now wedged in her mum's door. The woman frowned, as though she couldn't understand how this happened. Her car stopped, but Botticelli's kept rolling. It was so quiet, almost peaceful for a moment, until the car jolted. Neve's head hit the back of her mum's seat as a spray of water flew past the windows.

Precious seconds ticked past in slow motion. Water oozed through the door seals. Mum was lying down and the car was all buckled over the top of her. The car floated, like a big broken boat. Muddy water gurgled over the lip of mum's broken window.

And then Carlos screamed.

Water rushed in too fast. Faster than Neve's frantic heart, and faster than her fingers could release Carlos's seatbelt.

Only this time, the screaming face in the nightmare was Rowan's.

The same panic raced along the surface of her skin now and raised horrified goose bumps in its wake. What if Chelsea really had skipped town, like Micah said she would? Neve might never see Rowan again. She paced the short span of her office, flicking a pen against her chin.

"Mikey wet his pants again. Can you watch the kids while I— Is everything all right?" Annemarie frowned in the doorway.

Neve struggled to regain her composure. "Everything's fine. You change Mikey. I'll watch the kids."

There was nothing she could do about Chelsea or Rowan right now, and making herself sick with worry wasn't helping. Perhaps after work, she'd check in on them.

Chapter 8

It had been a day of futile conversations and pointless driving around, but Micah refused to give up. For the second time today, Micah stopped at the general store. It was late afternoon, and a man in overalls was pumping fuel into a battered ute. Matthew Stokes Farrier was printed on the side of the canopy. The guy eyed the Bentley, and Micah cursed for the hundredth time that he hadn't picked up a modest hire car.

He took a deep breath and approached the farrier. "Good afternoon. Sorry to bother you, but I wonder if you know Chelsea Matten?"

The guy's face tightened with suspicion as he gave Micah the once over. "I might. Who's asking?"

He went with the same story he'd been using all day. "Here's the thing. We used to be school sweethearts, and I heard, through Facebook, that she is living in Turners Gully. I was here for business, so thought I'd look her up."

"Yeah, I know Chelsea. Moved into the area not long ago. One of them sheilas who complains 'bout how noisy the cattle are and how slow the tractors are."

"Yes, that sounds like her. Do you know where her house is?"

Matthew Stokes shoved his free hand in his pocket and hunched his shoulders. "Can't say I do. Only seen her at the store now and then. Sometimes she's with a big bruiser of a bloke. I think she's got a kid at the kindy too. Might want to try there."

"Yeah, I'll do that." Micah turned away but swung back. "I don't suppose you've seen her today?"

"Nah, mate, but if I do, I'll tell her you were looking. What did ya say your name was?"

"Thanks, but don't worry about it. I'm leaving town tomorrow."

Back inside the Bentley, he dialled his PA. "Emma, I know it's last minute, but I'm going to have to stay in Turners Gully longer than expected. Could you organise to have a hire car dropped at the B and B?"

"Okay. I'll organise the usual—"

"No. I want something ordinary. Nothing from the prestige range."

Emma took down the address without further question.

It was five o'clock, and Micah hadn't eaten since the coffee and croissant from the general store that morning, but instead of hunger, his intestines had this awful feeling of being sutured into a tight ball. With every person who hadn't been able to help him today, and every road he drove down without sighting Chelsea, he felt progressively sicker. And still he was no closer to Rowan.

The kindergarten would be closed by now, but he'd do one last walk by before calling it a day.

A text message beeped. The hire car would be delivered early tomorrow morning. Emma was a saviour.

Then his mobile phone started ringing. Emma must've forgotten something. When he glanced at the screen, it was a private number.

"Kincaid," he said,

"I'm ready to meet you and sign the divorce papers. I know I've messed you around, Mikey, but I'm tired of all the drama. It should be easy to organise, seeing as I signed a prenup."

"Chels, if you'd stopped to look at the agreement I had drawn up a year ago, you would have seen it was very generous. There's nothing more important to me than taking care of my family and you'll always be that, whether we're married or not."

She sighed. "Everything seems clearer when I talk to you."

"I wish you'd done it a long time ago and saved us both the angst, but let's just move forwards, shall we? How do you want to do this?"

Big engines rumbled in the background.

"Um, I have to go, Micah."

"No, don't go until we've worked something out. At least give me your phone number."

"I'll call you tomorrow and make a time to mee—" She gasped. "Dave, what are you doing?"

"They're coming," a deep voice growled.

"Chelsea?"

Nothing.

The hairs prickled on the back of Micah's neck as he shut his phone.

What the hell just happened? Something's not right here.

One minute Chelsea was being cooperative, and the next it sounded like a male cut off the call. And those were definitely big motorcycle engines he'd heard in the background.

He banged his fist on a fence beside him, and a dog yapped madly, so he kept walking. If Chelsea really was in trouble, he was powerless to help her. And that meant he was failing Rowan too.

He headed through the park adjoining the kindergarten, along a dirt track, under willows and over a footbridge, and then paused in the shadows. There was a glow inside, and a familiar figure stepped in front of a lit window. Neve was working late. He could knock on the door and talk to her, but what was the point? He felt in his bones that Chelsea hadn't shown up with Rowan. Neve would be none the wiser. He had to hang his hopes on Chelsea finally doing the right thing.

As he turned to retrace his path, a car at the other end of the kindergarten forecourt caught his attention. Someone was sitting in a twin-cab Toyota Hilux with no interior light on, leaning against the headrest. Odd place for a kip. Maybe Neve had an overprotective boyfriend.

Micah shrugged, went back to his car, and headed for the sanctuary of his cabin.

• • •

Neve fidgeted with a paperclip. Chelsea hadn't brought Rowan to kindy today, and she hadn't phoned. What if she never saw Rowan again? There was always plenty to do around the kindy, but the real reason she was working late was the hope that Chelsea—or Micah—would call.

She glanced at the wall clock: 6:30 p.m. She was kidding herself. She packed crayon pots onto the shelf and flicked off the office light.

I'd feel if Rowan needed my help, wouldn't I? Not that it would make a difference if I don't know where he is.

She pulled his latest painting from the wall. A sunny scene of rolling hills with spotted cows drinking from a river. Her eyes fixed on the blue water, and it slowly transformed to murky brown. For a moment, she was transported back to the helplessness of swirling, murky water and fighting for her life. Carlos had been thrashing an arm's length away. Her fingers fumbled for the clasp on his seat belt ...

No amount of screaming had stopped that car from sinking.

Rowan's painting slipped from her fingers. She was powerless again, although this time he wasn't even her brother and she didn't have a right to help him. He could be anywhere.

Today Chelsea's phone had gone straight to voice mail. The first time, Neve had left a message. Not her problem, she reminded herself, but it left a bitter taste on her tongue.

Tony would be anxious that she wasn't home yet, so she locked up the kindy and held up the bundle of keys to catch the streetlight, so she could see which one belonged to the car door. Just as she managed to slide the key into the lock, a shiver of dread raised the hairs on her arms. There was warmth behind her. Like body heat. The last gasps of dusk cast irregular willow tree shadows across the car park. The air smelt damp as the temperature dropped in the valley and the first tendrils of mist lurked at the edge of the creek. Her breath came in a short gasp, and she spun around.

Too late. Thick arms pinned hers to her side, and she froze. The pervasive stench of beer curled up her nostrils and down her throat, making it hard to breathe. The arms around her were as thick and solid as iron bars. No point struggling against someone bigger and stronger; better to wait until she could gain the upper hand. Tony had insisted on preparing her for every eventuality; now she just needed to keep her head and use her training.

She shivered as warm breath trickled down her neck.

The voice was deep and calm. "Stay nice and still now and be real quiet. I'm going to have a little chat with you; make sure you don't do anything stupid."

Her mind spun. It didn't sound like this ape wanted to rob her, so why was he here?

"Chelsea wants to make sure you're not planning on involving the police or letting that prick Micah know where she is. You're not, are you?"

Chelsea sent this ape? That meant the woman was still in Turners Gully, and probably Rowan too. If she didn't want Neve to call the cops, Chelsea must be up to no good. Neve shook her head.

"Good girl." His syrupy voice dripped onto her like sticky tar. "If you keep your nose out of our business, then you won't get hurt."

"Hurt?" She thrashed. *Why would they want to hurt me?*

The ape's grip didn't budge. "Now, don't go getting all flighty on me. Just nod your head if you're going to keep out of our business."

She nodded. "Is Rowan coming back to kindy?" With any luck, it sounded like something a concerned teacher might ask, not the desperate plea that came from a nauseous place in the pit of her stomach.

The ape shook her and growled. "You don't need to know that. Just pretend like you've never heard of us, right?"

That was twice he'd referred to Rowan, Chelsea, and himself as *us*. Not a hired hand then. This must be Chelsea's boyfriend. What was his name?

"Dave." *Oops, didn't mean to say it aloud.*

He spun her around, threw her back against the car, and slapped her across the face. Hard. Neve fell sideways. Gravel tore at the palm that broke her fall, and she shrieked.

Shit, I need to get out of here without pissing him off anymore.

He loomed over her, his black T-shirt straining over swollen muscle, and bellowed, "You forget that name. Forget all of us. Got it? This has got nothin' to do with you."

Neve held a palm to her stinging cheek. Dave's face was in shadow, but there were silver highlights in his hair, a tiny stud in his left earlobe, and tattoos clawing up from his collar. She was sure she'd recognize him if she saw him again, and he was going to be in a whole world of pain if she got her hands on a weapon of any kind. She surreptitiously reached for her handbag—there was always a baton in there. Tony made sure of it.

Dave twitched towards the movement and kicked the handbag under the car.

She tried to distract him. "Micah just wants to see his son."

"Don't you worry your pretty little head about Micah. I have a plan for him. Just keep your mouth shut, or you're going to get more trouble than you know what to do with." He grunted, obviously satisfied that she was cowed, and disappeared into the shadows at a jog with a long ponytail swinging across his broad back.

She scrambled to reach her handbag, her hands shaking, found the baton, and brandished it at the shadows. A car engine caught and headlights flared by the road.

Leaping to her feet, she ran on shaky legs, but tripped on a bush. A white twin-cab ute turned, but the number plate was a blur through her brimming tears as the vehicle bumped over the curb and revved up the incline of Potter Road. All she caught was the first letter: *V.*

Crap! What the hell was I doing letting him slap me? Tony taught me better than that. The first chance she had to put all those bloody drills into practise and she wimped out.

It took a few tricky manoeuvres to extricate herself from the grasping limbs of a westringia bush, and then she stood alone in the dark, shaking like the nearby willow canes in the wind. If only she'd fought harder. Dave had caught her by surprise, but that didn't mean she was going to play his game.

She retrieved her handbag and held tightly to the baton. The car keys were hanging half out of the lock, and it took her a few tries to reinsert them. Inside, she locked the doors, rested the baton on the passenger seat, and started the engine. She wasn't sure where she was going yet; she only knew she didn't want to stay here in case Dave returned.

She headed in the opposite direction from home though. Tony couldn't see her like this.

At the top of the hill, a light fog clung to the ground, reflecting her headlights and making the shadows at the roadside ominous. Neve turned right and soon pulled to the verge. Jack's Shed was a hundred metres ahead.

Her heart still thundered behind fragile ribs, and her eyes felt like they were propped wide with toothpicks, like in the "don't drive while you're drowsy" billboards that gave her the creeps. There were no streetlights along this road, but a cold, white light shone through Jack's kitchen window.

There wasn't any point in coming here. If Jack saw her in this state, he'd worry. Even worse, he might mention it to Tony, who'd go ballistic. But where else could she go?

She sat in the dark car and let tears stream down her face. Head resting on the steering wheel, she screwed up her mouth against the ache of emotion. Her shoulders heaved, and she wrapped one arm around herself to stop the tremors. With the other hand, she searched the glove box for a travel-pack of tissues.

When the tears finally subsided, she wiped her eyes and blew her nose.

Get a grip, Neve. Don't just sit here, do something.

She restarted the car and pulled a U-turn, again, with no idea where she was going. She just drove, and the car decided which way to turn.

It didn't make sense that Chelsea would send Dave to threaten her. Neve hadn't given any indication that she'd go to either the cops or Micah, and yet Dave had promised to hurt her if she did. It seemed like an overreaction. The type of defensive behaviour someone might demonstrate when they felt guilty, but what were Dave and Chelsea guilty of?

Micah's story looked like it had more merit than she'd first thought. She ought to know by now to trust her intuition.

A tall figure at the side of the road leapt into the glare of her headlights, and she stomped on the brake pedal, eyes wide ... and then released the breath she'd been holding. Just a kangaroo.

It bounded out of sight, and she edged the car forward, tapping a finger nervously on the wheel.

One thing was for sure, she didn't want a Neanderthal like Dave anywhere near little Rowan. She'd never forgive herself if something happened to the boy. If Chelsea was still in Turners Gully, there was one person who had a right to know. This had nothing to do with Neve's job at the kindy or her responsibility to Chelsea. Dave had made it personal.

The problem was, she'd left Micah's business card at work and had no idea where he was staying. It might not even be in Turners Gully. Someone like him probably hired penthouses by the week, but the city was a long way to drive. No, it made sense that he was staying nearby, which seriously narrowed his choices.

It wouldn't take long to go back to her office and get his number, but she'd be alone in the dark. Exposed. She glanced at her watch. The turquoise numerals glowed seven twenty. The general store would be closed. It would be pointless to doorknock all the local bed-and-breakfasts, but the winery had rooms. If someone she knew was on reception, they might tell her if Micah was in one.

What she really needed was to see a familiar face before she went home to Tony's inquisition. He'd know something was wrong the second she walked in the door.

The car snaked along the country road, pushing through the fog like an icebreaker. Around the next bend, Neve spotted a familiar wrought iron lamppost. From it hung a lit sign that read Cabernet Bed-and-Breakfast. Without hesitation, she turned into the driveway and climbed the steep hillside until it flattened out and circled a classic stone fountain.

Neve went around to the side door of the main house and used the brass knocker. There were light footsteps from within, and then a shadow appeared behind the stained glass door. It cracked open and then swung wide.

"Neve, what are you doing here? Is everything all right?"

"Hi, Mrs. Travaglia. I just thought I'd drop in on Bron."

"Come on in, it's freezing out there. Bronwyn's in the study."

Neve followed her best friend's mother down the long corridor to the back of the house. Bron had her feet tucked under her and a book in hand as she sat by an open fire.

"Surprise," Neve announced without enthusiasm.

"Neve! It's great to see you." Bronwyn bounced off the couch and pulled her into a tight hug against her slender body. "What the heck are you doing out at this hour on a Friday night? Don't tell me"—she raised a hand—"working."

"Sort of." Neve's chin quivered and tears welled. She couldn't help it, Bron always got under her defences.

"Oh hell, what happened?" Bron steered her to the couch and snatched a box of tissues from an oak bureau. Her brows pulled together. "Is that a mark on your cheek?"

Neve touched the place where Dave had hit her. "Oh, I— I wasn't looking where I was going and bumped into the doorframe. Silly me." She balled her hands by her side to hide the abrasions on them.

I shouldn't lie to Bron. We share everything. But it might not be safe to tell her too much. The situation was kind of confidential, and Dave was dangerous.

"Just start at the beginning," Bron urged.

Just how far Dave was prepared to go was anyone's guess, but involving Bron would be a mistake. "I'm overacting, really. Just a lousy day at work."

"Damn those rug rats." Bron gave an exaggerated pout. "There's nothing like four-year-olds to bring you down to size."

Neve couldn't help but giggle.

Bron broke off a row of Lindt dark-orange chocolate and handed it over. "I was going to call you tomorrow anyway. You won't believe who's staying here. Only *People* magazine's Sexiest Man Alive."

Neve stilled. The hairs on the back of her neck bristled.

Bron leant forward. "I know, right? And the ninth wealthiest person in Australia. I have no idea how much money he's got, but it must be a gazillion and he's staying in our little B and B."

Neve swallowed the lump stuck in her throat. *Rich man. Here.*

Bron punched her shoulder. "And gorgeous like you wouldn't believe. Well, I'm not looking a gift horse in the mouth, let me tell you. I'm making sure our bachelor of the year gets the very best *personal* service." She laughed.

"Great. What's Richie Rich's name?"

"Micah Kincaid. You know, of Kincaid Industries."

Neve's quiet gasp must've accompanied a pasty complexion, because Bron frowned again.

"You okay?" she asked.

Actually, Neve felt like throwing up. "I'm not feeling very well, so I might head home. Catch you tomorrow, okay?"

"Umm, sure. Are you okay to drive?"

Neve nodded and made a beeline for the back door. Bron waved as Neve got into the car and crawled along the driveway. A swarm of angry and confused wasps in her head were too noisy for her to think clearly. There wasn't any good reason to run away, but she wasn't sure she wanted to get involved in this shit.

But I already am, and Micah has a right to know. Rowan could be in danger. What was she saying? Of course he was in danger if Chelsea was hanging around with a bruiser like Dave.

She touched her cheek. Heat still radiated from where he'd struck.

At the end of the driveway, gravel had spilled onto the road and glinted in the headlights. On the verge, straw-like grass trembled in the breeze. As the car idled and minutes passed, the darkness pressed in on her safe cocoon and made her pulse sprint.

It was bullshit to be this shaken by one bloke. If she'd been paying attention to her surroundings, Dave wouldn't have gotten the upper hand, and she would have taken him down.

It wasn't unusual for a parent with limited visitation rights to behave badly, but physical violence from someone *with* the child was just ludicrous. It couldn't hurt to warn Micah about how dangerous Dave was.

She put the car in gear and did a three-point turn. The journey back up the driveway seemed longer than usual, and the tires were so loud on the gravel that any minute now, Bron would stick her head out and demand to know why Neve was back. Instead of parking in front of the big house, Neve followed the divergence to the right, where there were six cabins. A four-wheel drive was parked in front of Cabin 1, then an empty parking space, a Volkswagen, and a tan Bentley. Surely it couldn't be this easy to find him.

Neve parked, got out of her car, and pressed the door closed gently so it wouldn't alert anyone. She glanced at the main house, but there was no movement. The Travaglias probably thought it was one of their guests.

Soft, yellow light from the porch of Cabin 4 made it easy to pick her way across the loose stones.

The ninth wealthiest person in the country. *Hells bells, he could buy a whole tribe of kids, or his own security force to track one down. But here he is in person.*

It was hard to hear over her conflicting thoughts as she climbed the steps.

I can't break my confidentiality agreement. Can I?

She stood in front of the door, fingers resting on the knob. Took a step backwards. Paused. And then reached again.

Chapter 9

Micah swished the razor in warm, soapy water and ran the back of his hand up his cheek. A razor always did a better job than the electric gadgets. He pulled the plug, rinsed the basin, and pressed a hand towel to his face.

He rolled his eyes at the knock on the door. No doubt it was the overly helpful Bronwyn Travaglia again. He sighed and went to open it.

"Neve?" Dread settled deep in his stomach as the look in her eyes registered. Something wasn't right. "What happened?"

"Umm." She chewed her lip. "I think Chelsea is still in Turners Gully."

"Do you want to come in and tell me about it?"

Her wary eyes scanned the room and returned to him. Slowly, she nodded.

He waved her to the stiff floral couch. "Give me a minute."

As fast as he could, he wiped the remnants of shaving foam from his face and ran his fingers through his damp hair. He looked left and right. Damn, his shirt was hanging on the back of the dining chair.

When he stepped from the bathroom, Neve had her head in her hands. He was by her side in a second, hovering his hand over her back, wanting to comfort her but not sure how far to go. A light pat would suffice.

"Are you all right?" Obviously she wasn't.

Neve shook her head as her flushed face appeared from behind her shaking hands. He draped an arm tentatively across her shoulders, maintaining a polite space between them. They stayed in the awkward embrace for several minutes.

When she cleared her throat and wriggled, he immediately slid to the opposite end of the couch.

"Neve, what's wrong? Is it Rowan?"

"Sort of ..."

Her silence made the thundering in his head louder. "Did something happen to Rowan?"

"He's all right, I think."

"How do you know Chelsea is still here?" He leant forward, urging her to respond.

"I tried to call her today, but no one answered. So I thought you were right, that she'd done a runner. Then I was working late and—"

He studied her face as she swallowed; puffy red-rimmed eyes and flushed cheeks highlighted a welt across the delicate skin.

"Chelsea's boyfriend paid me a visit."

Dave paid her a visit and ...

"Did he *hurt* you?" Micah got to his feet, fists clenched. He shouldn't have involved her in this.

Adrenaline hurled through his veins as Neve explained what had happened in front of the kindergarten, and what Dave had said about involving the cops.

"Jesus, Neve, I'm sorry."

This was getting out of hand. Only a bloody coward would hurt a woman. And if Dave could do that, then it wasn't much of a stretch to believe that he might hurt a child. This guy needed to be taught a lesson. Yes, that was exactly what Micah would do. He'd get Rowan the hell away from Dave, and he'd give Dave the opportunity to pick on someone his own size.

• • •

Neve stood as Micah shook his head and paced the room. She touched her still-stinging cheek, and a burning desire to rip Dave limb from limb heated her cheeks.

Micah's attention locked onto her face, and all of a sudden he stepped into her personal space. He traced a finger down the side of her face. "Did Dave do this?"

She nodded. The corners of Micah's eyes tightened.

"It's all right. At least we know they're nearby," she said.

The set of his jaw showed how *not* all right he thought it was, but he didn't comment. Instead, he took hold of her wrist and pulled her against his firm chest. She went rigid, but as she counted his heartbeats, she relaxed against him. There was a faint menthol scent on his freshly washed skin. The white singlet beneath her cheek revealed soft hair at the top of the scooped neckline and smooth, muscular arms. This hug could be hazardous.

Micah pulled back and frowned at her. "Why are you suddenly helping me?"

She shrugged. "Rowan shouldn't be anywhere near that bastard."

"Agreed. So what are we going to do about it?"

This was the moment of truth. Depending on what she said, she could lose her appointment at the kindy. It was her only way of interacting with children, and she needed that, seeing as caring for Tony didn't leave much time for a love life. Losing her job would be painful, but losing Rowan ... That was unbearable.

Whatever stories Chelsea had told, she couldn't be trusted. No innocent party sent a thug to rough someone up in a dark car park. Neve wouldn't be intimidated.

"I think we should call the cops and let them pay Chelsea a visit," she said.

Sandy Vaile

"I don't want to risk involving the police. Experience tells me Chelsea will run. Besides, I don't think this is her doing. We should talk to her face to face, before this goes any further."

"We? If you think I'm going anywhere near Dave again, you're mistaken."

Micah's shoulders drooped. "You're right. I'm sorry for getting you involved in this mess. You shouldn't have had to deal with him. How about you give me Chelsea's address and we go our separate ways?"

She held his stare. "I don't think that's a good idea. You're going to end up in jail, and I'll be sacked. Why didn't you just get a custody order in the first place?"

"I'm an idiot, okay? I honestly didn't think it would come to this. I've always taken care of my family. Chelsea had anything a woman could want, I thought. Anyway, it's a moot point."

She worried her bottom lip. What he was asking was too much, but Rowan needed her.

"For all her failings, Chelsea is a good person," Micah said. "But I've done everything I can to help her, and now I need to be in my son's life whether it's the best thing for her or not. I spoke to her again today, you know, and there's something strange going on. I think she's in trouble."

"Why would you think that?"

"We got cut off."

"You mean the phone cut out?"

"No, I could hear her arguing with someone—I'm assuming Dave—and then the line went dead. Damn it, this is all my fault. I should never have threatened to get full custody."

She raised a censured brow at him.

"I lost my temper." He shrugged.

"Well, you can't buy your way out of this mess. You and Chelsea are going to have to sort this out in court, for Rowan's benefit."

63

"I'm still not keen on dragging her through the courts. People usually do that for money, and I have plenty to take care of her. It would only create fodder for the gossip mags. Anyway, I'm convinced it's Dave putting ideas into her head."

"She'll call again."

"I can't just wait around and hope for the best anymore. Tell me where she is."

Neve shook her head. "The best course of action is to call the cops."

A red tide moved up Micah's throat and cheeks. "You can't expect me to do nothing."

"I understand your frustration—"

"How could you possibly understand? My child was stolen from me, and right now you're the only thing standing between me and him." Sweat beaded on his brow; his lips were set in a hard line.

Neve tensed and held his accusing glare. Perhaps appealing to his natural parental instincts would help. She watched closely for signs that Micah was going to lose his cool. His jaw was clenched, but then the fire in his eyes diminished by increments until his hands finally relaxed.

"If you weren't going to help me, then what was the point of coming?"

"I am helping you! I've given you information you didn't have and recommended you call the cops. If you go barging into Chelsea's house and back Dave into a corner, what do you think will happen to Rowan?"

"Neve." Micah reached to touch her arm. "It's not going to put Rowan in danger if we just drive past. Once we confirm they're still there, we'll call the police, okay?"

It seemed fair. Neve lifted her foot as a draft from under the door curled around her ankles. The chill went all the way up her spine. If she didn't help Micah, she was as good as handing Rowan to Dave.

She nodded.

"My car's out front." He pulled a shirt on and grabbed a leather jacket and car keys.

As Neve turned to follow, she saw the wall clock. "Shit, is that the time?" She pulled up her sleeve to double-check her watch. Tony would be worried. "Let me just make a phone call."

There were three messages on her mobile, and Tony picked up on the first ring.

"Where the hell are you? I was about to come and look for you."

That's all she needed, for Tony and Micah to come face to face. It was bad enough she was helping a poor little rich boy, without Tony knowing about it.

• • •

Neve's long braid swayed across her back as she turned away from Micah. It was a futile effort at privacy in the small cabin.

"Calm down, Tony," she said into the phone. "I'm sorry I didn't call earlier. I ... got carried away at work. I've decided to have dinner with a friend."

Micah watched her smile as she spoke, as though trying to make the perky tone convincing. Interesting that she wasn't telling this Tony guy the truth but obviously felt uncomfortable about doing it.

"I'm at Bron's house. Okay, love you."

Of course, Tony must be her boyfriend, or husband, although she didn't wear a ring. Micah had found her so appealing that he hadn't stopped to think. With those European looks and passion, obviously she wouldn't be single.

Once she finished the call, he held the cabin door open, but she wouldn't meet his curious gaze as she passed through.

A buoyant fog hung in the air, deadening the sound of their footsteps on the gravel. He hastened to open the passenger door for her.

Neve directed him along the winding country roads, and he maintained a tight grip on the steering wheel as he concentrated on the narrow ribbon of bitumen ahead. The glare from the headlights reflected from the dense mist, so he had to squint, and with no curbs or even lines marked, the going was slow.

With the windows up and the heater recirculating air, the atmosphere in the car became saturated with Neve's powerful scent, like eucalyptus leaves crushed between his hands, only sweeter. The internal space seemed to shrink, encased by fog. Micah cracked the window open.

He glanced at his companion's hands, balled on her lap. Maybe she wasn't as oblivious to the tension in the cab as her calm face suggested.

As they reached the top of the hill, the haze thinned. Micah made a sharp left onto Sugar Loaf Road, which curved and then straightened out.

"That's the house." Neve pointed.

The road was too narrow to park at the side, so he travelled a couple hundred metres to where the verge widened. He got out, but Neve remained in the car, so he walked around to the passenger side and opened her door.

"Are you coming?"

She chewed her bottom lip for a moment, then got out of the car and followed him down the hill. Out of the corner of his eye, he saw her shiver.

"Don't you have a jacket?"

"I didn't expect to be out so late." She rubbed her palms up and down her arms.

Micah took off his leather jacket and draped it over her shoulders.

"I don't need it," she insisted.

"I was too warm anyway," he lied.

As they stood at the top of Chelsea's driveway, Neve slid her arms into the sleeves and zipped the front. Micah pressed his lips together to hide a smile.

The glow from the distant city backlit a huge square beyond the trees, shrouded by wisps of suspended mist that threatened to clutch at their ankles and drag them into the gloom. He didn't state the obvious—there were no lights on and no cars in the driveway—but he refused to believe it meant no hope.

Chapter 10

Neve watched Micah rub his sternum. What was going through his mind? His son's disappearance, despising Neve for letting Chelsea get away, Dave's fist raised above Neve's face. A shiver twitched up her spine that had nothing to do with the cold night air. The welt on her cheek throbbed.

"I'm going to take a look," Micah said and headed down the driveway.

She leapt after him and tugged on the back of his shirt. "I don't like this," she whispered. "It's trespassing."

"You don't have to do anything you don't want to. Here." He pulled keys from his pocket and handed them to her. "Go back to the car. I promise I won't be long."

"I doubt Chelsea is hiding in a dark house, and you said we'd call the cops if we found anything."

He sighed. "We haven't found anything. Look, there's no way in hell I'm leaving without at least trying to get a clue to where she's gone." He continued towards the silhouetted residence.

Neve cursed under her breath. If he came across Dave, he'd need her help, and this time the thug would not get the drop on her.

Fog coiled at the base of native trees on either side of the driveway—the perfect hiding place for someone like Dave. She picked up the pace. As they got closer, double-tilt garage doors and a pillared portico materialised from the dark cube. Micah paused on the porch by a pair of potted money trees with elegantly plaited trunks. His shoulders were tense as he stared at Chelsea's house.

If anyone comes home, I'll just say I was worried about Rowan, so thought I'd look in on him. Yeah, right.

Micah took another step, and she held her breath. For a moment, it appeared he might climb the steps and ring the doorbell. He bent to check under the coir mat. Surely, he wouldn't break in, but who knew what he was capable of? The man was on edge. At least the neighbours were far away enough that they wouldn't see them around the house.

She crept onto the porch and touched his arm.

He swung around, an arm raised in a defensive stance. "Shit!" He let his arm drop. "What the hell are you doing sneaking up on me like that? I thought you were going back to the car."

She narrowed her eyes. "I didn't want you to do anything stupid. Well, more stupid. I'll help you look around outside, but I won't be a party to breaking and entering."

"It's not breaking and entering if you have a key. Anyway, there isn't one." He jumped down from the porch and peered through the front windows. Neve followed. What little of the dark interior she could see looked inhabited: furniture, potted plants, and a pair of slippers. They moved around to the back of the house and peered through the kitchen window.

Micah gasped. She followed his line of sight to a small pair of trousers hung over the back of a chair. His eyelids twitched, his nostrils flared, and he turned away, seemingly to admire the million-dollar view of suburban lights along the coast, except his stiff neck and the rapid rise and fall of his shoulders gave him away. This was a man in pain.

She stepped towards him, then stopped. It might be better to give him space; after all, *she'd* been the one to help Rowan slip through his fingers.

If only they knew for sure whether Chelsea and Rowan were still living in the house or had fled Turners Gully. Perhaps if she showed him that Chelsea's car wasn't there, Micah would be happy to leave. She glanced at Micah's back as she headed for the garage. It wasn't a drive-through, so there was just a wooden door set in the back wall. Her mouth was dry, palms slick, as she turned the handle. The door creaked open.

Micah turned. "How did you know?"

"A few months ago, Rowan left his favourite plush monkey at kindy, and I knew he wouldn't be able to sleep, so I offered to drop it to him. Chelsea said they were going out, but the door at the back of the garage was always unlocked."

Micah jogged over and stepped inside. "Damn it, no cars. I'm too late."

"Okay, so they're definitely not here. We should go."

Micah moved towards an internal door.

"Don't," she yelped. Hell, this wasn't what she signed up for when she knocked on his cabin door.

"Why would they leave the furniture, shoes, clothes? It's still early. They might have just gone out for dinner," he said.

"Let's get out of here before someone comes home," she pleaded.

Micah tried the handle.

"That's it. I'm out of here." Neve didn't wait to see if the door was locked. She ran around the house and up the long driveway, pushing through the burn in her thighs as she hiked up the incline. By the time she reached the car, she was gasping.

Her speedy retreat kind of lost its potency when she realised she'd have to wait for Micah or he'd be stranded there.

Tempting.

God only knew what he was doing in Chelsea's house, leaving fingerprints, breaking stuff. Dave could come home any second. Sweat prickled her forehead, so she opened the leather jacket to let some of the cold night air in and peered down the dark road in the direction she'd come.

Just when Neve had convinced herself it would be better to start walking back to Turners Gully, Micah's tall shadow appeared at the roadside. His hands were shoved deep into the pockets of his jeans, head bowed. He didn't look at her as he stood by the driver's door.

"You have the keys," he said flatly.

"Oh!" She searched the pocket of his jacket and tossed them over the car.

He pressed a button. Orange hazard lights flashed and the door locks clicked, but Micah continued to stand there.

"Okay, well, you seem to have this under control, so if you could take me back to my car ..." She opened the passenger door but hesitated.

Micah tilted his head to one side, his voice barely a murmur. "I am so far from having this situation under control that it's giving me an ulcer." A long, miserable sigh rushed from his lips, and he glanced over his shoulder, towards Chelsea's house.

"You're going to come back when I'm gone, aren't you?" In the dark, she caught the glint of his eyes but couldn't read his face.

"You really stuck your neck out for me tonight. Let me repay you by buying dinner." He glanced at his watch. "If we hurry, we'll make it before the pub stops serving."

"You know when the pub shuts?" She couldn't imagine him slumming it with the locals.

"I ate there last night. I'd like to hear your ideas about how to move forward with Chelsea."

"I don't think that's a good idea." Dinner with Richie Rich wasn't on the cards. She was already too involved in this mess. It was time to step aside and let Micah and Chelsea work it out between them.

His mobile phone rang. "Hang on a minute." He pressed it to his ear. "Kincaid."

Then he went very still. Alarmingly so. Neve walked around the car but couldn't hear the voice on the other end of the line.

"Yes, I understand. No, I won't. Yes. Of course I will. When?" He pressed the end button, but his mouth remained open.

When Neve couldn't stand the suspense any longer, she touched his arm. "Who was that?"

"Dave said that Chelsea will sign the divorce papers and hand over Rowan on Monday"—he turned expressionless eyes to her—"if I deposit two million dollars into a bank account of his choosing."

"Holy shit!" Bile rose in her throat. "They want you to *buy* him?"

It was unimaginable. Bloody Dave; she'd rip his arms off and beat him with them for thinking he could sell Rowan, but what she really wanted to ask was whether Micah would pay. Bron had said he was loaded, but two million dollars?

"Hey, do you think she knew we were at her house?" Maybe Chelsea had been hiding inside the whole time or had cameras set up. *Crap, now we're in trouble.*

Micah was unresponsive, his breathing shallow and a sheen of sweat coating his brow. Her work persona took over.

"Micah, you need to put your jacket on."

She took it off, and he was passively helpful as she slipped his arms into the sleeves and pulled it over his broad shoulders. At least her residual body heat would help warm him.

"Perhaps we should go back to your cabin so you can get warm?"

This time he turned to frown at her. "Huh?"

"You're cold, might be going into shock."

He shook his head. "I'm okay. Rowan is nearby."

"Yes, that's great, but I think you ought to sit down."

Obviously he was disturbed by the idea of having to come up with such a large sum of money, so there was no way she was letting him get behind the wheel. She snatched the keys from his hand and climbed into the driver's seat. She'd never driven a car with leather seats and a polished wood dash before. So this was how the other half lived. It took a couple of minutes to adjust the mirrors and the seat that was pushed back a mile. Apparently long enough for Micah to defrost.

"Where are you going?"

"I'm going to take you back to the cabin and make a cup of tea, and we can figure out what to do next." She turned on the heater.

"I need something a darn sight stronger than tea," he said. "Besides, I promised to buy you dinner."

"I don't need anyone to buy my dinner, but I am tired and hungry and could do with a stiff drink myself."

At least a little colour had returned to his face. With a flick of her wrist, she motioned for him to go around to the passenger side, and he didn't argue. She put the automatic into drive and cruised back over the hill to Turners Gully.

It was nearly eight thirty when they squeezed into the last available park in the dirt lot across the road from the Oak Hotel.

The old stone building sat well above street level, on the high side, with a second-storey perched on top and a side room that used to be the stables. She walked briskly beside Micah as they crossed the road and took the stairs to the alfresco area, where tables were nestled under broad Crown Beer umbrellas. She held her breath until they were through the cigarette smog.

He held the door open for her.

"G'day, Neve," the regular Friday waitress greeted them, and none too subtly checked out Micah.

Neve refrained from rolling her eyes. "Hi, Belinda."

"Wow, out on a week night."

"Very funny. We're just grabbing a quick drink."

Micah cleared his throat. "Actually, we were hoping to get a meal, but I think we're too late." He made a show of checking his watch.

Belinda looked like she might melt into a puddle on the floor from the voltage of his charm. "The kitchen hasn't served the last meals yet. Let me check for you." She adjusted her hair and trotted off.

"Oh, please," Neve mumbled.

Micah shrugged. "What? There's nothing wrong with asking. You don't get anything in life by sitting on the sidelines."

Belinda returned. "Chef said it's not a problem. I've got a nice quiet table in the back room."

Quiet table? "No, we—" Neve hurried after Belinda. That's how small-town rumours started.

The back room was built into the side of the hill, with a low ceiling and rough stone walls. Micah pulled Neve's chair out.

As Belinda bent to light the tea light candle on the table, she jiggled her eyebrows for only Neve to see.

"We're just friends," Neve whispered.

"Sure you are," Belinda whispered back. Then she winked and added at a normal volume, "Here are the menus, and the specials are on the board there. I'll give you a minute, Mr.—?"

Neve cut her off. "Thanks, we'll let you know when we're ready." No need for introductions. It's not like he'd be in town long. As soon as he bought what he wanted, he'd breeze on back to the rat race.

Micah raised an eyebrow in query. "I'll order us those drinks, shall I?' He didn't wait for an answer but strode across the room and leant against the bar like he owned the place. The countertop was made from a thick length of two-hundred-year-old red gum with bark still adhered at the edges. Strangely, Micah seemed as at home here as she imagined he would be in a boardroom.

While he studied the collection of Australian coasters above the bar, Neve studied him. Now that he was clean-shaven, to say he was good looking seemed like an understatement. His face was round and youthful, his body lean and powerful. Tight stonewashed denim clung to athletic legs and a firm butt. His hair looked carefully haphazard and was the same rich brown colour as the leather jacket.

Thirty-two years were enough to make her biological clock tick loudly, but it didn't mean she was desperate. She'd never wanted a man who could buy her the world. Only someone who would look at plain old Neve and see the world.

Old Tom—one of the regulars who was perched on a stool in the front bar—waved through the service window. Micah waved back.

How the hell do they know each other?

Micah returned with the drinks.

"I took you for a wine connoisseur." She tapped a nail on the side of the brandy balloon.

"I am, but with the week I've had, I thought we should skip straight to the hard stuff."

"You haven't seen the wine cellar. It's impressive."

"Maybe another night."

Not likely considering he could leave town at any minute.

"You know the locals?" She nodded in the direction of the front bar.

"I sure have chatted to quite a few in the past couple of days. They all seem to know you though."

"What? You've been asking about me?" Her hands snapped onto the tabletop.

He pushed a placating palm towards her. "Hang on a minute. I asked about Chelsea, but no one knew much about her. They did, however, say that if Rowan attended kindergarten, I should talk to you."

God, I'm such a dope.

Not that she cared what he thought, of course. She was strictly here to help Rowan.

Belinda arrived and pulled an order pad and pen from her back pocket. She fluttered her eyelashes at Micah and jotted down their orders.

What the heck was a small town kindy teacher supposed to talk to a zillionaire about? It's not like she knew jack about fancy cars or high maintenance wives. Really he didn't need her. He could pay a bunch of professionals to help him. Sure, he'd had her worried for a minute after Chelsea's phone call, but he looked calm and collected now. Awkward.

Stick to small talk. "So, do you have other family, besides Chelsea and Rowan?"

There was a slight twitch at the corners of his eyes, and he folded his arms. "Sure. A sister who's married with children, a brother who is a pilot and travels the world, and then there's Mum, who lives with me in Sydney."

"Doesn't living with your mum cramp your style?"

"I guess it should at my age, but we get along just fine."

"You didn't mention your dad. Is he still alive?"

"Not to me." His jaw tightened for a moment, and then he tilted his head from side to side and relaxed. "Thanks again for helping me." He cupped the brandy balloon between both hands and swirled the caramel-coloured liquid around the glass. "Tell me again why." He looked at her with such intensity that she couldn't turn away.

"Burnt sugar," she murmured.

"Burnt what?"

Crap, did I say that aloud? "Umm, you have the same coloured eyes as Rowan. That's how I knew you were his father."

His expression softened, and the longer he stared into Neve's eyes, the harder it was to breathe.

"You seem to genuinely care about Rowan. As though he's more than just one of your charges, I mean."

"He reminds me of my brother, that's all."

"Your brother's only four? He must've been quite a surprise for your parents."

"No." This wasn't something she wanted to get into with him.

"Oh, you meant Rowan reminds you of your brother when he used to be that age. Does he live in Turners Gully too?"

Well, he asked for it. At least once people knew the truth, they stopped with the questions.

"My brother and mother died twenty years ago in a car accident."

Chapter 11

Neve's eyes became expressionless, and her mouth hardened. Could he shove his foot any farther into his mouth? There were a million questions on his tongue, but she was clearly a private person, and he of all people should understand that, so he left them unspoken and sipped the cognac.

After a few minutes, he decided to break the silence with general chitchat. "So, how long have you worked at the kindergarten?"

"Six years, two as the director. I love it." Her eyes sparkled. "I'm so lucky to work there, and they're a great bunch of kids. I guess because we all live in the area, we're like one big happy family. Even my staff live locally and have worked there for years." She sipped her cognac. "Wow, that's good."

"It's extra old."

"And that's desirable?"

He chuckled. "Twenty years in an oak barrel is why it doesn't burn on the way down like the cheap rubbish."

"I wouldn't know. I'm not much of a drinker."

"Well, XO cognac would be enough to convert a nun. What made you want to work in preschool?"

"It's all I ever wanted after"—she averted her eyes—"Carlos died."

He'd done it again. This was the first time he'd really *talked* to her, and she was fascinating, but with his rampant foot in mouth disease, it might be safer to shut up.

Belinda delivered their meals, hovering just a moment too long. He flicked the serviette across his lap as Neve pushed a chip around her plate.

So, Rowan reminds her of her dead brother. What was he supposed to make of that? It still didn't exactly explain why she was helping. There was something she wasn't saying.

She glanced up and caught him staring. "So, what else did Dave say?"

Back to business then. "I told you everything. I guess he'll phone with the bank details and a hand over location."

Neve flinched. "And that's what you want?"

Her expression was unreadable.

"Honestly? I didn't want any of this. When I married Chelsea, I meant it to be for life. When we had a baby, I meant to care for him until my last breath. Things don't always turn out the way we want."

Her eyes softened. "No, they don't. Can you, umm, raise that kind of money?"

He tried to read any underlying intent in her words but failed. Still, he had had a lot of practice avoiding women who started with gentle queries about how much money he had and graduated to hints about the gifts he ought to buy them.

"I'll manage it."

Neve frowned. Disapproval or calculation, he couldn't tell. She opened her mouth and closed it again, drawing his attention to her lush lips—deep pink, even without a stitch of lipstick on them. He was so used to being surrounded by women to whom cosmetics were a second skin, it was refreshing to meet someone who felt confident enough not to want to cover up. She was a classic head-turning beauty.

Their gazes met and held, and a tiny muscle under her eye ticked.

"Just like that, you're going to hand over two million dollars?" she asked.

And back to the money. "I don't have a lot of choice."

He would give Chelsea twice that if it meant having Rowan back in his life, but that wasn't any of Miss Botticelli's business. He'd built his business so that he could provide for his family, although he'd never dreamt it would come to buying his own child.

"Well, I guess you don't need my help anymore—"

"Hang on. What do you mean? Of course I do. I need someone Rowan knows to be at the hand over, becau—" His mouth snapped shut; he twisted his fork into the last piece of broccoli.

"You're afraid he won't recognise you," she said gently.

Micah nodded, still staring at his plate.

When she reached across the table and picked up his Blackberry, he grabbed her wrist. That little device held more vital information than his laptop.

"I'll put my number into your contacts so you can let me know what the plan is after Chelsea phones tomorrow," she explained.

He nodded and released her.

She touched his grazed knuckles with one finger. "What did you hit?"

He moved his hand to his lap under the table. "It's just a scrape."

Neve's cheeks tinted pink as she tapped buttons on the Blackberry and put it back on the table.

"Do you really think Chelsea will hand Rowan over? She *is* his mother."

Micah closed his eyes. "She's never been much of a mother, but I have to believe she'll keep her word."

She crossed the cutlery on her plate. "It's getting late."

"Yes. I'll drive you back to your car." He waved Belinda over, and she placed a black folder on the table.

Neve grabbed it before he could blink, and scanned the docket.

"I said I'd buy you dinner for helping me," he reminded her.

"I'd feel better if I paid for my own meal."

"As you wish."

Neve fished in her purse for the correct money. Even someone who was as outraged at his wealth, as she seemed to be, would usually jump at the chance for someone else to buy their dinner. Not this independent dynamo.

Thanks to the low visibility, the drive back to his cabin was tedious, the streetscape haunting in the shroud of fog. When he cut the motor in front of Cabin 4, they sat listening to the tick of the cooling engine. The seat leather creaked as he turned to face her and found she was already studying him.

Her gaze travelled from his hair, across his face, and down to his lips, as intimately as the touch of a finger. It rested there, and he wanted to hold her, like he had in his cabin, to smell the honey scent in her hair, run his palms down the silky skin of her arms, and press against her warm body.

Not a good idea.

Think of something to say. Anything to keep her from going home.

Her lips parted, and he made a herculean effort to break the spell and get out of the car. She followed his lead.

"Thanks for having dinner with me," he said.

"Call me when Chelsea gets in touch."

She shivered.

"You're cold again." He took off his jacket and held it behind her. This time she hardly hesitated before shrugging into it. Neither did it escape his attention when she inhaled deeply.

"I'm curious," she said. "Where do you live? Is it a penthouse in the city or something?"

"Not a penthouse. I like a garden. I have a house in Sydney, on Victoria Street in Watsons Bay, actually." That would give her something to think about.

"Oh."

"This fog's thick. Will you be all right to drive? I mean, do you have far to go?"

Her eyes narrowed. "I'll be fine."

As guarded as ever. Micah watched Neve's station wagon coast down the hill and lost sight of it in the viscous haze. "Drive safely," he whispered.

There was something intriguing about the petite bombshell, but she was too secretive for his liking. People didn't do anything unless there was something in it for them, which begged the question: What did she hope to gain? He'd love to find out where Miss Secretive lived and what this Tony guy was like.

Don't be a fool. Look at the trouble you've had with the woman who promised to cherish you forever. The last thing you need is another one that can't be trusted.

All of a sudden, he scrambled for his mobile phone. His heart thundered as though something horrible had jumped from the moist foliage and said, "Boo." He scrolled through the phone contacts to N: Neve Botticelli. He let go the breath he'd been holding when he saw her number. For a moment there, he thought she'd played him.

• • •

His silk-lined jacket draped over her, Neve was enveloped in Micah's body heat and spicy cologne. She shivered again, but this time it was an unwelcome tingle of desire that coiled through her. This day was full of surprises. There was no denying he was handsome and he loved his son, but ... as tempting as the man might be, she hadn't missed the flash of gold on his finger. His wedding band was a glaring reminder to rein in her wayward thoughts.

Tony was standing on the verandah, strangling a beer stubby when she arrived at the house. She slipped off Micah's leather jacket and tossed it in the foot well of the car. Tony would hit the roof if he knew she'd spent the evening with a bloke. Not just any bloke either; the ninth richest in Australia. How had she gotten so far from her comfort zone in one short day?

"It's pretty late. I was worried," Tony said.

She kissed him on the cheek and went inside. "I called to tell you where I was, and it's not that late." She glanced at her watch. "It's ten forty. You should get a clock."

"Can't see the point in watching life tick by."

"You don't have to watch it, Tony. Clocks are handy."

"Don't need one."

Of course, he was right. It didn't matter what time of day or night it was, Tony could pick it within half an hour. Years of living a regimented life in the army, no doubt. She swapped her shoes for Ugg boots and heard Tony shuffle into the kitchen and fill his favourite yellow teapot. It had a hand-formed gum nut on the lid, and the handle was a branch. Clay gum leaves were pasted to the side. Neve had made it during art class when she was eleven years old, for Father's Day, and Tony insisted on glazing and firing it.

"The gas cooktop would be faster," Neve said.

"Doesn't taste the same."

It was rubbish, but she'd given up trying to win that argument long ago. Besides, he seemed a bit on edge, so she shouldn't goad him before bedtime. Not if she wanted to sleep through the night. She wrapped her arms around his waist and rested her head on his shoulder.

"I'm thirty-two years old and I'm home safe, Tony. I need to go out now and then."

He sighed. "Sorry, love. I worry, that's all. Did you have a nice time?"

"Yeah, they serve a mean schnitzel at the pub."

"Hey"—Tony brushed a fingertip across her cheekbone— "what happened here?"

Bugger, I forgot about that. "I walked into a low branch at the back of the kindy, that's all."

He frowned and studied her for a long moment, as though trying to use a Jedi mind trick to extract the truth. "How's Bronwyn?"

"Umm, she's good."

"Smells like she started wearing men's cologne."

Neve felt her cheeks heat, so she hurried to the pantry and fossicked for leaf tea, staying long enough for the blush to subside. Damn Tony for being so observant.

She still couldn't believe she'd acted like such a wuss and cowered in front of Dave. After all the training Tony had put her through over the years, she'd frozen at the first opportunity to put it into practice. Pathetic. Next time she would put up a fight.

Chapter 12

The sun hadn't long crested the eastern hills when Micah took a plastic key tag from a lanky hire car agent who reeked of smoke and whose yellow teeth were surrounded by a web of fine lines. The man's curious eyes moved from the gold Bentley in the driveway to the plain slate-coloured Corolla and back, but he didn't ask.

It didn't take Micah long to adjust the seat and mirrors to suit and meander down the hill to the Turners Gully General Store. The best part was, not a single person did a double-take when he climbed out of the little sedan. Exactly the effect he was hoping for.

He went inside and flashed a high wattage smile at the blonde behind the counter.

"Good morning, Beth."

She giggled. "Good morning, Mr. Kincaid. Coffee and croissant?"

"Thanks."

He'd bought the same breakfast three mornings in a row now, a tactic he'd employed in countless other towns around the country to get to know the locals. Sooner or later, someone would give up a useful piece of information. Why was it then, when he should be focused on finding Rowan, he couldn't stop thinking about Neve Botticelli?

The farrier he'd seen pumping fuel yesterday walked into the shop and nodded at him. What was his name? Micah pictured the battered ute and the sign on the side.

"Good morning, Matthew." His gift for putting names to faces had been a blessing in the business world. Everyone liked to be remembered.

Matthew nodded. "You're still in town then?"

"I liked it so much I decided to stay a few more days."

"You find Chelsea Matten?"

"I've spoken to her."

Matthew readjusted his family jewels and then reached for a carton of milk in the fridge.

"Here you go." Beth blushed as she handed Micah a warm ham-and-cheese croissant in a brown paper bag and a take-away coffee. "Have a nice day."

"Say, Beth, you don't happen to know Neve Botticelli, do you?"

"Of course. Everyone in Turners Gully knows her. Why?"

"I was just wondering if she lives far out of town."

"Oh, I couldn't tell you exactly. She keeps to herself."

Quite a feat in a small town. So much so that it pointed toward some considerable effort. Maybe enough to be suspicious.

"Yeah, because of Loony Tunes." Matthew sniggered behind a rotating rack of magazines.

"Loony Tunes?" Micah handed Beth a twenty-dollar bill and turned to face Matthew.

"That's who she lives with, Loony Tunes Tony."

"You shouldn't call him that, Matt." Beth frowned. "It's not nice. And Neve's a good person for taking care of him."

Micah wasn't following this conversation. "How so?"

"It's none of our business," Beth said. She handed Micah his change and turned to fill the pie warmer with pastries.

Matthew selected a farming magazine and plonked it on the counter with the milk. "A sheila like that shouldn't be stuck with a crazy old bloke is all I'm saying. I'll have a chocolate doughnut thanks, Beth." He turned to Micah. "It's like Tony's brainwashed her."

Beth swatted him with the magazine. "Don't be silly."

Micah opened his mouth to question him further, but a family bustled through the door and crowded the counter.

So, Neve's boyfriend, husband, whatever he was, was older and a few cents short of a dollar. Curious. Especially intriguing after the way she'd looked at *him* in the car last night. He was sure she felt the magnetism between them. The way her gaze had roamed across his face and alighted on his mouth. It had stirred all kinds of erotic ideas and taken a huge effort not to carry her into his cabin and kiss her senseless.

As if he needed any more complication in his life. Not to mention this was a woman who clearly hated everything he'd worked for. So why the hell was Neve Botticelli helping him?

Matthew waved on his way out of the store, and three children fought for space as they pointed at the lollies behind the glass-fronted counter. The noise was ear-shattering, and it looked like the family would keep Beth busy for a while, so Micah retreated to the hire car. Finding out about Neve's private life wasn't a priority.

He'd spent half an hour on the phone last night with his accountant, organising the money for Chelsea. You'd think the surly bastard was giving away his own money the way he'd carried on. But he couldn't make the transfer without the bank details. He checked his watch for the hundredth time that morning—only eight o'clock. *Come on Chelsea, just phone already.*

It wasn't fair for her not to trust him. *He'd* never betrayed anyone. And why he couldn't just deposit the money into her usual account was an anomaly he didn't like. After all, Dave had made the phone call, so it might be an account only he had access to.

How could their relationship have turned so sour? Four years ago, Micah had been nobody's fool, but despite Chelsea's polished exterior, there had always been something vulnerable in her eyes. He'd just never imagined the depth of her insecurities or the extent of her restlessness. Maybe, if he'd been home more instead of working, she wouldn't have gone looking elsewhere in the first place.

With the benefit of hindsight, it was easy to see that Chelsea had triggered his protective instincts. Once he knew about the abuse she'd suffered, it was impossible for him to walk away. After all, childhood deprivation was the one thing they had in common.

He checked his watch again. Bugger this waiting; he may as well do another drive-by of the McMansion. He pulled a U-turn and dawdled through the pretty township. The stone cottages nestled in the deep valley were interspersed with modern dwellings. He wouldn't mind visiting again when all this was over.

The dirt verge at the top of Sugar Loaf Road was still damp from the evening frost, and soil flicked from the tires into the wheel arches. He angled out of the car, dusted croissant flakes from his jeans, and strode down the hill. This time he didn't have the cover of night, but it didn't matter. He strolled down Chelsea's driveway like he owned the place.

Through the kitchen window he could see a glass wall clock with no numbers on it, just four black lines at the quarter marks— more embellishment than practicality. Typical of Chelsea; she was always worried about how she looked to other people. After a lap of the building proved that nothing had changed since last night, he paused to appreciate the view he was paying for.

A niggling concern wriggled sluggishly through his veins. Was it possible that Chelsea had only ever been interested in his money? That she picked *him* for that very reason? He'd never believed it ... until Dave demanded two million dollars. Of course, there was one thing Micah could offer that she might not find elsewhere, and that was simple unconditional acceptance.

On his way back to the car, he stopped to check the mailbox. A handful of junk mail, a letter to the householder, bingo! A letter addressed to David Wilks.

Back in the warmth of the car, Micah dialed his long-suffering PI. "Shannon, I've got something I'd like you to look into."

"I thought you were on your way home."

"Decided against it. I've been in touch with Chelsea, or rather she's been in touch with me."

"Wow."

"I know. Anyway, looks like she's still with the boyfriend and I have a surname. Could you look into David Wilks?"

"Do I want to know how you found his last name?"

"Probably not."

"Okay. I'll get back to you tomorrow."

Micah hunkered down and glared at Chelsea's house. This time he was going to find her. He could feel it in his bones.

• • •

As Neve drove home from the supermarket, she mentally counted backwards on the clock to figure out what time she needed to get the lamb shanks in the oven. It wasn't often she had an excuse to make a special meal, so she was going the whole hog tonight for Jack. The weather had turned out to be glorious and, although the sun was weak, it was toasty warm behind the windscreen. Hopefully, Micah had spent the night in his cosy cabin, and not prowling around Chelsea's house in the fog.

She'd given the situation a lot of thought in bed last night. Chelsea might be selfish and avaricious, but surely she wouldn't put her own son in danger. It was true the woman wasn't affectionate, but Rowan had always been clean, well fed, and happy. There'd never been any indication he'd been mistreated.

Perhaps if she dropped in on Chelsea, they could talk woman to woman about working this out with Micah. It couldn't hurt to try, and she had a couple of hours before dinner had to be in the oven.

Ten minutes later, she turned her car left onto Sugar Loaf Road and cruised slowly past a grey sedan parked at the side of the road. She passed it before her brain registered the figure entrenched in the front seat, and she stomped on the brake.

Hauling the car around, she parked behind Micah and their eyes met via his rear-view mirror. His expression tightened. When he didn't make a move to get out, she walked to the passenger side and got in. He didn't look at her, but there were purple shadows under his eyes.

"Don't tell me you've been here all night," she said.

He scowled. "And good afternoon to you too."

"Micah, what are you doing? You can't sit out front of her house twenty-four hours a day."

"I slept at the B and B last night, if you must know."

"Oh, good. So I take it Chelsea's not home?"

He shook his head.

Neve waited for him to elaborate, but he was silent. "I was expecting your call this morning."

"I didn't have anything new to tell you."

"She hasn't called? What do you think that means?"

"Who the hell knows, but the sooner I get the bank account number, the sooner she'll get her money," he said in a weary voice.

"So, you haven't got anything better to do than sit in your car and watch Chelsea's house until you pick up Rowan on Monday?" She was thinking aloud more than anything. If Dave came back to the house, Micah could be in trouble. Sure, Micah was muscular and confident, but Dave had the edge with raw crazy.

Micah stared out the window as though she hadn't spoken. His face was turned towards the window, and the reflection was of a tormented soul.

"Look, I'm busy tonight," she said, "but I'll make you a deal."

His attention snapped back to her.

"If you stay away from Chelsea's house, I'll hang out with you tomorrow."

"You'll hang out with me?" The corners of his mouth lifted minutely.

"Well, it looks like you've reached the bottom of your suitcase, so we could go over the hill and go shopping, seeing as you're going to be around for another couple of days. Do we have a deal?"

"Sure, why not?"

"So, you're going back to your cabin now?"

"Yeah, or the pub."

"Do *not* drink and drive," she warned. There was *nothing* she hated more than drunk drivers.

• • •

Micah stared after Neve's taillights. He *really* wanted to know where she lived, and it had crossed his mind that she might know more about where Chelsea and Rowan were hiding than she'd let on.

Don't be stupid. She wouldn't help you if she were working with Chelsea. Then again ... maybe she wasn't working with Chelsea exactly but wouldn't tell him if she'd had contact.

Information was power. It couldn't hurt to know more about Neve. He turned the key in the ignition and threw the Corolla into drive.

Chapter 13

Micah lost sight of Neve's station wagon on a crest and tapped the brake, searching the road. Nothing. His heart beat double-time. Then he sailed past a side road and caught a glimpse of the white vehicle.

He swung his car into a U-turn, ignoring the squeal of protesting rubber. There was a fork in the road and no sign of her down the long straight to the left. So he headed right.

This road was narrower with twists and turns and bushes crowding the bitumen. Then it turned to dirt. He eyed the ruts. This wasn't a road; it was a four-wheel-drive track. It'd be just his luck to get bogged so Neve would have to rescue him.

The car crawled forward, its underbelly scraping along the soil ridges, tires losing traction in the mud. Just as he considered giving up the tail, he rounded a clump of blackboy grasses and jammed his foot on the brake.

Neve was parked a hundred metres ahead and was out of her car. Thankfully, an overhang of melaleuca partly obscured his vehicle. He cut the engine and held his breath.

Play it cool. If she spots you, she's liable to throw you a beating, or at the very least a hand gesture and some colourful language.

She opened a metal gate, drove through, and then got out to shut it again. Once the station wagon disappeared into the scrub, he let go of the breath he'd been holding and looked around. Not enough room to get his car right off the track. There was, however, a dead end a short distance ahead, so he got as close to the vegetation as possible. Not much cover, but it would have to do.

After keeping watch for an hour, the sun was setting and he needed a leak. This must be Neve's home, but he couldn't see anything. He wasn't going to learn anything about Ms. Sneaky sitting in his car. So he got out and took a leak behind the nearest bush.

Standing on the track, apparently in the middle of nowhere, he felt exposed. Was he really going to trespass? That was the kind of thing creepy stalkers did, not respected businessmen. Then again, he'd strayed a long way off the path of what was expected of him, in his quest to recover Rowan.

There'd been a time when he'd deluded himself that he might even convince Chelsea to come back; his picture of the perfect family needed a mother and father. Now he doubted a perfect family even existed. All he wanted was to hold his child in his arms, to soothe him when he cried, and teach him about free electricity and sound investments. It was his right as a father, and Chelsea had stolen it from him.

Neve's part in this was still undefined, and the only way to know for sure was to follow her. He stood in front of the gate. No sign of a house through the dense trees. The surrounding area was quiet as he lifted the chain from its peg, stepped through, and resecured it.

Geez, you're really pushing it this time.

Needing information wasn't much of an excuse, and it was highly unlikely that Neve had Rowan secreted away. No, this expedition was more likely to be a case of curiosity killed the cat.

The dirt track of a driveway fell away from the peak of the hill and curved to the right. The eucalyptus trees on either side weren't dense, so he moved into them in an effort to keep out of sight, but the undergrowth was a tangle of fragile kindling that cracked underfoot. Why anyone would build a house so far from the road was a question he wanted answered.

When the track forked, he stood for a good five minutes considering the correct choice. Obviously, the best option was to go back the way he'd come and get the hell out of there. But he'd given up hoping for best options. He moved off to the right.

• • •

"Dinner's nearly ready, and Jack will be here any minute. Can you set the table?" Neve called.

Tony patted her shoulder and bent over the cast-iron pot to inhale the rich aroma. "That smells fabulous."

She drew in a big gulp of the flavoursome steam too, and saliva pooled in her mouth. Braised lamb shanks with her secret ingredients: balsamic vinegar and five-spice. The heavy iron lid settled into place with a clunk, and it took the two of them to lift the pot back into the oven.

The deep, melodic clang of cowbells sounded faintly.

Tony stilled with one hand on the cutlery drawer.

Neve tilted her head to the side and listened, then touched her dad's arm. "Jack?"

"He wouldn't stray from the track." Tony's dark eyes looked ominous.

Cowbells were attached to various traps he had set up around the property. His version of an intruder alarm. They occasionally caught animals.

The bells sounded again, and this time Tony didn't hesitate. He grabbed the hunting knife strapped under a dining room chair and ran for the door.

"Lock the door," he called over his shoulder.

Like hell she would.

Tony's paranoia meant he was always expecting a military invasion. More likely he'd trapped an animal and would put it out of its misery swiftly. It was the improbable scenario she was worried about. If Dave had found her ...

She slung a quiver of arrows over her shoulder, snatched the bow from its wall mount by the door, and raced after Tony.

It wasn't dark, but the sun had sunk behind the hill and long shadows blurred the edges of the scrub, making it appear more menacing than she knew it to be. She couldn't hear Tony's footsteps ahead, but knew she was going in the right direction when the bell clanged again.

Men were shouting, and through the trees she spotted Jack's ute.

"Step back, Tony," Jack yelled.

The men were a hundred metres away, crowding something that hung from a tree.

Tony yelled, "What the fuck are you doing on my property?" There was a thud and a grunt.

Jack moved between Tony and the thing. "I know who he is, now back off!"

Not an animal then. She knew Tony wouldn't let anyone hurt her, but Neve wasn't taking any chances with Dave on the loose. With a dozen metres to go, she reached over her shoulder, drew an arrow, and nocked it. The bow was taut and aimed at the writhing person, suspended upside down.

Her foot snapped a twig, and Tony whirled to face her, knife raised and a wild look in his eyes. It took a moment for recognition to halt his defensive, and he lowered the knife.

"Stay back, we've got ourselves an intruder," he commanded.

"Listen to Jack. He knows me!" another male voice croaked.

The back of Neve's neck prickled at the familiarity of the sound. She sidestepped Tony and gasped. Micah's feet were ensnared in a noose, his long body dangling above the ground. There was something very wrong about seeing this proud man incapacitated.

The whites of his eyes were bright in the fading light, and their gazes met.

Confident there was no danger, she relaxed the bowstring and dropped the arrow back into the quiver.

Tony's fist clenched and his arm tensed for another punch.

"Stop that!" Instinctively she positioned herself between Tony and Micah.

"This bastard is going to tell me what the hell he's doing sneaking around my property."

"Tony, stand down. He's not a threat," Neve yelled.

He frowned. "You know him?"

"Stand down." Neve snatched the blade from Tony's hand. "Geez, he's just a man, not the Vietcong! Give me a hand, will you, Jack?"

"Who the hell are you people?" Micah said.

She'd never intended for him to see the way she lived, but the time for secrecy was gone. Like her day needed more damage control.

• • •

Jack threaded his hands under Micah's arms, and Neve raised the knife.

Oh shit! Micah followed the rise of her arm and grimaced as the serration on the knife's blade glinted. She brought it down with one strong blow, and he closed his eyes.

A solid blow knocked the air from his lungs as he hit the ground. Jack's hold had cushioned him from the full force of the landing, but still every rib and muscle ached. The sweet tang of blood coated his tongue.

A thick rope lay slack at the base of the tree. There was nothing but concern on Neve's face. Of course, she'd cut him free. For a moment there, he'd thought …

His gaze flashed between the faces of his captors, ending with the crazy Italian they'd called Tony. So this was Neve's partner. The guy was thin and scruffy and much older than he'd expected, but boy could he hit.

Tony stepped forward, and Micah rolled out of Jack's grasp and clambered to his feet. A sudden wave of vertigo made him list to one side, and he dropped to his knees.

"It's all right, Micah. No one is going to hurt you anymore." Neve crouched beside him.

"That guy's a lunatic!"

"*That guy* is my father."

If it had been physically possible for a jaw to drop to the ground, Micah was sure his would have. Now he could see the family resemblance in the eyes and nose. That explained why she felt compelled to look after him, but it still didn't make sense. Neve seemed like a strong, independent woman. Why would she put up with such a violent arse?

One of her slender fingers traced his lip and came away bloody.

"Let's get you cleaned up," she said as she stood and flung the hunting knife towards a tree.

Micah followed its trajectory to where it quivered in the bark. Bloody hell, he was in way over his head with this lot of weekend warriors, vigilantes, or whatever the hell they were.

She offered him a hand, but he hesitated. Then Jack offered a hand too. Together they pulled him to his feet, and he shrugged off their offers to help him reach the nearby ute.

"I'll take him to the house," Jack said. "You'd better make sure Tony's okay."

Micah grunted. "Tony? I'm the one he just used as a punching bag."

Jack crossed his arms. "If I were you, I'd keep my mouth shut until asked a question."

Micah's gaze didn't leave Neve as she followed the crazy Italian into the bush. He wanted to tell her not to go, but his body felt rubbery, his mind hazy. Maybe he should go after her for protection. Then again, he'd just seen what she could do with a weapon. Perhaps she'd be okay after all.

After another minute of trying to spot her between the dark trees and a sigh from Jack, Micah climbed into the passenger seat. Jack started the engine, and they bumped along the track.

Within a minute, they stopped in front of a shanty and Jack got out of the car.

"What is this place?" Micah croaked.

"This is Neve and Tony's house. We're going to sit and have a nice, civilised chat about what you're doing here."

Micah shook his head.

"Don't worry, Tony won't hit you again ... unless he doesn't like your answers."

Jack opened the passenger door, giving Micah no choice. When Micah stepped down from the ute, the ground rolled and he held tightly to the door handle. Hanging upside down was overrated. Once he had control of the light-headedness, he shuffled forwards. Inside the house, he eased onto the couch.

"I suggest you think real hard about how you're going to explain yourself." Jack leant against the wall and stilled.

The way he surveyed his surroundings while standing watch gave the appearance of being relaxed, but his focus reminded Micah very much of the eagles he'd seen at the Silverton Wind Farm site. Ready to strike at a moment's notice.

Micah didn't have the energy to leave even if he wanted to. Tony had knocked the shit out of him; no wonder the locals called him Looney Tunes. He couldn't believe Neve lived with someone so unstable. And what was he supposed to tell the bastard? It wasn't like he had a good reason for being on the property. If they called the cops, he'd be locked up for sure and wouldn't have a hope of meeting Chelsea's deadline.

Then again, Tony seemed more like the kind of guy to beat someone to death rather than involve the authorities.

Chapter 14

Micah scanned the small living room. It wasn't a lot bigger than the caravan he'd lived in as a teenager. Three of the walls looked to be mud brick, with the back of the room solid rock, slick with moisture. Most likely the hillside, seeing as tufts of grass had taken root in crevices. Hell, this was more like a bunker than a house. Surely Neve didn't actually live here. A thin reed mat was tossed over the cement floor, and there was a line of shoes by the door, under weapons that hung on hooks. Raw wooden beams supported the low ceiling, and the faint smell of stale smoke emanated from the worn fabric of the couch.

The rich aroma of a mouth-watering stew drew his attention to a side room. Through a doorless opening, there was a small dining table and bunches of herbs were strung above the window.

Someone's boots stomped outside, and he held his breath. Jack tensed.

Neve entered first, her eyes wary. She touched Jack's arm. "Dad's okay."

Jack visibly relaxed. Bloody hell, they were all worried about Loony Tunes.

Tony loomed in the doorway, a murderous glare locked on Micah.

"How about you put the kettle on, Tony?" Neve suggested. "Let me see to Micah's wounds before we talk."

"Good idea," Jack added.

Tony shut the front door. "I'm *not* leaving you alone with him."

"*I'm* not going to hurt her," Micah growled.

Neve sighed. "*Nobody's* going to hurt me. Make the tea, Tony." She disappeared into another room, but Micah kept his gaze on Tony, and the old man reflected mistrust right back at him.

He saw movement from the corner of his eye, but it was still a shock when something warm touched his forehead, and he grabbed it. A warm flannel dangled from a delicate hand, and his gaze travelled up to Neve's raised eyebrows. He immediately let go, but Tony was already in his face, his bony fingers like a vice around Micah's throat, lip curled, teeth clenched. Micah tried to knock the resolute hands away.

Neve barely moved, but the side of her hand connected with Tony's windpipe. There was a grunt, and he stumbled back, gasping. Micah rubbed his throat too.

"Keep your hands off him, Tony, or we're going to have a serious problem," Neve said.

A peculiar emotion flashed across her father's face, very close to betrayal. The old man took a couple of steps back, and Micah let out a tense breath.

Neve sat on the couch again with a tube of cream on her lap and held up the damp flannel. "I need to wipe your face, okay?"

He nodded. As she wiped the rough cloth across his skin, her face was so close he felt himself falling into her dark irises, down the straight line of her nose, and over the gentle curve of her lips. Her hair was different too. Tight spirals frizzed around her face, and it made her look carefree.

Not once did she meet his probing gaze, but when she leant forward to dab the cream on his top lip, she held her breath. Despite the dangerous fire in Tony's glare, Micah was surprisingly calm, and he had no doubt it was due to the composure that radiated from Neve. No wonder she was so good with children.

"Okay." She straightened. "Let's have that cup of tea, shall we?" She hustled Tony and Jack into the kitchen.

Micah crossed his arms and stayed on the couch. He wasn't keen on having the shit beaten out of him again, but he still didn't have any good answers for their questions.

"You too," Neve called over her shoulder.

He made his way into the tiny kitchen on dragging feet. Neve pointed to the dining table, where Tony and Jack sat on the far side. Micah pulled a chair a metre from it—well out of Tony's reach—and sat down. Tony looked menacing, but Micah glared right back. His eyes stung from staring by the time Neve placed four steaming mugs and a carton of milk on the table, breaking the spell.

She took the last seat. "So, what are you doing here, Micah?"

There was a guarded look in her eyes, and he felt guilty for putting it there. He sipped the tea, stalling. "I wanted to know where you lived. I'm sorry. I should have stopped at the gate."

"You think?" Tony's chair hit the cement floor with a crack. Jack was quick to grab his arm.

"*Sit down*, Tony," Neve snapped.

"I don't know why you're treating this bastard with kid gloves," Tony growled. "He just admitted to stalking you."

"This is Micah, the guy I was telling you about."

"Rich bastard. More reason to teach him a lesson."

"What is it with you nuts and money?" Micah slapped his hand flat on the table and leant forward. A challenge.

Jack intervened. "That's not important. What we want to know is why you were snooping around after our girl. For God's sake, sit down, Tony!"

Tony righted his chair and sat back down.

Neve turned her attention to Micah again. "Why did you feel compelled to know where I live?"

He shrugged.

"You don't think I have Rowan, do you?" She sounded appalled.

He lowered his gaze.

"I can't believe you think I'm in cahoots with Chelsea and Dave, after ..."

Micah sagged against the chair. "I— I don't know what I was thinking. Bloody hell, I guess I wasn't thinking at all."

"That's a crap explanation," Tony grumbled.

"Micah has been under a lot of stress." Neve placed a hand over Micah's on the table and looked him in the eye. "Although that doesn't give you the right to waltz in here uninvited, I promise that I don't know where Rowan is, but I'm going to help you find him."

He nodded. It was obvious now that this wasn't the kind of place Chelsea would hide out. Neve really was helping him. The back of his eyes stung at the idea of her generosity, and he blinked hard. Still, he didn't understand why, and that made him nervous.

Glancing at Tony was a mistake. His murderous glare was locked on Neve and Micah's joined hands, so Micah extracted his and wrapped it around his tea mug.

"What were you going to do once you found Neve?" Jack asked.

Eyes down, Micah told the truth. "I just wanted to see her."

Out of the corner of his eye, he saw Tony's hands clench and figured he'd be getting round two of his beating any minute now.

"Let me show this guy the door," Tony said.

Neve stood and placed a hand on her father's shoulder. "Nobody's going anywhere just yet. Have you eaten today, Micah?"

His stomach grumbled as he thought back. "A croissant and coffee at the general store this morning."

"Well, dinner's ready. You may as well stay and we can all get to know one another a little better. Tony, you can mash the potatoes."

Tony huffed and went to the stove to help Neve lift a cast-iron pot. A swirling cloud of meat-moistened steam whooshed out when she lifted the lid.

"That's a wood oven." Micah stated the obvious, and everyone ignored him.

"That smells fabulous." Jack rubbed his belly. "Hey, you won't believe what was on the news this morning. There have been another two cars stolen this side of the hill."

"What's so unusual about that?" Micah asked.

Neve turned from the stove. "That makes half a dozen in the past month, and not one has turned up again. What does that mean?"

"Nothing good," said Jack. "If it was kids taking them for a joyride, I'd expect the cops to find them burnt out. This is different. Organised maybe."

After an awkward and mostly silent meal, the atmosphere in the Botticellis' kitchen was wound tighter than a steer in a rodeo holding pen. So no one disagreed when Jack swirled crusty bread across his plate to mop up the last of the casserole juices, licked his fingers, downed the last of his cabernet sauvignon, and announced that he would see Micah back to the bed-and-breakfast. It was a better outcome to the evening than Micah had guessed would play out.

At the front gate, Jack turned to him. "Son, I hope this goes without saying, but don't come back here. You're damned lucky I found you before Tony did."

Micah grunted. "His fists made it loud and clear. Anyway, I'm sorry. I hope I haven't made things, umm ... difficult for Neve."

"What do you mean?"

"Well, I don't know what kind of hold Tony has over her, but I'm worried he might hurt her."

"Are you now?" Jack's eyebrows lifted. "Look, I know what they call Tony around here, but he's not as bad as he seems. A little paranoid maybe—"

"Understatement of the year."

"—but Neve is safe with him."

"Does he have a mental problem or something?"

The gnarled old bloke sighed. "He suffers from post-traumatic stress disorder and likes to keep to himself. There's nothing wrong with that, until some nosey bastard oversteps the line."

"Yeah." Micah averted his eyes. "Isn't PTSD something soldiers get?"

"Exactly. Tony did three tours in Vietnam. The last one really messed him up, and after ... some personal losses, he just couldn't get his shit together. Neve's good for him."

Sure, the death of Neve's mother and brother was a huge loss, but she hadn't turned out like Tony. "But is Tony good for her?"

"I guess I hadn't thought about it like that, but yes, I think he is. They are the only family they have left."

"And Neve is his caregiver," Micah murmured.

"Neve is a loving daughter." Jack chewed his lip like he was searching for the right words. "Most of us don't get to choose the path our lives take."

"Most of us, meaning unlike me."

Jack shrugged.

"You don't know shit about me, Jack."

"I'll give you that. So how about you get to know Neve away from her home for a while? Neither of them need the aggravation you caused tonight."

Micah brushed imaginary fluff from his thigh. "Sure."

"And you're going straight to the Travaglias' B and B and staying there for the rest of the night, aren't you?"

"Yes." He sighed and then got out to open the gate before driving off in his rental car.

Jack tailed him in the ute, all the way to the bed-and-breakfast. If Jack and Neve had let Tony rip Micah to pieces, he would have deserved it. Neve might be relentlessly kind, but why would she want to go out of her way to help him, especially seeing as she and her father clearly had a problem with his wealth? Nobody did anything for nothing. Rowan looking like her brother just didn't seem like enough.

There must be something he was missing, and he'd best be alert for it.

• • •

Once Neve said good night to Tony and was finally alone in her library, she booted up her laptop and typed "Micah Kincaid" into the Google search bar. There were many pages with articles about the sale of his luxury yacht, his influence over the CFS Retail Trust, reports about his stocks and shares, a *Forbes* profile, and an article he'd written with recommendations for small businesses to survive the current economy.

She clicked on a *Wikipedia* page link. It was weird that he was only thirty-five years old. Hardly older than her, and yet he'd achieved so much. What drove a man to work that hard? Could just be luck, or maybe he'd been born with a silver spoon in his mouth. At the top of the page was a photo with a debonair Micah in a tailored suit, followed by his net worth of $2.4 billion.

It took her a while to digest that and move on.

There was precious little about his childhood, although the word *underprivileged* was used, so it didn't appear that he was born into money. Interesting. And then there was quite a bit about his talent for saving ailing businesses. Phrases like *environmental advocate* and *devoted family man* were used to describe him. He'd even been awarded a Medal of the Order of Australia for his work with homeless people.

Hell, he's practically a saint. A very rich saint who I've agreed to join in human procurement.

After scrolling through several more pages, a YouTube link caught her eye. It was an interview on *A Current Affair*, and Neve found herself riveted to the screen as his resonant voice spoke with passion about renewable energy resources. His eyes never left hers. Micah Kincaid was charismatic in the extreme. No wonder he'd done so well in the public arena.

He seemed different face to face though. The confidence was there, but he was more down to earth than she would expect from someone who lived his life in the media spotlight. She'd seen the Louis Vuitton and Bentley, but there was a chance he didn't live the high life all the time, right?

She typed Victoria Street, where Micah said he lived, into Google Maps. Using the earth view, she navigated along the coast and snooped at some of the houses. *Holy shit.* The properties were big, with pools and jetties, flanked by a sandy beach.

The life he inhabited was light-years from her own.

Next, she searched real estate in that suburb and nearly choked. The first property looked like a dive and read "offers invited over $1.8 million." When she found a property for sale on Victoria Street, she slapped the laptop shut.

Hell. No wonder two million bucks doesn't faze him.

She'd experienced firsthand just how far wealthy people would go to get what they wanted. Well, she wasn't going to be collateral damage this time. Rowan was the one she was here to help, and she'd keep her eyes wide open for Micah's deception.

Chapter 15

Neve swung the skipping rope, the balls of her feet hitting the concrete with a rhythmic scuff that she paced her breathing to.

Micah had sent her a text message earlier:

We still on 4 shopping?

It could be perceived as ballsy or just plain stupid of him to want to see her after everything that had happened yesterday. Then again, the guy really did need clothes and it didn't have to be more complicated than that. No doubt he was only thinking about how he needed her to be there for the hand over with Rowan and wanted to keep on her good side. Either way, it would be nice to hang out with him away from all the drama in Turners Gully.

"I'm pretty sure that rope isn't going to give you any more trouble."

Neve missed the next jump and her feet tangled. "You gave me a heart attack, Jack."

He tossed her a face towel to rub over her brow and neck. "Didn't expect to see you today."

"I need to work off some frustration after last night." Wasn't that an understatement.

"Anything you want to talk about?" he asked.

She shook her head, and he turned to leave.

"Wait! Tell me honestly, what do you think of Micah? I know he made a serious mistake yesterday, but do you think he can be trusted? I've said I'll help him, but ..." Her chest heaved as she tried to catch her breath.

Jack raised his eyebrows. "Are you asking for my permission to see this guy?"

"No, of course not. I'm just helping him get his son back. It seems like he's had a raw deal with Chelsea running him around. Besides, he's married."

"Look, honey, I think it's great that you're helping him. You're an intelligent woman who can make her own decisions, not to mention you could probably knock him on his arse if push came to shove." He draped an arm around her still heaving shoulders. "Don't let Tony's overreaction stop you from doing what you feel is right. Do you want to do a couple of rounds in the boxing ring?"

"Actually, I have a few errands to do at the shops this morning." She hoped the flush of exertion would hide the guilt on her cheeks. "Do you mind if I use your shower?"

"Not at all, love."

• • •

She felt calmer after a workout and hot shower. She'd thrown a silk blouse and slacks on instead of her usual jeans and tee, and rummaged in her handbag for perfume. A swipe of pink gloss across her lips and mascara along the tips of her lashes. Done.

Down the hill, the local Country Fire Service station sounded its test siren, as it did at ten o' clock every Sunday morning. The familiar sound reminded her she was part of a community, something that was easy to forget if she spent too much time isolated with Tony. Her stomach did a little flip at the thought of seeing Micah again; must be all the drama of last night.

She was almost to her car when she heard Jack's boots on the gravel.

"Looking fancy for a shopping expedition," he commented from behind.

Her heart leapt into her throat. "I'm going to Marion, so I don't want to look like a dag."

"Okay, have fun."

She waved and slid into the car. It was just her luck to have two of the keenest military-trained men in the country looking out for her. How was a gal supposed to get away with anything sneaky? It was no wonder her teenage years were so sheltered.

Today of all days, Bron had invited Neve to hike in the Onkaparinga Gorge, so she'd told her that Tony needed her at home. Neve had *never* lied to Bron before Micah came into her life, and didn't like what it said about her involvement with him, but a promise was a promise. She couldn't tell Bron about what was going on, especially if it might put her friend in danger from Dave.

That's why she'd told Micah to meet her at the kindy. The deviousness of it all was burning its way up her esophagus.

It was right on ten thirty when she pulled into the kindy car park and found Micah leaning against his hire car.

He slid into her passenger seat. "Are you sure you still want to do this? You don't have to, after ..."

"I'm afraid of the trouble you'll get into if I don't keep an eye on you." Her lips twisted into a smirk.

They stared at one another for a few seconds, and he nodded. He had a cut over one eyebrow, another on his lip, and a broken capillary in one eye. No doubt Tony had left other bruises she couldn't see. Even though Micah had done the wrong thing by trespassing, he hadn't deserved the full force of Tony's wrath. She put the car into reverse.

It was a gauche journey over the hills and down to the Marion shopping complex. Neve rarely went there—she hated the harried people vying for parking spaces and shouldering her in the mall.

Inside, the shopping centre was a blaze of lights, colour, buzzing noise, and cloying perfumes. The sensations brought on a heart-racing instant of anxiety. Perhaps Tony was rubbing off on her after all. A few deep breaths and she had it under control.

Micah frowned. "You all right? I thought women liked shopping."

"I'd rather poke a hot skewer in my eye, but you need clothes."

She weaved through the leisurely shoppers and into the first men's store they came to. It wasn't until she had a couple of T-shirts in hand that she stopped.

"Sorry, I'm used to shopping for Tony. I know they're not Louis Vuitton."

"Isn't there somewhere that isn't a chain store? Armani, Ralph Lauren, Thomas Pink?"

"I suppose David Jones department store might have something."

Before long, he was armed with jeans and shirts that were worth more than Neve's weekly wage.

"How about you select some polos while I try these on?" Micah said.

What did she look like, a personal shopper? It wasn't like she knew anything about designer labels, other than they were a waste of money, so she stuck to the brands he seemed to like. Arms loaded, she faced three floor-to-ceiling change room doors. All occupied.

"Micah?" she called.

"I'm in here." A door cracked open and then swung wider.

She handed over the garments, cheeks flaming as her unwieldy gaze dropped from his face and snatched a brief but noteworthy appraisal of a snug white tank top and sleek, freckled shoulders. The same warm tingle she'd experienced Friday night went up her spine. There was no need for clothes when you looked that good in underwear.

She spun around, headed for the safety of the mall, and landed on a vacant bench seat. It provided a tiny life raft in the middle of the chaos. With her eyes closed, she tuned out the chaos and centred herself. All of this was so far from her norm. She didn't do frivolous shopping. It would have been better if she really had spent the day with Tony and made sure he was okay. He hadn't slept a wink last night, after having his peace of mind destroyed by Micah.

Instead, she was shopping.

"I thought you'd ditched me."

Her eyes snapped in the direction of his voice. "Coulda, shoulda, woulda, but you know where I live now."

His smile vanished, and he turned to study the nearest shop window.

"I was just kidding. You got them to cut the tags off then?"

He was wearing new, black denim jeans and a snug, long-sleeved grey T-shirt.

"You approve?"

"Nice." Her eyes lingered on his chest again.

The rush of pleasure on his face was unexpected and unwelcome, but she wasn't the only one ogling him. A huddle of teenage girls scrutinised him in unabashed detail.

One stepped forward. "Excuse me, are you Micah Kincaid?"

He straightened and a warm smile lit his face. He looked confident and approachable. The perfect public persona.

"Yes, ladies. How can I help you?"

The girls erupted into a fit of giggles, grabbing one another's arms and flashing goofy smiles. "I told you," one whispered. "*People* magazine's Sexiest Man Alive."

Neve nearly choked.

The original spokeswoman spoke up again. "Like *wow*. What are you doing here?"

"Unfortunately, I really have to get going, ladies, but it was lovely to make your acquaintance."

"Hey, that's not your wife," another girl said as she eyed Neve.

"No, just a business colleague." Micah didn't bat an eyelid as he told the fib.

Oh well, it wasn't Neve's place to contradict him in front of his fans. Worshiping the rich and famous was a sport for some; it just wasn't one that she was interested in. Money and good looks made him exceptional, not necessarily worthy.

"Can we grab a pic?" another young fan asked.

Phones were already being focused on Micah, and his awkward grimace didn't deter them in the least. Next, the girls took turns huddling up next to him while their friends took more photos.

When Micah started backing away and saying good-bye, Neve wordlessly followed him along the mall. The giggling behind them faded, and Micah moaned.

"I'm sorry about that," he said.

"You don't like having your photo taken?"

"It'll be on social media within minutes."

There was a pink tint to his throat that she didn't understand. "I guess that kind of thing happens to you every other day in Sydney."

"I guess, but it doesn't mean I enjoy it."

Neve chewed her lip. "Don't you like being the owner of a successful business? I mean, you built it from the ground up, you should be proud of that."

He missed a step and frowned. "I had hoped to keep it low key around here, you know, while I'm dealing with all this stuff with Chelsea. How did you know I built my company?"

"Google."

"Well, I guess you know *all* about me now." His mouth pinched tight.

No doubt he lived with daily invasions to his privacy.

"I don't think for a minute that I know the real you."

"I would have answered any questions you had."

"I'm sorry."

He sighed. "I *am* proud of what I've built, but being in the spotlight is just a necessity I've adjusted to."

She nodded. Something to ponder as they continued along the mall.

Micah tapped her arm and pointed to a women's clothing shop. "Do you want to buy anything while we're here? My treat, seeing as you drove."

She grimaced at the crop tops, hipster pants, and strappy dresses clinging to bony manikins in the window. "I don't need you to buy me clothes, and I don't spend money unless I really need something."

It didn't matter how appealing Mr. Kincaid was; she wasn't for sale. She was helping him because Rowan needed her.

• • •

The venom in Neve's voice was the same as when she and Tony had commented about people with money. To her, money obviously equated to immorality. It was such bullshit, and he'd ask her about it soon, just not in the middle of a shopping mall where an argument was likely to end up on social media.

"I'm well aware that you don't spend money on yourself, and apparently you aren't in the habit of accepting gifts. I assume you do have to eat though, so where should we have lunch?"

Her lip pursed.

"How about Thai?" he said.

"Really? That's my favourite too. The Casuarina restaurant is just around the corner."

"Neve!"

Micah looked up to see a middle-aged blonde woman waving. Neve shot forward and embraced her. Behind them, two children broke from their father's handhold and rushed to hug Neve's legs.

She stooped to their level and gave them a couple of minutes of undivided attention, listening intently to their stories about ice creams with funny faces and new toys. Speaking of which, he needed to buy a truck for Rowan.

"She's wonderful with children, isn't she?" the blonde woman said. "I'm Mary, and this is my husband, Ron."

Micah shook their hands. "Nice to meet you. I'm Micah."

He returned his attention to the children. They seemed to accept Neve as one of them, and it was no wonder. Who wouldn't want the tenderness in her eyes directed at them? What he wouldn't give for his son to have a mother like that.

Neve straightened. "Did you introduce yourselves?"

"Sure did," Mary said.

Micah might have imagined it, but he thought Mary raised one eyebrow at Neve and flicked her eyes in his direction. No doubt the rumour mill in Turners Gully had been turning overtime with an outsider like him in town.

"We had a brilliant time in Port Broughton," Mary said.

"And I found a huge jellyfish," the young girl announced.

"Okay, you can tell Neve all about your holiday at kindy on Tuesday. We need to get a present for Uncle Nick's birthday."

They said warm good-byes, and Neve led the way to the restaurant. The waitress seated them in a quiet corner and took their orders.

"I want to buy a present for Rowan, and he likes trucks," Micah said. "Could you help me pick one out after lunch?"

"Sure. I know exactly what he likes."

"Yes, I guess you know a lot more about him than I do now."

"I didn't mean ..."

"Don't worry about it. I'm glad he's had someone like you in his life. I can't wait to hear him chatter about all the things he's been doing."

"He certainly is a special little boy." She smiled.

It was obvious she meant it. Rowan was special to her. More so than the other students, but why? It couldn't be just a physical likeness to prompt her to get involved in the shit storm that was Micah's private life. He wanted to trust her enough to rely on her, but he just couldn't. Trusting people only gave them the opportunity to deceive you, so he needed to figure this out.

"Neve, I wanted to ask you about your brother. You said Rowan reminds you of him." He left the query hanging, hoping she'd let him into her private thoughts. But the longer she pushed a straw around the rim of her glass of orange juice, the less likely he thought an answer was.

"I don't like to talk about it, but I guess you have a right to know." A muscle in her jaw twitched. "Some rich bitch was coming home from a Melbourne Cup lunch after too many champers and ploughed through a stop sign. T-boned Mum's car and sent it through a fence and into a dam. I survived, they drowned. Carlos was nine."

He laid his hand over her cold one on the table. "I'm sorry. That must've been really traumatic. How old were you?"

"Twelve. That's why I had to live with Tony."

At least now he knew how entrenched her hatred of wealth was. He'd never stood a chance. It also explained why she was both trapped by and needed Tony. The reference to a "rich bitch" still didn't quite make sense though. "So you don't like people with money because one killed your mum and brother?"

Her lips and brows scrunched into an unwelcome scowl. "Of course I hate the person who killed my family, but not just because of what she did that day. She never showed any remorse."

"But what's that got to do with her being rich?"

"Rich people think they can do whatever they want." Her hand curled tightly around her glass of juice. "And they're right. The rules of society don't apply to them. With enough money, they can get away with anything."

"Now hang on. It's not fair to generalise about the morals of everyone with money."

"All she cared about was keeping herself out of jail."

He could see the intensity of prejudice in her frigid eyes, born of years of believing her own propaganda, but it didn't give her the right to tar him with the same brush.

"That may be so for the woman who killed your brother, but saying everyone with money is the same is about as mature as me saying I hate kindergarten teachers because they're wannabe school teachers. One person does not represent a whole group."

Crimson blotches appeared on her cheeks, and the drinking straw between her fingers bent.

He plowed on. "In fact, I would go so far as to say that you don't hate money so much as you're jealous that you don't have it."

"That's bullshit and you know it," Neve said through clenched teeth.

She was on the edge of her seat, no doubt ready to bolt any second.

"You're prejudiced. I get that, but think about it in logical terms for a minute. *One* woman used her money for the wrong thing. No one else with money has actually done anything bad to you, have they?"

She scowled. "I won't let that happen."

"But apparently one person is enough to damn me. You know, I haven't done anything to deserve this animosity."

"No well ... I'm entitled to my opinion." Without another word, Neve was on her feet and headed for the mall.

Chapter 16

Neve wasn't used to playing chauffer—seeing as Tony rarely left the property—and Micah had been taciturn since their tense lunchtime conversation. She glanced sideways at him, unsure if she was pissed off that she'd been stupid enough to tell a virtual stranger her family secret or because he'd turned it around and made it about him. Either way, it was good they'd be going their separate ways once she dropped him off.

Of course, now that she'd had time to calm down and think, all kinds of witty retorts came to her. Micah had caused her trouble. He'd gotten her involved in this mess with Chelsea and Dave, and he'd caused Tony all sorts of anguish after following her home. Then again, he did a lot of good things with his money too.

His mobile phone buzzed regularly, but this time he stiffened as he read the message. After jamming it back into his pocket, he scowled out the window.

"Bad news?" she queried.

"No. Bank details from Chelsea." With a small turn of his face away from her, the subject was closed.

She swung her station wagon into the kindy car park and jammed on the brakes.

"Where's your car?"

"What the ..." Micah leapt from the car and ran to the footbridge, turning circles as he searched for a vehicle that clearly wasn't there.

"Did you organise for the hire company to pick it up?" Hopeful at best.

"Bloody hell, that's all I need." He kept the string of expletives low as he walked away from her and pulled out his mobile phone.

Neve sat in her car with the door open while Micah paced with the phone pressed to one ear and his other arm gesticulating irately. She pitied the poor person on the other end. It took at least fifteen minutes before he tucked the phone back into his pocket and came to stand in front of her.

"I'll have to go to the police station to report it stolen. Should I order a cab?" He gave her a resigned look.

It would make her look like a total bitch if she didn't drive him, but face it, being involved in *one* of his problems was enough. Setting foot inside a police station wasn't her idea of a pleasant end to the day. She didn't have a problem with him involving the police per se, so long as she didn't have to get up close and personal with any of them.

Micah threw his arms open to hurry her response. She couldn't leave him stranded.

"I'll drive you," she said.

"I appreciate it. There isn't a lot going right for me this week."

Micah got back into the car, his hands stiff in his lap as they headed back over the hills and onto the plains.

"You know, you said you'd answer any questions I had," Neve said.

"Mmm."

"Google also said that you did it tough as a teenager. How so?"

He crossed his arms, and there was a long silence. "It's not the kind of story people want to hear about a successful business man. Besides, I try to keep my private life private."

So that's where they stood. A professional relationship. "But I want to understand what drives you."

He sighed. "I told you my father left Mum bereft. Well I had a lucky break while I was working on a mine site and got to learn all about running a business from a pro. Two years later, I bought my first business and turned a profit. I wanted to make sure that no one ever took everything away from me again, and fortunately it turned out I had a talent for turning ailing companies around.

"Before long, I owned a bunch of companies. Money breeds money." He twitched one corner of his mouth as though in apology. "A few years later, I heard that my father's business had fallen on hard times, so I bought it and sold off the assets until there was nothing left, but I couldn't bring myself to put all of those people out of work, so I redeployed them to my other businesses. Every last one, except my father."

Vengeful Micah wasn't something she could picture. "Remind me not to get on your bad side." It was meant to be a joke, but the mood remained grave.

"Are you sure this is the closest police station?" he said. "It seems a hell of a long way."

It wasn't far enough in her opinion.

"Turners Gully used to have its own, but it closed along with most of the rural stations, years ago." She turned left at the traffic lights and into a small car park. "Here we are."

She rolled her shoulders. Geez, Tony's Big Brother paranoia must've rubbed off on her more than she realised. Micah was old enough to go in without her anyway.

He slid out of the car and waited.

Neve cracked her window down. "You go in. I'll be fine here."

He frowned. "You're not coming in? It's hot in the car."

Yes it was. "I'm not a puppy," she grumbled, but there wasn't any good reason for her not to go in, despite racking her brain for one. *It's just a police station. They help people all the time. Nothing to worry about.*

After a deep breath, she got out of the car and led the way along a cement path, past boxy windows and a curve of cubed glass that towered the full height of the building.

"What's that?" Micah pointed to an expanse of white netting over the roof.

"To keep the pigeons off," she explained.

The two-storey red-brick building wasn't anything impressive, or even appealing, but it was certainly free of bird poo. She rolled onto her toes and came to an abrupt halt with her nose millimetres from the automatic doors. Slowly, they slid aside.

An air-conditioned breeze blasted against her bare arm, raising goose bumps, but it was ineffectual farther inside the glass lobby, where it was equivalent to a hothouse. She felt like fruit poaching in a preserving jar, which wasn't helped by the nervous sweat that had broken on her brow. An ingrained paranoia of authority was impossible to ignore.

"You all right?" Micah squeezed her elbow. "You look pale."

"I think I'll wait over here while you make the report." She wandered over to the black plastic chairs pressed against the outside wall and perched on the edge of one. Ten minutes tops before either the moulded plastic felt about as comfortable as stone or she sweated enough to slide right off it.

Micah stood in line behind a guy wearing grey tracksuit pants with holes in the knees, a stretched yellow T-shirt, and thongs— the cheap rubber kind. Neve smirked when she saw Micah sniff and take a step backwards.

A young woman taking her turn at the counter blew a pink bubble and pulled down the back of a barely there dress. The gum snapped back into her mouth as the officer behind the counter typed. There were three service windows, but only one officer.

She leant back and rested her head against the warm wall.

Five minutes later, the bubble woman bounced out the door and tracksuit guy shuffled forwards. The officer gave him the once-over and asked a question that was swallowed by the design of the service window. Micah turned and grimaced in a show of apology for the wait.

Neve's gaze darted from each watchful black sphere on the ceiling, to the serving officer, to the Authorised Access Only sign on a side door. There was definitely someone watching her every move. An unseen breeze scurried across her skin, and she went to stand by the automatic doors to catch the chilled stream from the air-conditioner. She lifted the hair at the nape of her neck and let the breeze tickle the dampness beneath.

Micah checked his watch and shifted his weight.

There was no telling how long this could take, and every moment spent in the police station increased Neve's chances of being strip-searched or something equally unpleasant. Okay, that was unlikely, but she could self-combust from the stress and heat.

When the automatic doors slid apart and another victim stepped inside, Neve rushed towards freedom. Micah was on his own.

• • •

Half an hour later, Micah found Neve sitting against the wall of the police station, in the shade of a wattle tree. Thanks to her head tilted back and eyes closed, he could study the long curve of her exposed throat, the serenity on her face. Something flipped in his stomach. *No, she is only helping me because she feels compelled to.* It had everything to do with Rowan and nothing to do with him.

"Neve, are you okay?"

She opened one eye, and he held out a hand to haul her to her feet.

"Fine. I'm just not keen on police stations. How'd it go?"

"Nothing out of the ordinary. An officer lodged a report and seems to think the car will turn up soon enough. Probably some teenagers took it for a joyride. The hire company will deal with it now."

Neve dusted the back of her slacks. "Are you going to get a replacement car?"

"Seems pointless. The Bentley is still sitting at the bed-and-breakfast if I need it. Tomorrow Chelsea will get her money and I'll get Rowan."

There would be no further reason for him to remain in Turners Gully, but never seeing the feisty Neve Botticelli again wasn't a pleasant idea.

The journey back to the bed-and-breakfast was undertaken in silence. The atmosphere between them hadn't been right since he'd stupidly taken the bait about why she hated rich people. After everything she'd done for him, he could at least cheer her up. He wanted to; he just wasn't sure how.

When Neve parked behind Micah's Bentley, he turned and laid a hand on her forearm. "I know this whole situation is making things difficult for you, and I don't want to come between you and your family or friends. You don't have to come tomorrow."

"I told you I'd come to the hand over and I will."

"Look, it's only three thirty. I *could* still get into mischief," he said playfully.

She shrugged. "I'm sure you'll manage."

"Come on, I owe you a drink after driving me all over the place today. I have a nice local wine inside. Have a glass with me."

For a long minute, she considered him, and then her stiff demeanour relaxed a little, and she nodded. If they were going to work together to get Rowan back, then they needed to keep things friendly. But once he shared the latest information he'd had from Shannon, Neve might change her mind about her involvement.

• • •

Micah paused with the wine bottle tilted over her empty glass. "One more? I'd like to tell you what my PI found out about Chelsea's boyfriend."

"You have a private investigator?"

He shrugged. Buttercup-yellow chardonnay splashed into the goblet, and the sweet, fruity smell was divine. He handed her a glass and poured another for himself. They had been chatting for the past hour, and it was amazing how much they had in common, like an interest in sustainable living and eighties music.

It had been a good opportunity to study her: the way she twirled a stray hair curl around her finger when she was thinking or slipped off her shoes as she relaxed in his company. The worry lines on her forehead had smoothed, and his gaze couldn't help but follow the smooth skin down her throat and over her slender figure. A little of the pink lip gloss she'd brushed on after lunch still glistened, making her lips luscious and inviting.

She leant forward, cut a wedge of camembert, and layered it on a water wafer with quince paste. Her eyes snapped up, as though she felt him watching. The resultant blush was inexplicably satisfying.

"Shall I pick you up in the morning?" she asked.

Micah helped himself to the crumbly cheddar and a handful of red grapes. "I'll meet you at the kindergarten around eleven thirty. My PI dug up some interesting stuff on Chelsea's boyfriend. It seems Dave Wilks hangs out with some very bad people. He has a police record showing low-level crime like burglary and car theft, but recently he's also been linked to the Mutts bikie gang."

Neve nearly choked.

"You've heard of the Mutts, I take it?"

She dusted biscuit crumbs from her lap. "Hasn't everyone? They're into all sorts of illegal stuff. In fact, Jack thinks he's seen them going past his place recently. And you think Dave is hooked up with them?"

"It seems that way. Not the kind of guy I want around my son."

"Hell no." She was on her feet and pacing, shaking her arms out like a boxer waiting for the bell.

"I'm sure it will be all right," he fibbed. "Despite Dave's previous convictions, he's just a mechanic. My PI hasn't linked him to any drugs."

"Maybe he's into something more sinister and just hasn't been caught yet. You know, if Dave's in the area, it stands to reason the Mutts might have a clubhouse nearby. That's a horrible thought." She shivered.

"Not the sort of place you want in your neighbourhood." He stood, reached for her, but let his hand drop. Perhaps he should have kept the information to himself. It wasn't fair to make her worry on his behalf. "Anyway, my guy's going to keep digging. I didn't think there was any point in him flying over, considering this whole mess should be done with after Chelsea hands over Rowan tomorrow."

"You mean *your* mess will be over. If a gang of bikers are in Turners Gully, *our* mess is just beginning."

On her next pass, he grabbed her elbow. "Neve, even after I have Rowan, I'll do anything I can to help ... this community."

She looked at his hand and back to his eyes. He should let go. He would, any second now. A syrupy warmth radiated from her, drew him closer. A minuscule, uncertain flicker between her brows drew his attention to dark eyes.

"I promise to keep you safe," he whispered.

Her magnetic gaze dropped to his lips. No, he couldn't kiss her. It would screw up the plans they'd made and complicate an already tentative truce. Not to mention feed unwanted daydreams.

The pink tip of Neve's tongue trailed over her lower lip, and every logical thought fled from his mind.

Chapter 17

Neve tensed as Micah lowered his head a fraction. How could she so desperately desire a man who stood for everything she detested?

He paused, asking, their breaths colliding in a fiery stream, and she reached to brush her lips lightly across the warm silk of his. It was just the lightest brush of his lips across hers, but it was enough to set her on fire. His wine-fruity tongue darted out, and solid arms drew her closer. Time slowed as warmth wrapped around her and she kneaded sturdy flesh. She couldn't help but slide her hands around to the back of his neck and curl her fingers into his thick hair.

This was where she wanted to be.

There was a knock on the cabin door, and Neve leapt out of his scorching embrace. His hand reached across the space between them, but there was another knock and he let it drop.

"Who is it?" he called.

"It's Bronwyn Travaglia. My family is having a lamb roast for dinner and thought you might like to join us."

Crap! Bronwyn thought Neve was spending the day with Tony. It didn't relieve the guilt at all pretending it was a kindy matter. Well, Rowan was one of her students, but the tingle on her lips exposed the lie. Neve touched a finger to her mouth. Micah was a muddle of contradictions, and it was messing with her head.

"Sorry, I'm in the middle of something. Thanks for the offer," Micah said.

Neve swallowed the lump in her throat. Tony was mad at her, and now she'd lied to her best friend. This mess just got worse by the minute. Neve stared at the carpet, but Micah's warmth was close by.

"Um, I'm sorry about that," he said. "I shouldn't have ..."

What the—? "Oh what, so kissing the kindy teacher wasn't part of your grand plan?"

"Neve, don't be mad. It's just that, well, my priority needs to be bringing Rowan home."

What a prat. He couldn't backpedal any faster if he were rolling down a hill. Message received loud and clear. No matter the attraction between them, he belonged to someone else, and that wasn't any place she was willing to go anyway.

"I'd better head home," she said.

He walked silently beside her. At the car, she thought he was going to open the door, but he paused with a hand on the handle. Then he pulled a wallet from his back pocket.

"I'd like to at least give you some petrol money for today."

"I don't *want* your money."

He dragged his fingers through his hair.

"You know, I don't use my money to get my own way. I'm not like that."

"Did you forget I'm only here because you're buying a child for two million dollars?"

With a rush he was in her face, pinning her against the car with a hand on either side, his eyes narrowed. "I'm not buying any old child. I'm giving my wife what she wants so I can have *my child* in *my care*. It's not the same thing."

"Isn't it?" She ground her teeth.

Woah, he was so close that her body wanted him to close the distance and lean against her. No, it wasn't right or sensible to trust him. Least of all with something as precious as her heart.

He'd buy his kid tomorrow, and she'd never see him again. There was nothing in a place like Turners Gully for a man like this.

"Besides, the key word here is *wife*, isn't it?" she added.

The disgust in his eyes scalded her. Abruptly he growled and stormed to the cabin steps. With his back to her, he took a series of quick breaths.

"You of all people should know things aren't always as they seem," he said. After a few moments, his shoulders relaxed and his balled fists slackened. "You can't blame me for something that happened to you twenty years ago, but it doesn't matter, because after tomorrow, you won't need to see me again."

He strode inside, and she heard him slide the chain on the door.

Chapter 18

There were no kindy sessions on Mondays, but Neve often helped with playgroup in the morning. For the past two hours, she'd been glancing out the window every few minutes. There was still no sign of Micah.

Maybe he didn't want her help after their little tiff last night. Hell, with his resources he might have just decided to pay someone else to do the dirty work. No, that wasn't fair. It was obvious he cared about Rowan, and Chelsea, too, for that matter. He was either still madly in love with her or just plain crazy, and Neve wasn't sure which scenario appealed the least.

Then again, he might have gotten into a sticky situation last night. What if he'd gone looking for Chelsea on his own and found Dave? Various bad scenarios piled up like a clique of darts congregating around a bullseye. It was all she could do to stop herself from phoning him.

At eleven fifteen, all the kindy mums hustled out the door, and shortly after that, Neve said good-bye to the playgroup coordinator. As she shut down her computer, movement on the footbridge caught her eye. Micah strolled from beneath the willow trees and looked straight through the window at her. In the throng of playgroup traffic, she hadn't noticed the Bentley parked in the shadows.

Her stomach flipped with a strange mix of anticipation and anxiety. What a silly reaction. They'd only shared one kiss. It didn't mean anything, and it wasn't like she coveted a rich man. Sure, she was lonely sometimes, and he was ridiculously handsome, but it was a conscious choice to stay single. It made her life with Tony simpler. Besides, Micah wasn't any different from any other bloke, other than those delicious eyes and spicy scent, and then there was the passion and chivalry.

Okay, he might be a notch or two above anyone she'd ever kissed, but he still put his trousers on one leg at a time. Bugger, thinking about him without trousers was not an image she wanted when she was trying to keep her distance.

The front door opened before she got there, and Micah was backlit in the frame. His broad shoulders tapered to narrow hips and long legs, presenting a commanding presence that sent a shiver up her spine. He shifted a gift-wrapped box under his arm. The tipper truck they'd bought at the shopping centre.

Head bowed and voice low, he said, "I'm going to get Rowan now."

"Do you still want my help?"

His shoulders rose and fell. "I'll manage on my own if I need to. I always do."

Being given a way out should make her grateful, but she *needed* to know Rowan was all right, and if her presence would make him less scared, she had to go. Besides, Micah might be acting unruffled, but no doubt he was nervous as hell about the hand over.

"But you don't have to go alone. I said I would come."

Micah peeked from under those long lashes, with a miserable expression. "I'm sorry I involved you in this, but once I have Rowan, I promise I won't bother you again."

Neve shut her eyes tight. He was making a break, as she knew he would once he had what he came for. It wasn't a surprise, and she sure as hell wasn't going to let him know how much it hurt to hear it.

With no more than a nod, Micah turned and headed for the car. Wow, the Kincaid charm had completely vanished. She grabbed her handbag, locked the kindy door, and hurried after him. When he reached the back of his car, his shoulders shrugged up and down with a sigh, and he made his way to the passenger side and opened the door for her.

"Thanks."

They drove through several rural townships, turned left at the Meadows service station, headed towards Echunga, and that's when she got impatient.

"Okay, where are we meeting Chelsea?"

"An obelisk on the corner of Stock Road at Mylor."

"That's nearly to Stirling. Why so far away?"

"No idea. I'm past the point of asking questions."

"Maybe she's staying in Mylor."

Micah grunted. "Maybe she wanted to send me on a wild-goose chase so I won't know where she is staying."

Inside the township of Mylor, they passed a Care for Our Wildlife sign and slowed to fifty kilometres per hour. There was a Country Fire Service station perched on a rise, a row of early twentieth-century homes with picket fences, and a fodder shop. The front page of the newspaper was propped in a wire cage against a tree, and a tripod blackboard indicated the lunch specials at the general store.

Micah slowed as they approached a school crossing, and then pulled onto the grassy verge. Across the road was the obelisk. Neve scanned the intersection and squinted at the dense foliage along the creek.

Nothing.

When he got out of the car, so did she.

"What time are they supposed to be here?" she asked.

He glanced at his watch. "Twelve. We're five minutes early."

There was a constant stream of traffic passing on the main road and a tennis club two hundred metres away. Not a spot she'd choose for a secret rendezvous. Then again, perhaps Dave thought a public place provided Micah with less opportunity to deceive them.

The monument stood in the centre of a circular, paved area, bordered by squared-off hedges in brick garden beds. She wandered over to it and read the inscription: "Lest we forget 1914 – 1919. In memory of our boys who fell in the Great War." There was a list of names—local lads who'd given their all for their country. An Australian flag flapped above.

She wandered along the creek, searching the dappled shadows for hidden figures. With Dave involved, she didn't want to be caught by surprise again. Honeyeaters flitted through grevillea bushes, raising a cacophony of excited chirps as they feasted on the spidery blooms. It was a couple of minutes past twelve when she sat on a park bench in the sun to wait.

"Something's not right," Micah said.

"Give them a few minutes."

He stood with a rigid back, shifting his weight from foot to foot, looking ready to bolt at any moment. He didn't deserve to be tortured like this. Even a strong business tycoon needed someone to lean on every now and then. She swallowed her animosity and went to him, laced her fingers with his. Even with her gaze resolutely ahead, his head turn and searching eyes were palpable. A few minutes later, the tension drained from his arm.

He jerked when his mobile phone rang. "Kincaid."

Neve leant closer but couldn't hear the person on the other end.

"Where are you?" he barked.

She tapped Micah on the shoulder and mouthed, "Put it on speaker."

He nodded and pressed the button. Chelsea's familiar, whiny voice was loud and clear.

"I can't bring Rowan to you anymore."

"You bitch! I've transferred the money, now give me my son." The usual warmth in his eyes warped into something hard and wild. Neve backed up a step as a flush of rage raced across his skin.

"I can't," Chelsea whimpered.

"You mean you *won't*."

"I'm sorry, Mikey, I was going to hand him over today, honest I was." She sounded distressed.

"Where the hell is my son?" he yelled, pacing. "That's it, I'm involving the police."

There was the sound of a scuffle. A slap.

"Don't, Boiler," Chelsea cried.

A steely voice growled down the line, "I wouldn't do that if I were you, Kincaid."

It didn't sound like Dave. Neve and Micah exchanged a look.

"Who is this?" Micah asked.

"What's really important is that your wife and son are staying with me until I get what I want."

The underlying menace in Boiler's words sunk in slowly, and hairs prickled along Neve's arms. She gulped in oxygen, but it wasn't enough to stop her head spinning. Micah fumbled the phone but caught it before it hit the ground.

"Are you still there?" Boiler asked.

Micah grimaced. "What do you want?"

"Anyone can Google what you're worth, and I got to thinking Chelsea is aiming way too low. What's the point in asking a multi-billionaire for a couple of mill? You probably throw that kind of cash across the craps table in the casino. So, I want you to transfer ten million dollars into an offshore account. My very creative accountant here has set it up already."

"That's ridiculous. I can't get my hands on that much."

"Shut up," Boiler yelled. "I'm not asking."

"You idiot, my net worth is made up of assets and equities, not cash flow."

"Just get it done."

"I'm going to hunt you down like the cockroach you are and kill you with my bare hands if you hurt Chelsea or Rowan," Micah snarled.

The answering laugh from the other end of the line was chilling.

"What do you think I'm going to do if you don't pay up, Kincaid? Knock the little wife around a bit? Let the boys take turns with her?"

Neve laid a hand on Micah's arm as he turned beetroot red.

"If you don't come through, you'll need an excavator to dig them up. In fact, if you make me wait too long or even *think* about calling the cops, I might just send them to you in little pieces. Do we understand each other?"

Micah nodded, so Neve jabbed his shoulder.

"We understand each other," he said.

"Now, have you got a pen to write down the bank account number?"

While Micah patted his pockets, Neve produced a pen and pocket diary from her handbag and held them at the ready.

"Go ahead," Micah said.

Neve scrawled the number as nausea slithered through her belly. "What about Rowan?" she mouthed to Micah.

"I need to know Rowan's all right."

"I thought you might say that." Boiler's voice sounded far away as he called, "Get the kid."

Shallow breathing came down the line. "Um."

"Rowan, is that you?" Micah asked.

"Hello?"

The tiny voice reached into Neve's chest and twisted her heart inside out. Micah swayed beside her, and she reached out a hand to steady him.

"Rowan, it's Daddy. Are you all right? Are you hurt?"

"No."

"You're not all right?"

His hand squeezed the phone so tightly it creaked.

"I'm okay, but I don't really like it here. Mummy's acting funny—"

"That's enough." Boiler came back on the line. "I'll call you again tomorrow, when you have a better idea of how long it's going to take to make the transfer, but I wouldn't take too long." The phone went dead.

Micah threw his mobile, and it skimmed across the dirt like a pebble skipping waves at the beach, leaving a trail of sandy debris in its wake. He punched the nearest tree and let fly a string of curses as he shook his bloodied hand. Then he lurched, braced both hands on his knees, and vomited.

Neve clapped a hand over her mouth. The amount of money Boiler wanted was unthinkable. She couldn't even imagine ten million dollars, let alone one man being able to access all of it.

Rowan was going to die.

Chapter 19

With eyes focused on an imagined destination where his wife and child were being held hostage by vicious bikers, Micah dragged in a shuddering breath. What the hell was he going to do?

A light pressure on his shoulder radiated warmth across his back like a balm. Neve's hand. He looked down at her furrowed brow.

She took his face in both of her hands. "Micah, we'll get him back."

He gave a desultory nod, and bent to pick up the shattered remains of his mobile phone. The fury that had ravaged him moments ago had dissipated into numb disbelief.

Purpose flickered in Neve's eyes. "We need to talk to Jack before we do anything else."

He needed to be doing something. In the business world, he didn't trust his competition to play fair, and he wouldn't expect Boiler to keep his part in their deal. Micah's family was far too precious not to utilise every resource available to him, and if that meant Jack, then so be it. He headed for the car with long strides and was in the driver's seat turning over the engine when Neve hammered on the bonnet.

"You aren't in any fit state to drive safely, so get out."

"I don't have time for this." He glared at her.

"Getting Rowan home safely means keeping you safe too."

After a tense battle of glares, he cuffed the steering wheel, got out and jogged around to the passenger side.

It was an agonisingly slow journey as Neve stuck to the speed limit. Playing on repeat was the sound of the slap on Chelsea's cheek, her scream, Rowan's tiny voice, "I don't really like it here ..." He had to get them away from the Mutts, no matter the cost.

"They're holding Chelsea against her will." Micah's voice was raspy. "They don't trust her. What does that mean?"

"It means she's expendable," Neve said flatly.

"Bloody hell, I don't need to hear that right now." Once Boiler had the money, Rowan would be expendable too. *Crap, it's not her fault. She was only speaking the truth.* "Shit! Chelsea, you've really fucked up this time."

He reached across the console and placed a hand over Neve's. Instead of snatching it back, as he'd expected, she threaded her fingers between his.

Jack appeared in the doorway of the shed as they alighted from the Bentley.

"What are you doing here in the middle of the day?" he said.

Neve ushered Jack inside. "Something's happened and we need your help."

"Okaaay." He sounded cautious.

"Rowan's mother was supposed to hand him over to Micah today, but when she phoned, another man came on the line and said he's holding Rowan and Chelsea until Micah pays ten million dollars."

The gravity of the situation hung in the air like a noxious smell.

Jack rubbed the back of his neck. "I don't know which I believe less, that someone is being held hostage in Turners Gully or that anyone actually has that kind of money." He eyed Micah.

"That's the problem," Micah said. "I can't get my hands on it in any hurry. I need to find Rowan and get him out of there. You don't know what kind of people we're dealing with."

"And you do?" Jack's eyes narrowed.

"My PI found out that Chelsea's boyfriend is involved in the Mutts bikie gang."

"Shit! And you got Neve involved in this?" Jack stepped towards Micah, fists clenched.

Micah braced but held his ground.

Neve pushed between them. "Look, you two, we need to work *together* and work fast, so let's cut the macho bullshit." They both looked at her and nodded.

"The guy on the phone, Boiler, is probably in the gang too," Micah said. "I'll get my PI to look into it."

"They want money," Neve added, "and they're smart enough to know what Micah's worth, but too stupid to know they've asked for an impossible amount."

He tilted his head to one side. "Stupid, yes. Not impossible."

Her eyes bugged out. He crossed his arms and glared. It didn't matter that his money was the only thing keeping Rowan alive right now, she'd still hold it against him.

"You're telling me you *can* get ten million dollars?" Jack asked.

"If it means keeping Rowan safe, then I'll find a way. I have my own very creative accountant, but it might take a while."

There was silence for a few minutes, aside from a pounding in his head at the idea of what might happen if his accountant didn't come through.

"Well, it's obvious what we need to do," Jack said. "Go to the police."

"No!" Micah balked. "Boiler said we shouldn't do that. It's not worth endangering Rowan or Chelsea."

"Look, I don't know that I agree—"

"No police. Good God, he said he'd send them to me in pieces!"

Jack nodded. "I see your point. Okay, I have a buddy in the military who owes me a favour. If we could narrow the vicinity where they're holding Rowan, he might be able to use satellites to pinpoint the exact location. Even give us a picture of how many people come and go from the property. Then we'd be in a better position to make a decision."

"We could extract him." Neve's eyes widened, as though she was as surprised at the idea as the rest of them.

"What? No way." Jack put both hands on Neve's shoulders and looked into her eyes. "Right now, that would be more dangerous than sending the police in."

"I say we do what Boiler told us to do," Micah said.

Neve shook her head. "Look, we're getting ahead of ourselves. First Jack's guy and your PI should get as much information as they can about the Mutts and where they might be holed up. Micah, you need to find out how long it's going to take to get the money."

He nodded, pulled his mobile phone out of his pocket, and grimaced at the wreckage. Neve handed over hers.

"I guess I'd better order a new phone while I'm at it." Already dialling, he headed outside.

It was simple to organise the phone, but the accountant was more difficult to convince. He was about to head back inside when he dialled one more number.

"Shannon, I need you to get as much information about Dave and Chelsea's vehicles as you can, and look into someone called Boiler who might be a member of the Mutts motorcycle gang. And can you look into Neve and Antonio Botticelli, and Jack Burton for me?"

"Am I looking for anything specific?"

"Just a general background check, thanks."

Ten minutes later, he strode back into Jack's Shed. "It will take too long to sell any major assets, so my accountant is going to cash in stocks and shares, empty bank accounts. It's going to be a stretch, because I don't want to lay off any staff, but he's optimistic about pulling the funds together inside five days."

Jack hummed. "That's too long in a situation like this."

"I know, but it's the best I can do. Neve, you should pack a bag and get the hell out of here. I don't want you in any more danger."

"Ha! Why would Boiler even think I was involved? You're easier to find than me."

"I agree with Micah," Jack said.

"Shit." Neve paced. "If he finds Micah at the bed-and-breakfast, then the Travaglias could be in danger too. You should stay at my house."

"What?" Jack and Micah snapped in unison.

With hands waving in front of his chest, Micah backed away. "Are you nuts? Your dad said he'd cut my balls off if I set foot on his property again."

"That's not a good idea, love." Jack took her hand. "There's no way Tony would agree to it, and it would upset him no end. Micah can stay with me."

Neve took a deep breath. "It's like explaining things to four-year-olds. If Dave is involved with the Mutts and you've seen them driving past the shed, Jack, then the chances of them seeing Micah coming and going is too high. He'll stay at my place. I'll deal with Tony."

She stood with hands on hips, lips pursed, daring them to defy her.

"Great, I'll sleep with one eye open," Micah grumbled.

Chapter 20

After Micah took Neve to the kindy to pick up her car, they'd made a detour to the bed-and-breakfast to pick up his laptop and suitcase. It was surreal to lead the way along the rugged track that was her driveway, with Micah following behind in his car.

Breaking the news to Tony was going to be a challenge. No one else had ever stayed in their home, and he didn't take well to changes in his routine. Hell, she hadn't been thinking straight when she invited Micah to stay, but it was too late for backsies. It really made a statement about how desperate Micah was that he went along with it. After all, Tony *did* threaten his nuts.

She glanced in the rearview mirror. *I never thought I'd see the day when there was a Bentley at home.*

She got out of the car and signaled for Micah to wind down his window. "Stay here until I give the all clear. Got it?"

"Don't worry, I'm in no hurry to come inside."

"Chicken." A playful grin twisted her mouth.

Tony stepped onto the front verandah with a smile on his face, and then spotted Micah. He grabbed a broom that was leaning against the house and rushed forward.

Oh shit. She intercepted him with metres to spare and put both hands on his chest.

"What's that fucker doing here?"

"Stop, Tony. He needs our help."

"Like hell he does. I told him not to come here again."

Tony pushed forwards and she pushed back.

She lowered her voice. "Dad, just give me a minute to explain." She never called him dad, and it had the desired effect. Tony lowered his arms, searching her face.

Refusing to call him dad seemed trivial now, but when she had first come to live with Tony as a teenager, she'd so resented his primitive lifestyle that she'd directed all of the rage of losing Carlos and her mother at him. He'd given up trying to change her mind long ago.

Tony relaxed his shoulders and took a step back. "So what's Richie Rich doing here?"

"We went to the hand over this morning, and Chelsea didn't show—"

"His marital problems aren't your business, Neve."

"It's worse than that." Her hand went to her stomach as she explained the phone call and Boiler's demand. "Rowan is being held for ransom. I have to do something."

The tips of Tony's fingers made a scratching sound against his greying stubble. "I know how you feel about Rowan, and there's nothing wrong with helping Micah, but why does he have to come here?"

After a long sigh, she explained her reasoning just as she had to Jack and Micah. "The only place he'll be safe while we figure this out, is here, and *we* have the skills to help him if things don't go to plan."

"I don't like the sound of that. What kind of plan do you think there's going to be?"

"This is my home too Tony, and I need to do this. If you don't want to be involved, then I'll move out." That was a low blow, but there just wasn't time to spend talking him around today.

"Honey." It was a pained plea. He rubbed his temples and paced to the porch and back.

"It's only for five days," she said to soften the blow.

"I don't know what I'm supposed to do while Richie Rich makes himself at home," he mumbled under his breath, already heading for the tree line.

Neve waited until Tony had disappeared before waving Micah over. Well, he'd already seen the inside of her home and no doubt judged it as lacking. How much worse could living with him be?

It was Tony's house before hers though. *God I'm such a heel. Poor Dad doesn't need this stress.*

Inside, she ushered Micah into the kitchen. No backing out now.

"It's organised?" Micah asked.

"Yes, but as you can imagine, he's none too happy, and if you go near his bedroom, all bets are off."

"You're going to be here too, right?"

She laughed. "A big, strong bloke like you is afraid of an old man?"

"A batshit crazy old man who's trained to kill," he mumbled sullenly.

"Look, Tony has gone to cool off. It might be a good idea for us to grab something to eat now, so we can clear out of his way. Jack will be here later for a strategy meeting. What do you fancy to eat?"

"Dare I ask what you've got?"

"What's that supposed to mean?" She narrowed her eyes at him.

"I'm picturing kangaroo steak, rabbit stew, damper. Am I far wrong?"

"Don't be such an arse. Sit down." She pointed to the kitchen table and opened the door on the stove to toss a chunk of wood in. Then she fossicked in the pantry for what she needed, throwing the ingredients together while a cast-iron frying pan heated on stovetop.

The sensation of his gaze following her around the rustic kitchen was unnerving. She could guess at the kind of judgments he was making about her lifestyle, and now she was stuck with him for the best part of a week.

"Okay, I have to ask," Micah said. "You've got an electric light, but you cook on a wood stove, and that looks like a gas cooktop."

Tossing finely chopped vegetables into the frying pan, she kept her back to him.

"The bottled gas is for when it's too hot to put the wood stove on. There wasn't gas or electricity when I came to live with Tony, because he refused to connect anything to the grid—Big Brother phobia—but I was twelve years old and used to living in the real world, so we came to a compromise."

"I'd like to see your power set up." Micah picked up *Wind Power Workshop* by Hugh Piggott from a shelf beside the dining table. "One day I want to build a self-sufficient house in the Blue Mountains."

Neve put the knife down and turned to face him, head tilted sceptically. He'd better not be mocking her.

He smiled, and a tiny dimple folded into his right cheek, which changed his face from its usual businesslike intensity to something boyish that took her breath away. "I'm very interested in sustainable energies. Hard to believe, eh? In fact, I own several wind farms and am about to build the largest in Australia at Silverton."

Her house had a wind turbine. He owned farms of them. "I'll take you on a tour after this," she said.

Hearing about his interests from him was more compelling than reading it on *Wikipedia*. The ever-increasing enigma only boosted her curiosity, which really wasn't healthy considering he'd be gone from her life in less than a week.

• • •

"I'm not saying it'll be quite as simple as this place," Micah said, "but I don't want to bring a family up in the middle of Sydney."

He was thinking more of a semirural homestead on acreage where Rowan could run and play, even if there was little chance of him having siblings now.

The Botticellis' kitchen was simplistic, but he could appreciate the warmth of the timber, the functionality, and there were homely touches, like the herbs hanging from the ceiling and what looked like a handmade teapot. Sustainable living in its most basic form, and sustainability was what he was trying to bring to communities around Australia.

"It must've been really difficult for you being landed in such a primitive existence as a teenager."

"It's not primitive," she snapped. "Tony would have done anything for me back then, no matter how much it hurt him."

"And now?"

"He still would, but I don't need it now. I'm happy with our life. It's peaceful. There's Wi-Fi and power points on my side of the house when I need a bit of civilisation."

From the stiff way Neve held herself, she wasn't much enjoying having him lob in her private space. It had been a hell of a day all around, and the drama wasn't over yet. Not too many people would invite a virtual stranger into their home, especially with the additional complication of Tony. In truth, Micah wasn't convinced that staying at the bed-and-breakfast and being found by the Mutts would be any more dangerous than Tony Botticelli.

"Have you ever had a houseguest before?"

The chopping ceased. "Not really. Jack and Bron are the only people Tony ever trusted enough." She sighed. "I know how we live isn't normal, but I'm used to it."

"Define normal."

No chance of that. There was zero normal about this situation.

"Neve, it's just ... different from what I'm used to that's all." Way different. "Hey, not everyone needs a lot of stuff. I like having money. It provides me with amazing opportunities to help people less fortunate and to improve our environment. Not to mention providing security for my family."

"How's that working out for you?"

"Look, we're getting side-tracked here. I really appreciate what you're doing for me, Tony too. Is there anything I should know about him so I don't put my foot in it?"

"Mostly he just wants to keep me safe. Keep out of his way and you'll be fine. I read him the riot act."

A tremor shuddered along her arm. No doubt this was costing her dearly. None of this was fair on either of them. Tony was her whole life, and she was his. It said volumes about how much she cared about Rowan that she had become embroiled in this situation.

"Tony doesn't act like this to be mean, you know." Neve lifted the edges of an omelette in the pan. "He finds it difficult to cope with the outside world, that's all."

She slid a folded omelette onto each plate, added a handful of salad, and they tucked into their meals.

Several mouthfuls in, Micah said, "I'll try not to upset him. This is delicious, by the way."

"We grow most of our own fruit and vegetables and have hens."

Once they'd finished eating, Micah followed her on a tour of the house. It wouldn't take long considering the size of the place.

The first thing she pointed out was Tony's bedroom, the no-go zone. Now that Micah had recovered from the initial shock of the yellow-ochre walls, concrete floor, and sparse decor, he could see signs of Neve in the house. A potted plant by the window and a photo of a smiling family on the lounge wall. Obviously a much younger Tony with thick, black hair and softer eyes, his arm around a woman with pale skin but with the same oval face and almond-shaped eyes as Neve, who had two long braids over her shoulders, with green ribbons on the ends, and a cheeky grin. Her little brother was holding her hand and looking up as though she meant the world to him.

Neve cleared her throat, and he moved on.

"And this is my wing. Bedroom"—Neve pointed to a curtain-covered archway at the back of the house—"and library."

"Wow, that's a lot of books."

"Not a lot to do without a TV."

"I didn't notice. I don't watch a lot myself."

He could imagine her curled in the armchair, book in hand. The room even smelt of her, like walking through a eucalypt forest on a summer day. If he listened closely enough, he might hear the crackle of crisp gum leaves underfoot. In the corner was a black pot-bellied stove, and a thick floor rug in autumn colours gave the room a homey feel.

"Hey, I should get you something for those grazes on your knuckles and your lip," Neve said.

As long as the scrapes still stung, he wouldn't forget how dangerous his every decision had become, and that was critical. "It's nothing. I'll be fine."

Neve's mobile phone beeped. "Umm, someone named Shannon has information about Boiler for you," she said.

"Oh yeah, sorry. I gave my PI and PA your number in case of emergencies. Just until I get a new one. Hope that's okay."

"I guess so. You may as well wait until Jack gets here to share the info about Boiler. Then we can pool our resources and make a plan to find Rowan. Seeing as we've got an hour to kill, why don't we do a perimeter check and you can see the rest of the property." A shiver ran up his spine at the recollection of Tony's traps.

Chapter 21

Neve lead Micah outside to a shed attached to the end of the house and grabbed a key from a hook on the wall.

"Will you be okay to show yourself around the orchard and veggie garden while I check the fences?"

"Or I could come with you. I'm guessing it's a long way around the fence line."

Neve laughed. "It's two-hundred-acres, I'm not going on foot."

She ran her hands over a familiar shape in the dim shed and then pushed it outside.

"You ride a motorbike?" He looked impressed.

She shrugged. "I learnt back when Mum and Dad first got divorced and I only spent school holidays here.

"Is that a TT250?" Micah ran a finger across the handlebars.

"You know your dirt bikes?"

"I have a KTM Enduro 250 at home," he admitted. "It was all I could afford when I was a teenager, and going off-road on the weekend was the *best* fun. I've thought about upgrading over the years, but the Enduro has sentimental value."

"Okay then, you can ride Tony's bike."

She pushed a second motorcycle over to Micah, who wore a huge grin.

"They haven't been started in a while," she called over her shoulder.

Within minutes they were fastening helmet straps and stomping on gear levers. It had been ages since she'd been riding, and it felt awesome with the sun warming her back, hair whipping around her neck as she accelerated. Motorbiking was something she used to enjoy with Tony on Saturday afternoons, after his compulsory combat training drills, but they hadn't done it in a long time. Quite likely a direct result of her resentment about having to train for an implausible catastrophe. In retrospect, maybe she just hadn't thought of all the catastrophes that could occur, like the one that involved Rowan right now.

It was comforting to hear an engine behind her as they followed the fence north to the wide Onkaparinga River coming in from the east. The sheep they ran on the property congregated near a thicket of wattle on the lee side of the hill, and half-a-dozen cattle were scattered along the riverbank, uninterested in the motorbikes as they sheared the grass to ground level.

Even Tony in all his paranoia hadn't bothered to run a fence along the permanent river, which was the boundary here, although someone had once. Higgledy-piggledy fence posts teetered on the far bank with sagging wire, half of them swept away during the winter floods.

Micah came alongside as they rode along the top of the steep bank. "What are we looking for?"

She shrugged one shoulder. "Tony does this regularly, just to make sure nothing looks out of place."

They circled around a half-full dam, then followed the southern curve of the river to where a couple of dry watercourses joined it. Neve stood on the bike pegs and slowly negotiated the steep decline of the loose bank. The bridge Tony had built across the narrowest part of the river didn't look like much—arm-span-wide planks as it was—but it was durable. It had to be to survive the high watermark. She paused once they were across and pointed to a tangled mess of reeds and branches about six metres up a tree.

"That was the water level during the last flood," she yelled over the engine noise.

"Wow."

She kept the revs high as the bike slid around underneath her on the way up the opposite bank. At the top of the hill, the scrub thinned and ancient gums dominated dry paddocks. Micah blew past, a huge grin on his face. Who would have guessed that a multi-billionaire would be so at home on a dirt bike in rural Turners Gully, the serious situation with his wife and son notwithstanding?

The river snaked back and forth through the steep gully, appearing to be cut off at one point by a rock outcrop, but the water flowed in streamlets under boulders, along cracks, and between tree roots, until it threw itself carelessly over a final precipice and formed a watercourse again. At the bottom of the waterfall, Neve turned the bike off and kicked down the stand.

"Let's have a break."

Micah ripped his helmet off. "That was great!"

She grinned back. "You know what you're doing."

"No need to sound so surprised. I told you I have my own bike. Right now I'm thinking it's been way too long since I had that much fun."

They sat on slabs of slate, and she took her boots and socks off so she could dangle her feet in the icy stream.

"Good idea." Micah did the same.

She pulled two paper parcels from her knapsack and passed one to him.

"Crikey, I haven't had cake wrapped in greaseproof paper since I was a kid. You have a beautiful property, by the way. Do you need to check the fences, because of trespassers?"

"Occasionally, local kids climb the fence and have bonfires over that way." She pointed up the hill. "Tony even found dope plants in the scrub once, where it's dense enough to hide them but close enough to a road to be accessible."

"Sneaky. Did he harvest them?"

Neve pursed her lips. "Tony might be unusual, but he's not a stoner."

"I was kidding."

She wasn't sure he really was, but she let it go.

Micah twirled the gold band on his ring finger.

"You do that a lot, you know," she commented.

He let his hands drop to his lap. "I guess you don't think much of me, and this probably doesn't sound very convincing seeing as I kissed you, but I can assure you I haven't had a girlfriend since marrying Chelsea."

So, he takes commitment seriously; good for Chelsea, bad for me. But once he had what he came for, he would go back to his fancy house in Sydney, his important business meetings and expensive dinners with friends in high places. She didn't want any of that stuff, so would go back to Turners Gully Kindergarten, and wouldn't even have Rowan to brighten her day anymore.

• • •

"You still love her, don't you?" Neve's voice sounded melancholy.

This conversation was roaming into dangerous territory fast. He might be intruding in Neve's life, but that didn't mean he had to tell her everything about his, although she did deserve honesty after everything she'd put on the line.

"I told you, she's the mother of my son." He lay on the rocks with his hands behind his head. His voice was as soft as a sigh when he spoke again. "I tried so hard to make our marriage work, but it takes two people. Relying on others isn't something I'm used to doing"—he grimaced at the irony—"and I was foolish enough to believe marriage vows were enough to keep us together."

"But it's been a couple of years since she left, and you're still wearing your wedding ring. You must still love her."

Damn, she was tenacious. It wasn't easy to explain what had gone so wrong between Chelsea and him, but he wanted Neve to understand that he didn't go around kissing other women as a matter of course. "I'll always love her."

There was a sharp intake of breath by Neve.

"What I mean is that there was a reason I married her, but if I'm honest, I feel more like a protective brother than a husband." There was a long pause—*please, let Neve say something.*

She didn't.

"I know we're still married on paper, but ... I guess we haven't been husband and wife in a long time. I will always care about her welfare though." It sounded so final when he said it like that. The end of something he'd believed was real once upon a time. The expiration of the family he'd so carefully sculptured, nurtured and defended.

Neve was staring into the distance.

"She agreed to sign the divorce papers, you know. I had them with me when we went to get Rowan."

"Really?" Neve's voice went up an octave, and she finally looked him in the eye.

"Plus, it was easier to leave the ring on than answer a lot of questions from nosey acquaintances."

"Protecting your public image." She nodded knowingly.

"No, that's not it."

I can't tell her I've been carrying the bloody divorce papers around for a year. This has been staring me in the face all this time. Chelsea was never going to come back and pick up where we'd left off.

Micah took a moment to assemble his thoughts. Neve's chocolate-brown eyes stared into his, and the energy that surged between them every time they were close seeped through his glum mood. She had the most expressive face he'd ever come across. A perfectly shaped oval with full, luscious lips and a high forehead, but it was her eyes that were most compelling. Fine creases revealed her every emotion. Right now the inside edge of her brows was the tiniest bit taut, but her eyes were wide open.

"I want to understand," Neve whispered.

She deserved to understand, but it wasn't easy to explain something you didn't understand yourself. Like, if he said it aloud, his marriage really would be over, and he would be all alone. Just a thirty-something guy living with his mother. The life he'd worked so hard to build, expunged. He closed his eyes and leant back. "When Chelsea first left, I honestly believed that she'd— she'd see that the grass wasn't greener on the other side. That she'd miss the things I provided, maybe even miss me, and come back even if it was just for Rowan's sake. But she doesn't love me anymore. Maybe she never did."

When Neve didn't comment, he opened his eyes and examined her face for a clue to what she was thinking. There was none of the sickening pity he'd expected or contempt. She nodded and offered a cheerless smile.

"Our marriage was destined to fail from the start. We both wanted something the other couldn't give. I wanted the perfect family, and she wanted the kind of excitement you can't get in a monogamous relationship. If I'd known, I'd never have had a child with her. Money is truly a curse."

Neve sat straighter. "That's not true. You do a lot of good with your money."

His good deeds weren't a payoff for his failure as a husband though. There wasn't anything he couldn't buy for Chelsea, and it still wasn't enough. In one swift movement, he scrubbed his hands across his face and got to his feet. "Then Dave came on the scene, and it all went to hell."

• • •

Micah was reading in the lounge room of the shack, diligently avoiding Tony, who was reading in the kitchen. They hadn't been back at the house long when a car pulled up outside. Micah smiled at Neve's enthusiasm as she bounded off the couch and threw the door open.

"Hi, Jack." She kissed him on the cheek.

Jack stood on the back of his boots to get them off. "I see you're still alive," he said to Micah.

"So far."

"I bought the finest d'Arenburg Money Spider roussanne." Jack held up two translucent green wine bottles.

Neve giggled. "Money spiders are supposed to be lucky, Micah."

"Thought it might help smooth our planning," Jack added. With a flourish, he waltzed into the kitchen and glasses clinked.

"Shall we?" Neve beckoned to Micah.

Once the wine was poured and Jack and Tony had a dreadful looking bowl of lentils in front of them, Jack was the first to offer information.

"My boy in the army reckons he can look at recent satellite images and check out the activity, but it's too broad an area at the moment. If we can narrow it down, he can even locate specific vehicles."

Neve sipped her wine thoughtfully. "I can give a description of Chelsea's vehicle."

Interesting that she didn't mention Dave's Hilux. Given Tony's volatility, she probably hadn't mentioned her run-in with the thug.

"My PI, Shannon, is going to try to get the registrations, makes, and models, based on the names we have," Micah said.

"That'd be helpful." Jack said. "I'm going to get my guy to flag any and all motorcycles too. In the meantime, I'm going to do recon on the ground."

Neve touched Jack's arm. "Be careful."

It was a look of genuine concern they exchanged. Jack was part of her family, too, and Micah was putting everyone she loved in danger.

"I'll go with you," Tony announced.

Neve coughed up a mouthful of wine. "You're going off the property?"

Tony raised another spoonful of lentils to his lips. "This kid needs finding, right?"

"Right."

"Well, I'm not letting Jack go and do something stupid without me."

Jack grinned. "Yeah, if we're going to do something stupid, it may as well be together."

Neve laughed. Jack and Tony toasted to their success.

It was like being down a rabbit hole in Alice's wonderland without the benefit of the magic mushrooms. Amazing as it was that they wanted to help, this was Micah's problem and he'd be damned if he'd leave it to a couple of old fellas he barely knew. Okay, he knew they could throw a punch, but it was *his* wife and child on the line.

"I was thinking of getting Annemarie to cover me at work tomorrow," Neve said, "so I can search too. We'll cover more ground that way."

Tony's lips twisted his already gnarled face. "I don't want you going on your own, love. You don't want to bump into these guys."

"I won't be by myself. Micah and I will go together."

Tony shot eye daggers at Micah, so he feigned interest in the label on the Money Spider bottle. Best not to show any weakness or the wild animal would strike.

"We're just looking for a location," Neve said. "Two teams are better than one."

"I'll get a map then, and we can divide up the search area." Tony got to his feet.

Jack leant forward. "What else do we know about these people?"

Neve nudged Micah's leg under the table.

"Oh, um, my PI e-mailed me some info about Boiler." Micah opened his laptop and found the e-mail. "Apparently, he's well known to Adelaide police. He's one of the top dogs in the Mutts motorcycle gang—pardon the pun—and rumoured to be responsible for their automotive division." He smiled at the confused faces at the table. "Chopping cars."

Jack drummed his finger on the tabletop. "Hmm, there sure have been a lot of cars going missing in the area lately."

"Not least of all my rental," Micah said. "And Shannon sent a mug shot of Boiler too, so we'll recognise him—not that we're going to get within cooee," he added quickly.

Tony dropped a handful of maps on the kitchen table. "It'd be good to find this clubhouse, if it exists."

Neve proceeded to relate the whole story of Micah's ongoing search for Rowan, the money demand from Dave, and failed hand over. When she got to the part about Boiler getting on the phone, her voice strangled.

"I still don't understand why Chelsea would make us drive so far," she said. "Unless she was staying around there."

"It's not that far along the back roads from my place to Mylor," Jack said.

Tony flicked a well-worn topographic map open. Not something your average bloke kept lying around, but Tony was in no way average. Not someone to underestimate, that was for sure.

"Mylor is a location with multiple exits." Tony pointed at the map. "You can head to Stirling, Hahndorf, Echunga, and Cherry Gardens."

Jack nodded. "That's a good sign. Means we're on the right track."

"In that case," Tony said, "let's keep the search this side of Mylor for now. We'll have to be systematic."

Jack stabbed at the map with a knotted finger. "Here's my place. How about Tony and I check everything north of this line, and you two head south along the back roads from Mylor. Not much point in going farther afield yet."

"Um, Micah?" Jack chewed his bottom lip as though deliberating.

"Go on," he encouraged.

"Is it just Rowan you want to find or his mum too?" His eyes flicked to Neve.

Micah rotated the gold band on his finger. They were all awaiting his response. "People count on me to make the best decisions for them. I have to do what's best for them, even when they don't know they need protecting."

"We'll keep that in mind."

"I ought to hear from my accountant by then too," said Micah.

Neve stood. "Well, it sounds like we've got a big day ahead of us, so that's enough wine for me. I'm going to do a bit of reading and hit the sack early. We can rendezvous at dinnertime tomorrow."

"Sure, love." Jack tilted his face as she bent to kiss his cheek.

She turned to kiss Tony, whose suspicious eyes were on Micah. It didn't take a lot of imagination to figure out what was going through his mind: a picture of his daughter sleeping in the same room as a man he hated. Micah wasn't convinced it was a good idea either, especially after the kiss in his cabin.

"Good night, Tony." Neve squeezed her dad's shoulder, and he finally broke eye contact with Micah to smile at her.

"Good night, honey."

She bent and whispered, "I'll be fine."

With a flick of her head, she indicated Micah should follow. There wasn't any other choice really.

"Do you want to have a shower or use the Internet or something?" Neve said.

Despite being afraid to ask if having a shower meant standing outside under the hose, Micah took that option. Neve pointed to a door off the lounge.

"There are plenty of towels in there. Pretend you're camping." She sniggered.

Playful Neve was back—he liked her. Tentatively he opened the bathroom door and was faced with a tiny room. No bath, but at least the floor was tiled. An odd wooden louver in the ceiling caught his eye. Attached to it was a metal rod with a lever at chest height. He pulled the lever down and the louvers opened to reveal the night sky. Icy air rushed in, and he pushed it back up. The equivalent of an exhaust fan, no doubt.

At least the water was hot. The next problem was the two unlabelled bottles on the shelf. A thick white mixture that smelt like eucalyptus—like Neve, in fact—and a runny yellow liquid that smelt a lot like honey. Not the array of body, face, and hair care products he was used to seeing in Chelsea's bathroom, relegating his stuff to the floor. Who knew a woman could manage with two bottles?

There had never been anyone quite like Neve in his life before. He'd known smart and sexy women, but Neve was compassionate to a fault, and that body wasn't diet thin, but a compact package of lean muscle and feminine curves. Her lifestyle was ... intriguing, and she'd felt so good in his arms. So soft and sweet, with supple lips. Geez, if he didn't quiet this train of thought, he'd have to turn off the hot water.

Chapter 22

Neve had read the same paragraph half a dozen times and still had no idea what it said. Her mind swirled from Rowan's confused voice on the phone that afternoon, to the sound of a slap and Chelsea's cry, but it always returned to Micah. His round, boyish face belied the determined man she'd seen. It seemed much longer than five days since he'd walked into the kindergarten looking like hell and demanded to see his son.

He wasn't afraid of asking for what he wanted and was probably used to getting it too, but was clearly feeling the pressure of being separated from Rowan. At times it was difficult to remember where he came from. Times when he acted like a down-to-earth bloke, like when he was dining at the pub or sharing an omelette in her tiny kitchen.

Her mobile rang and she snatched it up.

"I thought you were going to call today," Bron accused.

"Oh crap, I'm sorry. It's been a hell of a day and I just forgot. Look, can we catch up tomorrow?"

"You can run, but you can't hide, Neve Botticelli."

Time to bite the bullet. "Actually, I've been helping Micah Kincaid with a kindy matter. It's about his son, Rowan."

"Your Rowan?"

"Yes, but Micah is his father."

"So that makes the fashion bitch his wife?"

"Estranged."

"Complicated," Bron said.

"I can't say too much, because Chelsea is involved with some bad people. That's why Micah has to get him back." Neve wasn't sure how much it was safe to tell. After all, it wasn't her information to share, but after Micah left Turners Gully, she still wanted a best friend who would speak to her.

"And you're helping him." Bron sounded dubious.

Neve gulped a fortifying breath. "Umm, he's staying with me until this is all over."

"What the hell? Things must be bad if Tony allowed that. Are you in danger?"

"No. Maybe. We're just being cautious."

"What have you gotten yourself into? Do you like him?"

After tucking a bookmark between the pages of her latest novel, Neve lowered it to the floor. There wasn't any way around Bron's probing. "I don't want to, but I can't help it."

"Who could? The man's gorgeous. Okay, I'll let you go, but only if you promise to call soon and tell me all about the mega hunk."

"I promise I'll call tomorrow."

"I know where you live if you don't. By the way, Mr. Kincaid got a mention in the online news today." Bron disconnected.

Great, now I'm alienating my best friend. I guess I should be grateful that she's even speaking to me after how unavailable I've been lately.

Neve read the paragraph in her book again.

"Damn it, this is pointless." The book slid onto the concrete floor with a slap, and she headed for the bedroom.

The radiant heat and damp eucalyptus smell hit her before he did. Literally.

"Sorry."

Micah had a hand on each of her shoulders, bracing against their collision, but it wasn't the impact that shocked her into silence. His athletic body was still warm and clammy from the steamy bathroom, and he wore nothing but a towel slung low around his hips. Any second now steam would erupt from her ears, and she'd whistle like a kettle. Good Lord, the man had shoulders to die for and abs ...

She let out a shaky breath. He hadn't let go or moved away. The rhythmic quiver of the pulse just below his jaw caught her attention, and she lost the battle to seek out his eyes. Molten sugar burned through her, all the way to her soul. She felt exposed in front of this man. He'd seen how she lived, copped a beating from Tony, and still had the courage to be here. Wide, strong hands slowly scorched a path down her arms.

She couldn't breathe. Couldn't run.

"Neve."

A whisper of warm breath followed her name from his mouth and his fingers entwined with hers. It was happening again. His gaze dropped to her lips, and she felt the magnetic pull. She should stop it. Oh, who was she kidding? She wanted him to kiss her more than anything right now.

Her eyelids closed at the first butterfly touch of his lips. Only two senses were functioning, and they were on high alert. Everything she could smell and feel was Micah. Warm lips, sweet honey in his damp hair, soft flesh, a tapered waist firm beneath her hands. Then she crept her fingers around to the hollow of his back and kneaded the hard muscles that wound up either side of his spine, splayed her hands across his broad shoulders, and anchored herself to him.

It had been so long since she'd touched a naked man; his warm flesh was sleek, divine. His tongue plunged deep into her mouth, and she welcomed it, clung tighter still. She loved the feeling of hot kisses and roaming hands. The explosion of emotions it unleashed left her giddy.

Neve let out a longing moan, and Micah tightened his arms as she sagged on rubbery knees. Her head lolled onto his shoulder, and his lips skipped along her jaw and down the side of her neck. A shiver of desire sprinted across her skin, and there was a heaviness she hadn't felt in a very long time between her thighs.

She wanted him.

"Neve." He breathed roughly against her neck, his hands gripping her buttocks.

His shaft pressed into her stomach should have brought her to her senses, but it only weakened her resolve. It didn't matter if he was all wrong for her. She was a grown woman, and she needed to feel him right now, skin on skin.

She moved a hand between their hips and tugged at the towel. Micah grabbed her wrist. Their eyes locked.

"I want you," she whispered.

His nostrils flared. "Oh hell yes, I want you, too, but ..."

"Why is there a but?"

"Neve, this isn't right. Tony's in the other room and ... and tomorrow you'll regret it. There's so much you don't like about me, remember?"

Slowly she shook her head. "Can't remember." Her palm was flat against his chest, with his racing heart pumping beneath it. Why did this have to be complicated?

There was a metallic clatter in the kitchen, and Micah recoiled. Tony was making his last cup of tea for the night. Of course they couldn't do this.

Her hands dropped, head bowed. "You're right."

"I wish I wasn't."

As unreasonable as it was, the sharp sting of denial pricked behind her eyes, so she shut them tight. She heard the scratch of the towel as he resecured it. Then he brushed her cheek lightly with his fingers.

"You are such an amazing woman—strong, sexy, intelligent—but we can't do this, here, tonight."

Now we're talking. He wasn't saying he wouldn't do this somewhere else, another time. It sounded reasonable. Her body wanted to believe, but ... tomorrow he would still be a multi-billionaire and she'd still be a kindy teacher living with Tony.

Oh hell. And there's the little problem of his wife. She sucked in a deep breath. "I'm going to bed. There's a camp bed on the floor for you."

She yanked the curtain back to reveal her narrow bedroom with the small wardrobe, double bed, and a bedroll right next to it.

"Shit." Micah exhaled the word behind her, his gaze fixed on the side-by-side beds.

Yep, it was going to be a long five days.

"You can sleep in the library if you'd prefer. I just thought ... in case Tony sleepwalks."

"Oh, sure. It's fine."

"Give me a minute to put pyjamas on. You ought to check the online news. Bron said you got a mention."

Neve disappeared behind her bedroom curtain and changed in record time. She unravelled her hair, raked her fingers through it as it rebounded into spirals, and then leapt into bed. Holy cow, how was she supposed to sleep a wink with Mr. Hot and Steamy lying right next to her? An ice bath would be in order if he kissed her like that again, and yet it was he who stopped the kiss.

The only one of them with enough sense to realise they couldn't carry it further. Not with Tony in the house or Chelsea in his life still. No matter how many times she reminded herself he wasn't right for her, merely being in the same room sent a thrill from her crown to her toes.

Chapter 23

Micah booted up his laptop and opened the local news website.

Please don't let it be about Rowan and Chelsea.

It was only a small article in the entertainment section: "Playboy Billionaire in Brawl?" And there was the blasted photo the teenage girls had taken at the shopping centre. Just as he'd predicted, it had gone onto Facebook, and now the media speculated about why he was in Adelaide, who was the mystery woman he'd been seen with, and how he got a cut lip. Drunken brawl over the new girlfriend seemed to be the favourite scenario.

He didn't care what they said about him, so long as it didn't affect his negotiations with Boiler or his chances of getting Rowan back safely.

"Okay," Neve called.

He shut down the laptop and flicked the bedroom curtain aside. Neve looked fabulous with a halo of frizzy hair around her face, lying back on the pillow. Way too inviting. He stood there fidgeting for a moment.

"Um, perhaps I should've bought some pyjamas at the shops. Do you mind turning the lamp off?"

Their eyes met. A whole conversation exchanged in silence, and then she reached across to the bedside lamp, and flicked the switch.

It was pitch black as he crawled under the swag canvas. It was surprisingly warm and comfortable, with a solid mattress to cushion the cement floor and a hooded sleeping bag.

He wasn't sure how much time passed. It didn't matter how comfortable the swag was or how exhausted he was, there was nothing relaxing about being in Neve's bedroom with her shallow breathing only a metre away. He desperately wanted to reach up and touch her. Run his fingers along her arm. Kiss her plump lips again. It didn't matter how much he'd meant his wedding vows to Chelsea or how long he'd tried to make their relationship work, enough time had passed to be sure it was over.

It was Neve whose very presence sent a thrill through him, and it scared the shit out of him. If he slipped into her bed, he suspected she'd welcome him, but it would just complicate their mission. Finding Rowan was his first priority, and pissing Tony off by sleeping with his daughter wouldn't help.

In an effort to release the tension from his taut body, Micah clenched and released one muscle at a time from his toes to his scalp. Finally, he sighed and let his weight sink into the mattress.

"Are you still awake?"

A faint whisper in the dark was all it took to instantly knot his muscles again. Neve was awake and practically lying next to him.

"I can't sleep," he told her.

The energy practically crackled around the room.

"Neve, I don't want to come between you and your father. If it causes too much trouble, tell me and I'll go back to the bed-and-breakfast."

"Don't worry, I've got Tony under control. I've been looking after him for twenty years. You can't break that kind of bond."

"That's good to hear. Family is more important than anything."

"Really?"

That single word conveyed all of her mistrust and false beliefs. The last thing he wanted was her pity for his dysfunctional family; besides, her prejudice was too deep-seated for her to see him clearly, so he changed the subject.

"Hey, I have to ask you about the flower-power choices in the bathroom," he said. "They aren't labelled."

She giggled. "I told you it was like camping. I make my own products."

"A woman of many talents. I think I used the wrong one on my hair."

"The eucalyptus soap is for your body. That's the white stuff."

"Got that right."

"And the runny yellow mixture is for your hair."

"But it smelt like honey and didn't lather."

"It doesn't need to lather, silly. It's like a shampoo and conditioner in one."

There was silence for a few minutes; she must have fallen asleep. Then something touched his cheek. Gentle fingers stroked his forehead, explored the contours of his face, and made him shiver as they glided across his lips and down his throat.

"Neve, tell me again why you're doing this."

Thankfully, she seemed to know he wasn't talking about touching him.

"You probably think it's silly, seeing as I'm just Rowan's teacher, but I adore him. I couldn't bear it if anything happened to him." Her voice flowed over him like warm honey.

"And you care for him because he reminds you of your little brother?"

"At first I could scarcely bear to be around him because of the likeness, even though Carlos was older when he died. Rowan's personality is quite different though, and I came to appreciate him for the person he is."

"Tell me about him, please. You've spent more time with him than me this year."

Her slender fingers continued to caress his neck and shoulders, soothing and exciting him.

"He's quiet, but he sees everything. Once I got to know him better, he trusted me enough to show his inquisitive side, but—"

"But what?"

"He's emotionally fragile. I don't think Chelsea's very affectionate, so I guess I try to make up for that."

He reached up and squeezed her hand. "You're a good person. Rowan's lucky to have you in his life. It isn't Chelsea's fault though. She had an abusive childhood. I knew that before I married her, but I didn't dream it would affect her ability to love her own child."

"You don't think she loves Rowan?"

"No, that's not right. She does love him, but has trouble showing it." He held his breath, hoping she wouldn't ask for more details.

He turned his head to kiss her palm, and she withdrew her hand.

"We'd better stay focused on what we have to do tomorrow," she said. "Good night, Micah."

Chapter 24

Someone was screaming. Micah sat up in bed, reached for the bedside lamp and felt rough clay walls. Where was he? The panicked shouts were from a man. Then a socked foot stepped on him.

"Sorry. Stay here."

It was Neve's voice. The bedroom curtain was ripped back, and he saw her shadow run from the room.

Don't tell me the Mutts found me here. "Neve!"

But she was gone. He fought his way out of the swag. Using the glow from the fire, he found the light switch. The shouting had turned to angry mumbling, and he followed the sound through the lounge room, stubbing his toe on the couch and hopping to the kitchen doorway.

There was even less light in here, but the voices were clear. It wasn't the Mutts.

"Dad, it's me. You're safe."

A thin silhouette held a knife. "Get out of my house!" Tony yelled vehemently.

Micah's fingers skimmed the rough wall, searching for a switch. He couldn't see enough to help Neve and didn't want to be on the wrong end of that blade. His heart thumped against his ribs as he tried to breathe through the panic.

There was some kind of scuffle.

At last his finger hooked onto something and the room flooded with light.

Tony's expression was ferocious as he blinked in the glare. The same serrated blade he'd brandished at Micah not so long ago was pointed at Neve, who was tensed for battle.

Adrenaline sprinted through Micah's veins as he searched the small room for something he could use as a weapon. He'd seen how fast the old man could move, so he didn't want to get within striking.

Tony's glare roved over Micah and then alighted on Neve, and his brow crinkled. "Neve?"

"Yes. You're at home and safe. Calm down, Dad."

Tony's eyes widened, his hand opened, and the knife clattered to the cement floor. "I didn't mean to." He dropped to his knees, head slumped into his waiting hands.

"It's all right, Dad." Neve knelt in front of her father and pulled him into an embrace.

Unwilling to move too far away, Micah snatched up the knife and put it on the kitchen bench. He leant against the rough wall in his underwear as Neve held her father and stroked his hair. Cold seeped from the cement floor into Micah's bare feet, and he shivered. It was impossible to know if the worst had passed or if the old man would erupt again.

Neve whispered soothing babble into Tony's ear as she rocked him like a child. It was unfathomable how she could be so calm when her own father had threatened her just minutes ago.

After a while, Neve helped Tony to his feet. She looked sheepishly at Micah. "I'm going to sit with him until he goes back to sleep. I promise I'll be all right."

She was either brave or just plain reckless. Freezing though he was, Micah followed her to Tony's bedroom. Neve supported her father as he shuffled back to bed. He dropped onto the mattress, and she lifted his feet, then tucked him in.

Tony whimpered. "I don't want to go to sleep again."

"I know, Dad, but I'll be right here. I promise you're safe. Go back to bed," Neve whispered over her shoulder at Micah.

No way. He stood watch until Tony's eyelids drooped as Neve continued to stroke his hair. The devotion in her eyes was that of a doting parent. Tony might seem like a badass at first glance, but it was Neve who had been taking care of him all these years.

• • •

After Tony had fallen asleep, Neve was surprised to see Micah still standing watch. In his underwear, no less.

"You're shivering," she said.

"I'm fine. How's Tony?"

"Sleeping."

He turned and went back to his bedroll on the floor. She climbed into her own bed and turned out the light. There must be so many awful things going through his mind right now: fear of being murdered in his sleep, confusion about the best thing to do for Chelsea and Rowan. What person in his or her right mind would stay in a house with someone like Tony?

Tomorrow he was bound to insist on returning to the Travaglias' cabin. Maybe it was the safest option. Maybe she'd overestimated Tony's resilience. If he bumped into Micah in the dark ... She shivered at the thought.

This situation might be more than any of them could bear.

As the silence stretched, images of Jack and Tony creeping about the bush with the Mutts swirled through her fatigued mind. It made her feel sick to think of the people she loved coming into contact with the gang.

If anything happens to Tony... Not after losing Mum and Carlos.

She clenched her fists and squeezed her eyes shut, but it didn't stop the tears that trickled down her temples and dampened the pillow.

Her vision blurred and nose clogged. She couldn't help a sniffle.

Micah's fingers felt for her in the dark. "Are you all right?"

There weren't words, so she just shook her head. Of course, he couldn't see it, but he stroked the hair off her face and rubbed circles on her shoulder. Instead of comforting her, his touch was like a release valve, and the tears streamed faster.

She sobbed.

"Tell me what's wrong," he pleaded.

With a gentle grip on her wrist, he tugged her closer. It seemed like the most natural thing in the world to roll off the bed and into his arms. Sturdy arms that cradled her against his bare chest as she wept.

"Neve, you're scaring me. What can I do?"

"I can't lose Tony," she said between sobs.

He hugged her tighter, rested his chin on top of her head. "I won't let anything happen to him."

A few minutes later, she shuddered in a couple of deep breaths and managed to get a handle on the waterworks. Micah tucked the top layer of the bedding over her, leaving a sheet between them, and continued stroking her hair. She couldn't remember this kind of comfort since her mother ...

"Maybe I didn't make this clear enough, Neve, but you shouldn't feel like you *have* to be involved in this. Not any of you. This is my problem, and I'd hate myself if anything happened to you."

She heard the honesty in his words, but it didn't matter. "I care about Rowan too much not to."

He nodded, and she rested her head on the soft curves of his chest, listening to his steady heartbeat and drinking in his exotic, spicy scent.

It was a long time before her heavy eyelids closed and her mind stopped swirling.

Chapter 25

Neve was blisteringly hot when she cracked open one eye. Something wasn't right. Why was she looking at her bed from the floor? And then she felt the tickle of soft chest hair under her cheek. She was tucked under Micah's arm, one leg over his thigh, snuggled inside his camp bed.

Oh hell.

What have I done?

Trying to move like a ninja, Neve slowly lifted her arm from across Micah's belly—his naked, washboard belly—and raised the blankets. She peeked down and breathed a sigh of relief at his boxer shorts. It was a toss-up what she should be most embarrassed about: blubbering like a baby, Tony's antics, or falling asleep on Micah. Obviously he didn't mind or he would have woken her.

What to do now though?

It was going to be difficult to extract herself without waking him. Little by little, she moved her weight backwards, intending to roll off. Micah shifted, hugged her tighter, and nuzzled her hair.

Oh boy. If Bron could see me now, she'd hit the roof. Not to mention Tony.

Geez, talk about giving a guy the wrong impression. Maybe tonight she'd suggest he move the bedroll into the library. He'd be warm by the stove.

She tensed as she used the arm under her to push upward. When she was half in a sitting position, she put her right hand on

Micah's other side. Now they were front on, with her suspended over him.

One more push and ... her thigh grazed an impressive hard-on. She stopped dead.

He rolled over and knocked her arm out from under her, so she collapsed on top of him. Micah blinked and rubbed his eyes with one hand, the other arm still wrapped around her.

He frowned. "What are you doing?"

"Nothing. I was trying to get up, and you knocked me over."

He looked a little bewildered but made no move to release her from his embrace. Her thigh was intimately aware of his condition, and it made every inch of her skin hyper-alert. Warm, pliable flesh, bare legs touching the length of hers.

Not good. Not good at all. "I'm sorry I crashed your bed. I must've fallen asleep."

"I've gotta tell you, at this moment I'm not minding at all." He grinned.

"If you'll just let me untangle myself ..."

"I'm not sure I can take any repositioning right now."

She slapped his shoulder but couldn't help a snort of laughter. "You're a pig."

"Darling, you're the one on top."

This time she thrust her arms straight and jumped to her feet.

It was better and worse. At least she was no longer pressed against him, but an almost naked, stunning specimen of a man was lying on his back in all his morning glory, smiling at her. What woman in her right mind would walk away from that?

A woman with a lethal father in the next room. "I'm going to make breakfast, and you'd better be dressed the next time I see you."

"Are you sure you don't want to stay?"

She grabbed the nearest clothes and raced for the bathroom, hearing a soft chuckle in her wake.

• • •

By the time oats were simmering on the stove, Neve had lost her appetite. Although she'd experienced Tony's night terrors many times before, Micah witnessing it left her feeling ... vaguely ashamed. The familiar mental fatigue associated with caring for Tony was now magnified by Micah's presence. There was no doubt that the situation had looked dire, but she knew without a doubt that Tony would never hurt her. She gave the white claggy mixture a savage jab with a wooden spoon.

"Everything all right, honey?"

Neve jumped at Tony's voice behind her, and the spoon clattered to the floor.

He placed a hand on her shoulder. "Sorry, didn't mean to surprise you. Um, I'm sorry for last night. About the knife too."

She kissed his temple. "We're good. Did you get some sleep in the end?"

"A bit."

She retrieved the spoon, washed it, and wiped the floor. "Do you want some porridge?"

"I'll have some fruit and feed the chickens." He grabbed an apple and a pear from a cane basket in the pantry and pulled on leather boots.

Neve knew he was hiding from Micah, not her. "Don't forget Jack's picking you up for your scouting operation soon. Be safe."

"Love you." His stubble prickled her temple as he kissed her good-bye.

The front door banged closed, and Neve stretched her arms above her head to release the tension in her limbs. The scent of Micah's spicy cologne lingered on her skin from their intimate encounter, unfurling a long dormant desire in her belly.

There wasn't any other sound, but she felt a presence behind her and a flush raced across her cheeks. She chanced a glance towards the doorway, and sure enough, there leant Micah with his arms crossed and yesterday's rumpled T-shirt on, looking like he belonged in her little home—not to mention looking smoking hot.

"Breakfast won't be long," she said.

His silent scrutiny was unnerving as she scooped porridge into bowls and popped the lid off the container of raw sugar. A rich molasses scent wafted out, bringing with it memories of Tony making this same breakfast for her as a child. The moment the sprinkled sugar hit the hot porridge, it started to liquefy and the sweet, warm steam wafted across her face.

It wasn't until the bowls were on the table and she was seated that Micah finally took a seat opposite her and sighed. Feeling awkward was unfamiliar territory, and she needed to get last night's incident out in the open.

"Micah, I'm sorry about Tony. It must have been scary to wake in a strange house to shouting."

"And knives." His hazel eyes bored into her. "Are you all right?"

"Tony would never hurt me."

"That's *not* what it looked like last night."

She grunted. "Look, I can take care of myself. Having you in the house triggered his night terrors, that's all."

"I thought I might be the cause, so it's probably best if I move back to the B and B today."

Exactly the response she'd expected. He was probably tired of roughing it anyway. It was no skin off her nose. No matter how decent he was, she had no plans to be a rich man's plaything.

But maybe it *was* time she thought more about her future and where it was going.

• • •

With a spoonful of porridge halfway to his mouth, Micah paused. He hadn't expected Neve's face to drop at the news of him moving out. In fact, he thought she'd be pleased, seeing as it was stirring up trouble between her and Tony.

"I feel like I'm putting you in constant danger," he explained. "We're looking for bikers, my son has been kidnapped, and now you have someone attack you in your own home. This has gone too far."

"Tony suffers from very vivid nightmares, but I know how to handle him." Her eyes glistened with indignation.

"I'm not trying to assign blame here. I just want to keep you safe."

One of Neve's hands went to her waist. "And why is that important, exactly?"

A five foot nothing chick trying to look imposing whilst sitting. He almost smiled.

"Hell, Neve, isn't it obvious?"

"It's obvious that you need to keep me onside to help you, but you don't need the accommodation, you don't need money, and you sure don't need help getting yourself into trouble ..."

Try as he might, he couldn't stop his teeth from clenching. "Damn it, even if I didn't fancy you, I wouldn't want to put you in danger. Look, there's stuff we need to get done today, so what's our first course of action?"

With her attention on her breakfast, she grumbled, "I promised to drop in on Bron, and you pick up your new mobile phone, but we'll need to take two cars if you're staying there."

This was a page right out of the *Men Are from Mars, Women Are from Venus* book. Did she want him to move out or stay? No doubt he'd be damned whichever way he went, and he couldn't ask her outright or he'd seem insensitive.

"We'll go together." Hopefully that left his options open and satisfied Neve. He'd have to come back to her house to get an update from Jack later anyway. "Do you mind if I just check my work e-mails before we head off?"

"I need a shower anyway." She stood, still not making eye contact.

"I'll do that." He took the bowl from her fingers.

Brooding about the danger Tony posed to Neve, and himself for that matter, he washed their breakfast dishes. Maybe if he stayed at the shack, it would help Neve by diluting the tense atmosphere that followed Tony around. Besides, he knew the domestic violence statistics: A woman was killed in Australia every week by the man she was living with. The assault didn't have to be between a couple.

Done. It was safer for Neve if he stayed with her.

Now for work. He'd neglected the business world too much lately, so no doubt there would be a multitude of crises clambering for his attention, and he needed Emma to clear his diary for another week. While his laptop booted up, he dialled his PA.

The sound of the shower spray drew his attention, and his mind drifted to a naked Neve. He grinned. Having a woman run from him could well injure a man's ego, and, let's face it, his attraction couldn't have been more obvious, but the hunger in her eyes this morning had been plain. She wanted him too. No matter how stoic she pretended to be, there was a hot-blooded woman just waiting for someone to release the tight bands constricting her passion.

Outlook opened and loaded 227 new mail messages. Great.

He flicked through them, deleting as many as he could, flagging others for future dates. There was one from his PI with the subject line: Muttley Enterprises Pty Ltd. He opened it and read the information about the registered business run by the Mutts. There was no street address, but the postal address was Mylor. Precisely where the hand over was supposed to be. It looked like they were focusing the search in the right area.

At first glance, the business was aboveboard, but it was easy to launder dirty money if you knew how. He needed to dig deeper, find something to use as leverage. He hit reply and sent Shannon further instructions.

Neve's mobile phone buzzed on the desktop and he frowned at the screen: Shannon. He'd programmed a couple of his key contacts in, seeing as his phone was out of action, including his private investigator's. He glanced over his shoulder. No sign of Neve, so he accepted the call.

"Hi, Shannon."

"Sorry to call so early, Mr. Kincaid, but I saw you were online. I see you've read my e-mail about Muttley Enterprises. I'll keep my feelers out for information about their current activities."

"Great."

"And I thought I'd better explain the background checks. Have you seen them?"

"Hang on, I'm just opening the e-mail." He glanced over his shoulder to check that Neve was still in the bathroom.

As his gaze skipped down the lines of the report on Neve, his chest relaxed and he breathed again. The woman was to be taken at face value.

Jack's report was similar with a host of war medals to boot.

On Tony's report, there were birth, marriage, and divorce dates listed, no second family or illegitimate children, but he did drop off the grid and ceased paying taxes shortly after his honourable discharge from the Australian Army, and he'd received a trove of medals for his three tours, but that was it.

"Where is his work history, army postings? There's not much here."

"My best bet is that his history has been sealed," Shannon said. "Could be he was operating with high-level clearance in Vietnam, or he's in the witness protection scheme."

"I see. Any way to dig deeper?"

"Not without a high level contact."

"Thanks, Shannon."

Okay, so the war hero theory made sense, but then again, if Tony was in the witness protection scheme, it would explain the isolation and paranoia. But Neve would have to know about it too, and she hadn't mentioned that little gem.

Mistrusting people was as natural as earning money to Micah, but this ... It was a lesson to be vigilant.

He put the phone down and reclined in the office chair, eyes staring blankly at the expanse of scrub outside. His teeth clenched. Enough people had betrayed him over the years, and he wasn't going to let Neve Botticelli be another.

To clear his mind, he headed outside and strolled along the firebreak out front of the shack breathing in fresh country air. It was time to get his head in the game and focus on today's mission. He had no idea how probable it was that they would find any trace of the Mutts, but it wouldn't be for lack of trying.

He turned at the sound of gravel shifting behind him, just in time to be thrown against the nearest tree. Tony had a handful of Micah's T-shirt, mouth set in a snarl, eyes wild.

Shit! The bastard's losing it again.

"If you hurt my daughter, I'll throw you a beating you won't forget. I can remind you what that'll be like if you've forgotten."

Micah threw up his hands. "No. No, I haven't forgotten." It was only natural that Tony was worried. "Look, if we see any of the Mutts, I promise to get her out of there."

Tony narrowed his eyes. "You're a selfish prick for dragging her into this in the first place, but it's what's inside I'm worried about."

"What?" Micah frowned.

"She's not one of your town girls that changes men like panties."

"I— I didn't think she was."

"Not that I have the faintest idea what's going on between you two, but I want to make sure we understand one another. My daughter doesn't need a rich, *married* man who is going to breeze out of her life as soon as he gets his kid back."

Micah hadn't realised anyone else had noticed the attraction between them, and some small part of him was impressed that Neve's feelings were obvious enough that Tony thought Micah could have any lasting effect on her.

"I don't intend to hurt her, Tony." The sincerity rang in his voice.

The house door banged, and Tony took a quick step backwards. They both turned as Neve crossed the clearing, wary eyes trying to figure out what was going on. She was wearing a khaki green tank top that clung to her breasts, camouflage cargo pants, and leather boots. Her hair was pulled back in the usual braid, and she looked like she meant business.

"I'm ready to go," she said.

"Good. It was nice chatting to you, Tony." A smile played at the corners of Micah's lips as he walked away. *Tony thinks Neve likes me enough to be concerned.*

Chapter 26

For the hundredth time, Micah glanced sideways at Neve. Even with the car windows cracked open, the space was filled with her sweet and evocative scent. She'd barely said a word, other than directing him down one road after another as she ran a highlighter pen along the road map spread across her knees. What on earth was her problem with him now? All they'd done so far this morning was pick up the new mobile phone Emma had overnighted to the general store. Perhaps she was ashamed about the incident with Tony last night, or she didn't like him saying he wanted to keep her safe by leaving her out of this mess with Chelsea, or maybe she'd just had enough of him in her personal space. After all, she was used to an isolated home life.

He envied her focus though, but now that he had her alone and relaxed, he wanted to talk. There wasn't any point relaying information about the chat he'd had with his accountant, or the information about the Mutt's property, because he'd only have to repeat it all for Tony and Jack later anyway. He'd rather talk about her.

"How much ground have we covered?" he asked in an attempt to draw her out.

"That's Mylor and Longwood done. We're onto Scott Creek next. All these dirt roads and dead ends are taking longer than I expected."

"Yes, but we have to cover them if we're going to be thorough."

"I agree, but we're not going to finish our side of the map today. Your car might be comfy, but I'm looking forward to standing up for a while."

"We missed lunch, so let's grab a bite to eat somewhere. What time are we meeting back at the house?"

"Not until dinnertime. That reminds me, we'll have to stop at the butcher on the way home, because I'm not used to having guests and there isn't any meat in the house. What do you like?"

"How about I make my special lamb ragout? Give you a night off. I might need some help with the wood stove though."

"It's like camp cooking." She grinned and elbowed him.

A radiant smile that melted the morning's tension.

"There's a great cafe at Stirling, about fifteen minutes away."

"Point the way, navigator."

They zigzagged through the hills and native scrub, past quaint cottages with ponies in the paddock and a Slow Down sign where a telltale trail of manure scarred the bitumen beside paddocks of dairy cows. When Micah spotted a yard full of rusting cars piled three high, he slowed. No, if the Mutts were chopping cars, there would be a lot less evidence than this.

"You know, with all the drama, I forgot to ask you about Bronwyn. I take it you're close."

"She's my best friend, and she's got a crush on you."

He felt her watching him and desperately wanted to look into her eyes, but kept his attention on the winding road ahead. "She recognised me the day I checked in to the bed-and-breakfast, you know. No doubt it's the idea of me she's got a crush on."

"Maybe, but there are more appealing aspects to Micah Kincaid than business magnate."

Somehow he didn't think they were talking about Bronwyn anymore, so he snuck a peek. One tire hit the dirt verge.

"Keep your eyes on the road!"

"Sorry. Anyway, whatever the reason for her crush, I'm not interested in Miss Travaglia."

"Turn left here."

Neve was quiet as they negotiated the final twists and turns into Stirling and found a car park on the tree-lined street. From her pinched expression, he'd hazard a guess that he'd put his foot in his mouth again, but how? Surely not because he didn't like Bronwyn. Maybe because he hadn't said he liked *her*.

"Hang on a minute. I need to load my sim into the new phone," he said.

"What, the world can't do without you for a few days?"

He shrugged. "I run a corporation that owns umpteen businesses. People need to contact me. And I need to be available in case Chelsea, or any other prick, calls about Rowan."

As soon as he'd put the old sim into the phone, there was a musical chorus of e-mails, texts, and missed messages, and then it started ringing.

"Crap," he said. "Never a moment's peace. Kincaid. No, I'm not. My mobile was damaged, but it's all sorted. You won't have any more trouble contacting me. You'll see it in your bank by the end of the weekend. Can I—"

"You look pale. Who was that?"

"Boiler wanted an updated," he said. "Thought I was trying to avoid him."

"You should've asked to talk to Rowan again."

"He didn't give me a chance."

"Don't worry," Neve said, "we've got time. We'll find them."

"Speaking of hunting bad guys, I'm curious about what exactly Tony and Jack did in Vietnam."

She shrugged. "They don't like to talk about it, but Jack was a sniper ..."

That explained his calm, patient approach to everything.

"... and Tony led covert operations."

What sort of covert, though? When the old man was calm, he had an air of authority. He stood with a ramrod straight back, his eyes pinched at the corners as they bored into you, and when he spoke it was a command. A natural leader. Information to file away for later.

They headed into the Organic Market, found an alfresco table, and ordered. When the quiche arrived, they ate in silence.

"Neve, is everything all right?"

She shrugged. Not a good sign. People never did anything unless there was something in it for them, and despite the tragic tale she'd told about Rowan reminding her of her brother, she was going way out on a limb, putting herself in danger, inviting him into her home, and causing rifts with her father and her best friend. There must be something Neve wanted out of this deal.

The delivery of enormous slices of carrot and walnut cake followed by frothy hot chocolates with pink marshmallows bobbing on the surface interrupted his train of thought. He dug in and groaned his appreciation.

"This is the best carrot cake I've ever had."

"It's made with love, and all the ingredients are organic."

"You're more environmentally conscious than most people I meet. It's refreshing."

"I guess I don't have much choice, living with Tony."

"So, what are your views if they're not the same as Tony's?"

She swiped at a chocolate moustache. "No, that's not what I meant. I care about how things are produced. I wouldn't waste my time making my own body products if I didn't believe in them."

He licked thick cream cheese icing from the back of his spoon, unsure if he should voice his current thought. *To hell with it.* "What do you want for your future?"

"What do you mean?"

"I mean, do you see a future away from Tony?"

As her lips skimmed the rim of her mug, she mumbled, "That's not possible."

"Explain it to me. I understand why he's so important to you, but not why you feel duty bound to take care of him forever."

"That's out of line. You've known me for a matter of days. I would have thought someone in your situation would understand life is never that simple."

"Touché. I didn't mean to drill you. It's gallant that you think his welfare is more important than yours."

"Gallant, yeah that's me."

"Well, *do* you think he's more important than you?"

She shook her head and crossed her arms. "Of course I don't, but Tony needs me."

"Are you sure?"

"What's that supposed to mean?"

"Well, he seems pretty self-reliant to me."

"I'm not using his illness as an excuse not to live my life, if that's what you're implying. I like the tranquillity of the bush and simple pleasures. We can't all afford the high life."

His nostrils flared. She'd barely taken an interest in his life and certainly didn't know him. "It always comes back to money with you, doesn't it? You're a money bigot. Or is it just an excuse to avoid facing what's going on between us?"

"There's nothing but finding Rowan between us."

He huffed. "You know what I mean, Neve. You kissed me back, remember?"

If looks could wound, he'd need a medic right about now. Pushing her out of her comfort zone was hurting her, and it brought a tight, panicky sensation to his chest. Maybe it was time to take this down a notch. There wasn't any way to force her to see that living in Tony's shadow wasn't any kind of life at all.

"Look, all I'm saying is that you are beautiful and smart. You deserve someone your own age to have fun with. When's the last time you went on a date?"

"We had dinner at the pub on Friday."

He shook his head. "That doesn't count. Going Dutch with the bill isn't a real date. You deserve someone to spoil you."

"Being independent doesn't mean I don't want someone to care for me."

"You're dead right. Everyone has different personal priorities. It doesn't mean that two very different people can't meet halfway. Compromise isn't a sign of weakness, Neve. When I woo a woman, I want to make sure she knows she's the centre of my universe."

She pushed her plate away with a corner of cake still intact and leant forward.

"Reeeally. And what other stipulations do you have for a *real* date?"

Despite the overdone sarcasm, her previous ire seemed to have passed, so he worked to keep the mood upbeat. He leaned closer too. God, her hair smelt fabulous, like honey drizzled on pancakes.

"There might be dancing or walking in the moonlight. I'd hold your hand and spoon-feed you a decadent dessert. Like a gentleman, I'd drive you home and escort you to your door. But that's where the chivalry would end, because I'd steal a kiss."

He grinned, and it drew a smile from her too, which softened her features.

"You wouldn't have to steal it," she whispered.

Ha! She'd wanted those kisses all right. There was something inexplicable and powerful developing between them—two people who were quite unsuited and should never have met. It was thrilling and frightening at the same time.

He reached hesitantly across the table and her eyes darted to his hand, so he rested his fingers on the corner of her plate.

"Do you want that?" He nodded at her leftover cake.

She giggled. "You have it. It never ceases to amaze me how men can eat like horses and look like that." She waved a hand in his general direction.

"And how exactly do I look, plump and cuddly?"

After a brief appraisal, she smirked. "Ripped and intense."

He nodded. "Nice descriptive words."

The gravitational force of her lips was dragging him in, and he knew she felt it too. Her dark gaze dropped from his eyes to his lips and lingered. She swallowed, and the tip of her tongue darted out, leaving those lips glistening. There was no way he could keep his distance when she was so unfairly alluring.

The shrill ring of her mobile phone made them both jerk upright.

"Hi, Bron. What's up?"

Micah feigned interest in the other diners while listening intently.

"Really? ... I see. What did you tell them? ... Good one. Thanks for the heads-up."

He studied the puckered skin between Neve's brows as she tucked the phone away.

"What did Miss Travaglia want?"

"Apparently a couple of reporters lobbed on her doorstep looking for you."

"Great." His mind went immediately to the teenagers who'd snapped a photo of him at the shopping centre. With that on social media, it wouldn't take the bloodhounds long to track him down.

Having a roving media contingent on his tail wasn't unusual, but right now it was more unwelcome than ever before. He didn't need to be stalked while he was involved in this delicate situation with Rowan. If they published anything saying he was in Turners Gully, it could quickly turn into a disaster. Worse still, the reporters might actually find out what he was doing there.

"Did they want anything specific?" he asked.

"Bron said they were just sniffing around. They wanted her to confirm that you were staying there and whether you were in town on business or a personal matter."

"I'll bet they did. What did she say?"

"Used the "no comment" and "client confidentiality" retorts. Apparently they didn't buy it, because they've set up camp in a van down the road."

"Damn. I'm sorry the Travaglias had to deal with that. Doesn't matter what paper or TV station they're from, they'll be well researched and familiar with all of my vehicles, so I won't be able to come and go in the Bentley or return to the cabin. I'm sure they'll get bored in a couple of days though."

"Does this sort of thing happen to you often?" Her eyes were intent on his face.

No point in sugarcoating it. "Yes. They can be devious too. I guess I'll organise another hire car."

"Don't bother. You can borrow my car, if you don't mind driving a heap."

"That's very kind. I'm sure I'll survive."

Bad timing though. It seemed like since he'd arrived in Turners Gully, his stench had lured all kinds of trouble to the township. Prying paparazzi was just another one to add to the list.

Not to mention the intimacy of a few moments ago was lost, which left him feeling hollow.

Chapter 27

Micah glanced across at Neve on the passenger seat, her eyes intent on the roadside vegetation, wind tugging at stray coils of hair around her face. He could stare at that face for hours. All of a sudden, she drew her head back and coughed, her tongue out in distaste.

"Good God, that was disgusting."

And then he copped the stench too: roadkill. It was the kind of pong that soaked into your nasal passages and needed to be scoured out. He held his breath until they were past, and then sucked in a huge lungful of clean air.

"I don't know why you need the window open," he complained. There was going to be a layer of road dust all over the leather interior.

Neve raised an eyebrow. "You can't hunt by watching through glass."

Hunting. That's what we're doing? It felt like the lions had the guns and he and Neve were the stupid meerkats darting in and out of holes. He rubbed his sternum.

So far, they'd traipsed up and down every minor road and dirt track from Mylor to Scott Creek. From the thick scrub abutting Mount Bold Reservoir and providing countless places to hide, to the tiny township of Bradbury, where many of the houses were set so far back he couldn't catch more than a glimpse of the rooves. The sun was starting its descent, and right now they were on some poor excuse for a dirt road that made the tires skate on the loose surface every time he avoided a pothole.

"This has been a disappointing search." Neve sighed. "Let's head home for now ... hang on, do you hear that?"

Micah slowed the car until it was stationary in the middle of the road, put his window down, and stuck his head out. An unmistakeable engine rumble bounced off the hills and trees, seeming to come from first one direction and then the other.

"Sounds like a motorbike," Neve said.

They waited another minute, as the sound grew louder and various pitches became discernible.

"That's more than one motorbike," he said.

The unique, throaty *pop, pop* of Harley Davidson pistons firing was familiar. "I'd swear they are V-twin engines." His pulse sprinted.

Neve's expression was alert. "Pull off the road just in case."

He knocked the car into drive again and the wheels spun as he wrenched the heavy car up a fire track. Fifty metres ahead was a wire gate with a sign on it that said Emergency Entrance: Scott Creek Conservation Park. He glanced around at the small clearing, where keen bushwalkers obviously parked to enter the recreational scrub via a stile in the fence.

The rumbling sounds were almost upon them.

"What if it's them? They'll see us here," Neve squeaked.

"Give me a minute."

He did a three-point turn and reversed as close to the permapine fencing as he could get. The car was pressed under the overhang of a wattle in full flower, and when he cut the engine, the hum of hundreds of bees filled the air. Powder-fine dust hung all around them.

Neve leant out the window. "It's hard to tell which direction they're coming from." She pulled back inside. "Why am I whispering?"

He shrugged. The snarl of multiple large cc engines was thunderous now and throbbed up through the floor of the car. Part of him hoped it was the Mutts, and another part prayed it wasn't.

"They're close."

A bike streaked past, chrome glinting in the sun, and a cloud of silt hanging in the air behind it. Micah slouched lower in his seat. A poor attempt at concealment. Neve's mouth made a silent O.

"That's a Fat Boy." He knew his Harleys, like any keen rev-head would. As each bike rumbled past, his heart pounded faster and faster.

Neve counted off beside him. "One, two, three, four. That's five bikes. I didn't see the backs of their jackets, did you?"

He shrugged. "I thought I saw the insignia, but ..."

"Are we gonna follow them?"

"Hell yes."

He turned the ignition key and planted his foot on the accelerator, skidding onto Scott Creek Road and retracing the path they had just driven. It was a struggle to keep the dust plume of the last bike in sight on the winding road, without getting so close that they'd be seen.

This was the break they needed, and he wasn't going to lose them or any chance at finding Chelsea and Rowan. It took every ounce of willpower not to just floor it. Roaring up behind them and maybe tapping the rear end of a Harley was a pretty tempting idea right now, but it wouldn't get him what he needed. It wouldn't keep his family safe.

The bush encroached on the roadside and dropped steeply on the left. Soon the gravel turned to bitumen. Apparently they had arrived amongst sufficient population density to justify a centre line, although he couldn't see any difference, and they hadn't seen another car since they'd given chase. The road was still too narrow for two vehicles to pass without one putting its wheels off the side.

Without the dust, Micah had to rely on the engine noise to maintain the tail, but it was deceptive. The drone reverberated around the hills, and he couldn't be sure where the bikes were. He pushed the car faster and noticed Neve clutch the edge of her seat. They hauled up a long hill, with a clear view for several hundred metres. No Harleys.

They're getting away from me.

His foot pressed harder on the accelerator, and Neve glanced at him. On the crest, a side road curved to the left. He hit the skids and they were thrown against their seat belts.

"Shit, which way did they go?"

Neve listened through the open window. "Sounds to me like they're on our left."

Micah nodded and swung the car up Yallunga Road, which quickly turned to dirt. They were far off the beaten track now, but the road base was solid—nothing that would put off the Harleys.

They climbed higher. At one point, the road was cut into the hill and the cliff face was held together by wire to prevent rock falls. They passed a gate and a couple of driveways but didn't spot any houses. Instead of lot numbers, many of the properties displayed names like Falcon's Nest and Eagle Croft.

"It's impossible to tell if they've turned off." He slapped the steering wheel.

"Stay the course," she insisted. "I can still hear them."

Adrenaline must be pumping through her veins the same as his, and yet she remained calm. In fact, she had an eerie focus.

The road wound through the bush, flattened out at the top of the hill, and ...

"Aw, hell." He took his foot off the accelerator. "It's a dead end."

"Let's backtrack to where we last had eyes on them."

"Do you suggest we just drive back and forth until we spot them?"

Neve narrowed her eyes. "No. I suggest that our search area is between here and when we last had eyes on them. Let's go on foot."

The decisive tone left no room for argument, and he'd do anything that would lead him to Rowan.

Micah did a three-point turn and parked the car beside a stand of white pines. He climbed out of the car and met Neve at the open boot.

"What's in the bags?"

She tossed a knapsack at him. "Snacks, drinks, first aid kit, sunscreen. You can put the map in there." Then she rummaged in a long, black duffle bag and withdrew a hunting knife.

He balked. "What the hell?"

She bent, pulled up one pant leg, and strapped the massive knife to her calf.

"It's illegal to carry a concealed weapon in Australia," he said.

"Yes, but we're snooping around to find a property owned by an outlaw gang. I'm *not* going unarmed."

"Neve, I'm not comfortable with this on so many levels."

Blood thundered over his eardrums. "If I think you're in any danger, I'm getting you out. We're not going to *fight* anyone, certainly not gang members."

An unsettling serenity had settled over her. Her actions were deliberate, unhurried. Even her voice was measured. This was a different Neve. Not the kindergarten teacher or Bronwyn's best friend or the woman who'd made him feel things he never had before. This version of Neve reminded him of her father, and that scared the crap out of him.

She closed the car boot and finally looked him in the eye. "There are some things I'm willing to compromise on. This isn't one of them, but I agree that the plan is to look around and get out. I don't intend to fight anyone. Think of me more as a Girl Scout. I'm prepared for any eventuality."

"I take it you know how to use that thing?" Of course she did. He'd seen her wedge a knife into a tree from ten metres.

Neve nodded. "Tony taught me well. Let's go."

Micah stared after her as she clomped towards the first driveway. After a moment's hesitation, he jogged to catch up. She might be the one with the training, but Tony would string him up by the balls if anything happened to her.

"So what's your plan? You're just going to march up to every front door along this road and ask if they're holding Rowan and Chelsea captive?"

She scowled. "I plan on being a little subtler than that."

"You should stand behind me when I knock," she said as a house came into view.

"What, so you can protect me with your knife?"

"No, idiot, because people are less likely to be threatened by a short-arse girl than a hulking bloke."

"Oh." He dropped his eyes to the limestone road surface and kept his mouth shut.

Neve stepped up to the front door of the red-roofed colonial and knocked hard. She took a step back and waited. After a minute, there was a soft scuffing sound and the door opened. A young blonde woman with dark shadows under her eyes looked them up and down. Neve had been right. The woman's eyes turned suspicious when she spotted Micah.

"I don't want any," the woman said, already stepping back to close the door.

A beatific smile lit Neve's face, but he noticed her foot slide forwards to stop the door.

"Oh, we're not selling anything," she said. "I'm really sorry to bother you, but we're kind of lost. I don't suppose you'd have a map of the area?"

The blonde reassessed Neve, and her face smoothed. "No, but I can draw you something that'll get you back to a main road. You're a long way from anything touristy."

"We were supposed to go hiking at a place called Scott Creek Conservation Park, but I think we took a wrong turn."

"Don't worry, you're not too far. I'd invite you in"—she glanced at Micah again—"but I just got my baby to sleep."

"Oh, we don't want to disturb the baby. I have a scrap of paper and a pen right here. It's so great of you to help us."

"Sure thing." The blonde leant the paper on a wooden shoe cupboard on the porch and started to sketch a map.

"It's a lovely area," Neve commented. "I bet you don't have to worry about traffic noise."

The woman glanced sideways and then kept drawing. "Only the odd tractor or truck."

"Do you get many motorcycles this far out?"

The woman shrugged. "It's pretty quiet, but there have been a few lately."

Micah was amazed at how quickly Neve managed to put the blonde at ease and engage her in seemingly casual conversation. The apprehension he'd harboured at the start of the journey eased as he watched her work. She'd be dynamite in a business negotiation.

Two-and-a-half hours later, Micah's feet burned from the heat of the road, but Neve had been right. It was better on foot because he could immerse himself in the scents and sounds of the area. They'd knocked on five more doors and spoken to two more residents. At three unoccupied houses, they'd looked in widows, tried doors, and, despite Micah's protests, she'd even entered outbuildings.

So far, nothing they'd seen or heard was suspicious. "That's a fire track for rescue vehicles. What does the map say?" Neve asked.

There was a metal gate with a permapine stile beside it.

He unfolded Tony's well-worn map and traced a finger along Yallunga Road. "It looks like about a kilometre of dirt before it joins another sealed road on the Cherry Gardens side of the hill."

She touched the padlock on the metal gate that blocked access to the track. It was intact, but the bracing metal strap had been torn from the permapine post, and one end of the crossbeam rested on the ground. Neve dropped into a crouch.

"What?" Micah said, coming alongside.

"Those are tire tracks," she whispered. "I'd say large cc motorbikes from the width of them. Look"—she bent over and lifted the loose end of the permapine post—"it would be easy to move this aside to gain access."

Micah tensed. "That's easily wide enough to ride a motorbike through." They were due a break, and this had to be it.

Chapter 28

Neve stooped over the mess of tire tracks. "These look fresh."

She stepped through the stile opening and pulled the crossbeam back into place after Micah. It was as though she could hear every lizard in the grass and bird in the trees, smell motorcycle oil dropped on the soil, feel the tickle of the breeze on her clammy skin. If they really were getting closer to the Mutts, then she needed to put everything Tony had ever taught her into practice, to make sure they both made it home safely.

A warm, dusty breeze whipped through the gully and stirred up dust twisters. *A perfect day for hiking through the scrub after dangerous bikers. Not.*

The track was a car width, clear of debris and the soil packed hard. About a hundred metres along, it branched left.

Micah referred to the map again. "Straight ahead is where it should go."

Neve glanced between the two roads. "The track to the left is more worn. We should go that way." Decision made.

The road twisted and turned through dense scrub, becoming narrow and rough in places. At least it was cooler in the shade of the trees. Neve stayed alert, listening for engines, voices, anything that might mean danger. A crow cawed and she jumped. Micah reached for her hand and gave it a reassuring squeeze.

It seemed like they'd walked for ages, but it was probably just because she was on edge.

"We've crossed Scott Creek twice now," Neve said. "Do you want to turn around?"

"I'm good." Micah trudged on.

Just when she was about to suggest they head back, the road did a weird dogleg and there was another gate with a broken style beside it. They climbed over and looked to the right, where the road curved past a little cabin, and then looked left down a driveway with no house in sight.

"What do you want to do?" Micah handed the map over.

"Right will join another road. I suppose in the name of thoroughness we should knock on the doors over here too."

He nodded and followed the nearest driveway up a gentle slope. A few metres along, Neve grabbed Micah's sleeve. There were the usual noises of wind rustling through leaves, rosellas squeaking, but then the sun glinted off a tiny black box fifty metres away. Right where the driveway curved. She pulled Micah into the scrub.

"What are you doing?" he whispered.

"Something's not right." She pointed. "That's a camera."

"Surveillance in the middle of nowhere. We should go back."

"No. We need to find out for sure."

It could be nothing more than a hobby farmer with more money than sense, protecting his assets. She needed confirmation of Rowan's whereabouts, before all of the sand in the hourglass settled.

• • •

Micah's stomach flipped like a fish in its death throes as he stared up the long driveway. It was the point where it curved to the right that bothered him. There was no way to know what was around the corner. He'd promised Tony he wouldn't put Neve in danger, although her father hadn't seemed worried about the physical kind at least.

He slid an appreciative gaze over her lean figure. The muscles in her arms were taut with anticipation, her body rigid, her eyes searching their surroundings. She didn't look at all panicked.

Neve turned to him. "You need to follow me and do exactly what I do. If they have cameras set up, there might be more."

"More?"

"Like motion detectors or booby traps."

"Perhaps I should go first."

"Don't be ridiculous. I know what I'm doing."

She started forwards, moving into the trees this time. Each step was carefully placed as she stalked like a cat, coiled and ready to fight or flee. He followed slowly, although not with as much stealth. Somehow his lightweight sandshoes made twice the noise of her heavy boots on the crisp undergrowth.

A few metres into the scrub, she began to move parallel to the driveway. It seemed there were cameras on the main entryway but nothing off the beaten track. Typical low-level security. It was looking more like asset protection and less like organised criminals. He breathed easier.

At the curve in the driveway a dusty, white, twin-cab ute came into view.

Neve grabbed his arm. "The license plate of Dave's ute started with *V*," she whispered.

There was only the one vehicle in the cleared parking space, and its registration plate started with *V*. Any number of utes might be similar, but he couldn't leave without knowing for sure and he wasn't going to wait for Neve to decide their next move.

The increased tempo of his pulse left him breathless. He couldn't stay hiding in the bushes if his family was on the property. He moved mutely past her, downhill from the parking area, and circumnavigated a large dam. This brought them around to the other side of the car, where he could see a huge olive-green shed, rainwater tanks, and the back of a standard ranch-style house.

"We need to get to higher ground so we have a view of the whole property." He whispered.

Neve pointed ahead. "Can you see the cameras on the corners of the house and shed?"

He nodded.

"They're all about watching what approaches from the driveway. Nothing around the back."

They moved around the shed and up a gradual incline to a rock outcrop overlooking the occupied area.

"Shit." Micah's curse was no more than an exhalation.

Chrome glistened on the western side of the house. A large group of Harley Davidson motorcycles in a circular clearing.

"I count fifteen," Neve said. "Someone either has a lot of biker friends, or the Mutts are here."

An electronic buzz made Micah start. Just a grinder inside the big shed, but it took several minutes for his heart rate to slow. From their vantage point, he could see a lot, but it wasn't enough to confirm what he needed to know: Were Chelsea and Rowan on the property?

There hadn't been any movement outside. "I'm going closer," he said.

Their gazes met, and her expressive brown irises conveyed everything she couldn't say; there were too many of them to safely take on. But then she nodded. Thank goodness she understood how much he needed this.

"Watch where you put your feet," she whispered, already moving down towards the back of the buildings.

The shed nestled against the trees, providing good cover right up to it. With his back pressed against the warm corrugated iron, Micah leant close to Neve.

"You go left, I'll go right," he said.

He shuffled sideways to the east and boldly hurried around the side. At the front, he peered around the corner, where verbal banter in deep voices drifted out of an open extra-wide roller door, but the words were indistinct.

The surveillance camera mounted to the corner of the gutter was pointed down the driveway, not at the shed entrance, and garden shrubs and a rainwater tank blocked the line of sight to the house, so he stepped briskly into the clearing, keeping close to the shed front. The tips of his fingers tingled and his legs felt heavy, as though his whole body was telling him not to do this.

"Hand me that drill bit, will you?"

Micah stilled. The baritone reply was lost in machine noise. Not Dave's and Boiler's familiar voices, but there were definitely two of them. The other dozen bikers and Dave could be anywhere on the property. Too many to take on. Too many to keep Neve safe. He could look inside, but he needed to remain concealed long enough to find Rowan.

The mechanics were grinding the shell of a car, and there was a pile of license plates and engine blocks to the side. Parts that had identifying features.

A boom of raucous laughter carried up from the house. No point going in gung ho. Better to lie low and peek in a few more windows. Figure out exactly what they were dealing with. He backed away from the mechanics.

• • •

There were voices coming from inside the shed. Hopefully Micah wouldn't do anything stupid. Holding her breath, Neve pressed a cheek to a dirty window frame in the back wall and turned her body slightly. There was a narrow plywood-lined room, separate from the main part of the shed, a door on the front and inside walls, a tallboy with a swimsuit calendar hanging above it, but no bikers.

As she crept around the side of the big shed, her boots were almost silent on the dolomite base, but her breathing was ragged in her ears. A quick peek around the corner confirmed that the camera was pointed towards the house. She'd be clear if she stayed by the shed wall.

There was the sound of a radio and muffled voices, but nothing close to her, so she stole a look around the front. The handle of the door to the narrow room was only a few steps away. If they were going to find Rowan, she needed to get inside and check it.

Go feet go! She slid around the corner and, totally exposed, wrapped a hand around the door handle. It started to turn when a scrawny bloke in overalls stepped through the open roller door farther along the shed. The air in Neve's lungs caught with the anticipation of a fight, but his back was to her as he bent his head and flicked a lighter.

"You'd better not let Boiler catch you slacking off," a voice said from inside the shed.

The hairs on the back of Neve's neck prickled at the name.

"I'm havin' a bloody fag. If we're gonna work fourteen-hour days, then I'm allowed a few smokos," the skinny bloke retorted.

"Brave talk for a mechanic."

Neve backed up a couple of paces, the stiff casing of the blade strapped to her calf a reminder that she had deliberately walked into a dangerous situation. She was almost to the corner of the shed when the smoker scuffed dirt with his boot in an obstinate show and started to turn. One leap and she was out of sight.

She sprinted away, rounded the back wall of the shed, and ploughed into a solid body. A scream bubbled up her throat.

"It's me. It's just me," Micah muttered, holding her tight.

Eyeball to eyeball, breathing heavily. Waiting for an attack. She couldn't give in to the temptation to let his closeness reassure her because any second now, she might be fighting for their lives.

A minute passed with no sounds of pursuit; a final shudder of adrenaline coursed through her body and left it on a relieved sigh. She sagged against him.

There were a hundred questions in his eyes, but thankfully he remained silent. She stabbed a finger in the direction of the dam and then pushed and cajoled a reluctant Micah to the other side of it. It wouldn't take long to reach the safety of the fire track.

A solid tug on her hand jerked her backwards. Micah stood with his arms crossed.

"What did you see?" he demanded.

"One of the mechanics mentioned Boiler, but I didn't see Chelsea or Rowan," she whispered. "There's nothing we can do right now. We'll have to come back."

"I'm *not* leaving without seeing if they're in the house."

"We don't even know if they're here. Be reasonable, there are fifteen Harleys and a ute. That could mean as many as nineteen men, and if just one is armed, we'd never make it out alive."

"I can't abandon them." He shuddered as though the thought of leaving was physically painful.

"Micah, it's crushing me, too, but we can't do this alone."

His teeth clenched. "*You* head back to the car, but I'm going to find Rowan and Chelsea." He turned his back on her and stomped up the hill again.

"And what do you think the Mutts are going to do if they catch you sneaking around instead of paying up?"

That froze him midstep. His shoulders heaved under the weight of indecision. It was all the opportunity she needed.

"Micah, we're going to find them, but we need to regroup. We know the Mutts are here, and Jack and Tony will help us, or we could get the cops involved."

"No. Boiler said no police." He turned to face her again. "What if they're in there, waiting for me to save them?"

The terror in his eyes was gut-wrenching; she felt it too. This might be their only chance. No, it couldn't be ... and besides, it was suicide to get closer to the house with that many gang members inside. The only sensible decision was to get out of there.

"We'll bring them home safely, but we have to be sure they're here first." The promise was worthless, but she would give her all to make it a reality. "Now is not the time."

Micah paled.

• • •

It took them forty minutes to get back to the car, and Neve's T-shirt was soaked with sweat. Micah hadn't said a word, and didn't complain when she opened the passenger door for him. After adjusting the Bentley's mirrors and seat, she cranked the air-conditioning up and rolled her shoulders to loosen muscles. She pushed the big car over the speed limit at every opportunity on the narrow roads.

Micah's arms were crossed in a protective huddle, and the farther they got from the Mutts, the more he hunched over. Neve pressed the back of her hand to his forehead and it came away damp. His skin was cool despite the ambient temperature, and his breathing was faster than it should be now they'd had time to rest.

He's probably going into shock. I need to distract him. "Hey, can you pass me the water?"

Mechanically, he fished in the knapsack and handed her the litre bottle. It was nearly empty, so she just sipped and handed it back.

"You need to drink something too."

He drained the bottle and dropped it onto the floor.

She laid a hand on his thigh and squeezed. "We're going to find them," she reaffirmed.

At last he looked at her. "I know." He shook out his arms.

That was the longest answer he gave all the way home. By the time she parked in front of the house, Neve didn't like the look of his grey complexion and listless eyes at all. The shock was shutting his body down, slowing circulation.

Before the key was out of the ignition, Tony was striding towards the car, with Jack close behind. "What took you so long? Why is Neve driving?"

She jumped out and ran around to the passenger side to help Micah. He was compliant.

"Is Micah hurt?" Jack looked them over as he assessed the situation.

"Not exactly." She pulled Micah into the house and the bathroom.

"What happened?" Tony demanded.

"Will you just wait? Go put the kettle on if you want to be helpful."

Her father retreated, mumbling something about babying a grown man under his breath. Jack stood watch at the bathroom door as she pulled Micah's T-shirt over his head and turned the shower on high.

"You're not getting in with him, are you?" Jack raised an eyebrow.

"Ha ha. I think he's in shock." Once the water was hot, she pushed Micah under the stream, jeans and all. "Can you keep an eye on him while I help Tony?"

"Sure, love." As she passed, Jack touched her arm. "Are *you* all right?"

It was a lie, but she nodded anyway. There was nothing all right about not knowing where Chelsea and Rowan were. Her eyes stung, but she blinked back the tears. This wasn't the time to let emotions get the better of her. Micah needed her to dig deep and use her training to come up with a solution.

Whatever she'd originally thought of Micah, he really was a decent guy. Seeing him with marital problems, hopes, and regrets didn't come naturally to her, but aside from being a business magnate, he was just a guy, who had fit into her life, her home, like he was custom made. Unfortunately, it didn't change the fact that he belonged in another social class.

"How's the tea coming?" she said in an upbeat voice as she entered the kitchen.

Tony nodded towards four mugs on the counter as he measured leaf tea into his favourite yellow teapot. By the thin line of his lips, he wasn't impressed about being banished to the kitchen. Neve wrapped her arms around his waist and kissed his cheek.

"Thanks, Dad. It's been a long day." He tensed momentarily. Oh yeah, she'd called him Dad. It sounded nice, actually.

Tony wrapped his arms around her and rested his chin on top of her head. The pot on the stove boiled.

"Just let me freshen up and I'll tell you everything," she said.

The bathroom door was shut when she passed.

"He's good," Jack said from the couch.

Neve headed for the bedroom with the intention of changing into clean clothes. Instead, she sat on the edge of the bed. What a mess this day was. She still didn't have a clue where Rowan and Chelsea were or how the heck they were going to safely retrieve them if they were with the Mutts. What if the reason they hadn't seen them was that they were already dead?

The idea was like a sucker punch to the chest. Her lungs wouldn't fully expand, and she couldn't seem to gasp enough air. Her heart was arrhythmic as she pressed her face into her hands to keep the image of a bloody bullet hole in a tiny body at bay. Her heart raced faster still.

No way. She wouldn't survive that kind of loss a second time.

It wasn't the same as before though, not just her trying to pull Carlos from a sinking car this time; she had Tony, Jack, and Micah to back her up. They were closing in on the Mutts and she wouldn't stop until ... it was over.

Chapter 29

Micah tossed his sodden jeans onto the shower floor and wrapped a towel around his waist. He nodded to Jack on his way to the bedroom, grateful the old man didn't rub his face in the fact that he'd been dazed on the way in.

The sight of Neve on her bed, hunched in on herself, set his hairs on end. He sat beside her, draped an arm over her shoulders, and pulled her closer when she shuddered. She'd been as good as alone this afternoon, dealing with him nearly charging into the biker's camp unarmed and then completely ignoring her while he wallowed in self-pity. She was so used to taking care of others, but had anyone ever taken care of her? Although, having Neve in his arms felt more like he was the one being comforted.

"You look exhausted. Why don't you take a shower? It certainly made me feel better."

"Yeah, I think I will. Can you tell Tony to pour the tea? I won't be long."

Yep, Neve Botticelli was nothing like any woman he'd ever known. What woman could take a shower and get dressed in the time it took to brew tea? Everything about her was at face value, just an undemanding woman who was prepared to do anything to help another human being. He ought to cut Tony some slack too. After all, she'd lived with him since she was twelve years old, so he must have had some input into the kind of person she'd become.

He headed for the kitchen and leant against the door jam, watching Tony place a stainless steel strainer over the mugs and pour tea through it. He stepped forward and tipped a spoon of raw sugar into one mug, grabbed a carton of milk from the fridge, and splashed some into all four. It felt strangely satisfying to know how everyone took their tea. He felt more comfortable in this mud-brick shack than he'd ever envisaged.

"My girl better be okay," Tony mumbled.

"Neve's taking a shower. She won't be long," he said. It wasn't the first time Micah had noticed how attuned Tony was to his daughter. The guy might appear zoned out at times, but he didn't miss any sign of Neve being off kilter.

He transferred the mugs to the dining table as Jack ambled in and took a seat.

"I can't wait any longer," Tony announced. "I gather from the long faces that you didn't find anything good." He dropped handfuls of almonds and dried fruits onto a plate.

"Contrary. We found the Mutts."

"What the hell?" Tony spun around. "Where are they?"

"I'll have to show you on the map, but it was about a kilometre off Yallunga Road."

Jack's and Tony's mouths popped open. Micah recounted the initial search and how they'd followed the fire track. When he got to the part about possibly seeing Dave's vehicle, Neve slid into the chair next to him and squeezed his thigh under the table.

For a moment he was totally diverted by the mouth-watering scent of the honey wash in her damp hair. She'd left it loose, and limp spirals fell around her oval face.

"You did the right thing by getting out of there," Jack said.

Neve's gaze didn't leave Micah's. "It doesn't feel like it," she whispered.

"There wasn't any more we could do without putting everyone in danger." Now that he'd had time to think, he knew she'd been right and he couldn't bear her beating herself up about the decision. "Don't worry. Boiler isn't expecting payment for another couple of days. We'll find them before then." His eyes flicked to Jack, who corroborated with a nod.

Tony slid the plate of nibbles in front of them, and Micah used the ensuing hush to figure out what his next move should be.

Who the hell knew how he'd won the loyalty of these amazing, quirky people, but he was glad he had. The dilemma was whether or not he should involve them in a rescue operation or keep them out of harm's way by hiring mercenaries for a snatch and grab. Maybe it was time to get the police involved. If he gave them the location, they'd go in heavy. Trained or not, there was always going to be a risk of someone he loved getting hurt.

Of course, the police would also want to know how he found the Mutt's property. That would be an awkward conversation. He could see the news headline now: Business Magnate Goes Rogue.

• • •

Neve popped an almond into her mouth, then grabbed her laptop from the kitchen bench, and slid it across the table to Micah. "You find the location on Google Maps while I bring the boys up to speed."

On a pad of lined paper, she sketched what they'd seen. "It's a long driveway, and we saw Dave's ute here. The land drops away below the car park, with a sizeable dam, and I spotted another house a little way through the trees. There are surveillance cameras." She pointed them out. "But none are pointed at the shed entrance, so they're more worried about uninvited visitors than protecting whatever is in the house. We didn't get close enough to see much, because the house is surrounded by thick bushes."

"I've got the map up," Micah announced.

"Switch to satellite imaging, so we can see the details."

He clicked on the screen and turned it so everyone could see.

Jack scrutinised the image. "One thing to remember is that this should be a stealth mission. In and out undetected. These guys are likely to be big and mean."

"And armed," Tony added.

Neve took a swig of tea to disguise a shaking hand. "If we take weapons, it will make us look like we intend to hurt someone, and we don't, right?"

Tony bit his lip. "No contact is preferable," he agreed.

She pointed at the computer screen with a pencil. "There's a big industrial shed here, and it sits right up against the trees with high ground behind it."

"That's the best place to set up reconnaissance," Jack cut in.

"And if there is any danger of contact, we get the hell out of there," she reminded him.

"But we'd be fools to assume our ideal scenario is going to run like clockwork," Jack said. "If we see Chelsea and Rowan, we need to try extraction there and then."

"No. I don't like that." The very idea of the people she loved coming into contact with the Mutts made her cringe.

Tony put his mug down. "I agree with Jack."

It was the first thing he'd contributed, but Neve knew he was taking in every detail. Planning covert missions had apparently been his specialty in the military, but they were dealing with civilians now, and they didn't have the right to carry guns. That didn't mean the Mutts wouldn't be armed.

"We need a back-up plan in case we have to get up close and personal," Tony continued.

"Dad, I think you're forgetting that Micah doesn't have any tactical training. I don't want him in danger."

"Hang on a minute!" Micah threw his hands up. "I can look after myself, and that's my wife and child in there." Micah said.

"It's not just about holding your own against these guys," Tony said. "Some of us *are* trained soldiers. We should go in first."

"Hey!" Neve slapped the table. "I am just as capable as any of you."

"I'm not saying that," Micah said. "I don't want any of you in danger. It's time to get professional help."

Tony grunted and then pointed to the map again. "What's the best way in?"

Neve tapped it. "We came in from Yullunga Road, but it's only a couple of hundred metres through medium-density scrub to Vickers Road. That's the way we should get in and out."

Jack drummed his fingertips on the table. "Two hundred metres is still a long way to drag a frightened woman and child."

Micah paced the tiny kitchen, an intense scowl on his brow. "That's the problem. I don't want any of you involved in this. I know I said we should go in, but I've changed my mind. Now's the time to bring in outside help. If I report stolen car parts on the property, the police will have probable cause to go in. A SWAT team could be in and out before the Mutts knew what hit them."

"Maybe." Tony crossed his arms.

Neve grabbed Micah's hand on his next pass. "I know you're frustrated, but we have to cover every aspect if we're going to find and retrieve them safely. There's more going on here than a hostage situation, and we just don't know how these thugs will react if they see us."

There was a frustrated sigh from Tony. "We can find them and get them out ourselves, without it coming to a fight. This is what Jack and I specialise in. There's nothing to say a SWAT team will do a better job, especially when they're bound by rules and regulations. Not to mention they're lacking one key motivator."

"What's that?" Micah asked.

"They don't give a shit what happens to your kid."

Micah stumbled back as though he'd been shoved.

Neve came to his defence. "This isn't the time for your suspicions, Tony. We are talking about the lives of real people."

"Are you insinuating I don't know the value of those lives?" Tony's brows pulled together in one shaggy menace.

She dropped her gaze to the tabletop. "Sorry, that's not what I meant."

"I think we all need to chill for a minute." Jack, ever the moderator. "How about we open a bottle of wine and make a plan?" He held up a hand against Micah's rebuff. "There's no point in rushing into anything when we still have time to make an educated decision. We need to weigh the pros and cons of involving the police, and sleep on it."

"No. We have to act now!" Micah punched a frustrated fist into the air.

"You're understandably emotional, but think about it; we don't even know for sure Chelsea and Rowan are on the property, and besides, the Mutts aren't going to do anything to them when they're waiting on their biggest payday ever."

Neve's stomach lurched. No matter what, she didn't want Micah going near the Mutts again. "It's too dark to take action now anyway. We'd be at a disadvantage and someone is liable to get hurt." Then she stared at Tony. "And I think the final decision should be Micah's."

Tony growled, and Neve braced for his lecture about how you couldn't trust anyone outside the family. His nostrils flared, and then the flat line of his lips softened. After a moment, he calmly got to his feet.

"Well, I don't know about the rest of you, but I need a beer at the pub."

Three mouths gaped.

Neve's eyebrows shot up to her hairline. "*You* want to go to the pub?"

"While it's full of locals?" Jack added.

"Doesn't look like anyone here's going to cook my dinner," he grumbled half-heartedly, already heading for the front door.

"I'll drive," Neve called, hot on his heels.

• • •

Conversations died when the Botticellis entered the pub. Micah stepped over the threshold behind them as every pair of eyes in the place followed Tony to the front bar. Even the chef stuck his head around the corner to see what had happened.

Wow, Tony really doesn't get out much, Micah thought.

"I'll have an Oak Burger and a Coopers Ale, thanks," Tony said in a booming voice.

Apparently that was a normal enough thing to do, and attention gradually returned to individual conversations. When a few of the locals raised their glasses and said "hi" to Micah, Tony and Jack did a double take. Neve just rolled her eyes and pulled up a barstool beside him.

"Hey, I'm going to call Bron and see if she wants to join us for a drink. I owe her one."

Huddled around a tall table by the window, the conversation turned again to what they'd seen on the property.

"They were removing identifying features from cars," Micah said. "Features you might want to grind off if you worked in a chop shop."

Everyone turned to look at him.

"I think he's right," Jack said. "That would explain the stolen cars and the remote location."

They fell silent as the waitress cleared their dinner plates, and then Bronwyn joined them. Propped against the windowsill, she waved a glass of vodka and orange at Neve and chatted about a local band and their salad gardens. Despite him being nothing but polite to her, there was a weird vibe coming off the woman and she'd barely spoken to him. Still, it was nice to see Neve having fun with her family and friends in a relaxed atmosphere. She lit up the room when she smiled, but her laugh ... that was something once heard, he'd always crave.

By ten o'clock, Micah knew he'd had more than enough beer. His stomach sloshed with the stuff as he followed Tony and Jack outside amidst rowdy farewells from the locals. A different scene than when they'd arrived.

"That was a good night," he whispered in Neve's ear, arm draped over her shoulder as they crossed the road to the dirt car park.

She giggled.

"What?"

She threw a nervous glance in Bronwyn's direction. "You're tipsy."

"Sorry." He withdrew his arm.

"It's not a criticism, just nice to see you smile."

Tony and Jack broke into a chorus of the '60s hit "Born to Be Wild" as they stumbled forward and slapped one another on the back.

Some place in Micah's blurry brain knew he should be appalled to be out having fun while Chelsea and Rowan were still missing. "Maybe we should've gone in tonight," he murmured.

"No, we shouldn't," Neve said. "Tomorrow we'll make a decision, when we've had time to digest all the information."

It took a concerted effort to walk casually around the car, and he swayed a couple of times. He dodged Tony as the old man fell into the back seat, still singing at the top of his lungs, and almost bumped into Bronwyn. She was inches from him with those intense, hard eyes.

"You'd better not hurt her," she snarled quietly.

Whoa. He tried to step back but landed against the car. He heard Neve's car door shut.

Bronwyn kept her voice low. "Sydney won't be far enough for you to run if you break her heart."

He didn't have a chance to respond before she spun around and headed for her own car.

Okay, so she's protective, not jealous. And here I thought Neve and I had kept our distance well tonight.

Maybe not.

•••

Neve waved to Bron as she pulled onto the road.

Even without alcohol in her system, she felt intoxicated watching three of her favourite people fool around. Her gaze was constantly drawn to the rear-view mirror, where Tony's rosy face was larger than life, his white teeth glistening against his olive skin as he laughed and crooned. Seeing him so jolly was like being twirled around the dance floor atop his toes as a little girl.

Tony and Jack broke into a rendition of *He Ain't Heavy, He's My Brother.*

She chuckled. Her legs ached from the long hike today, and she rolled her shoulders to loosen those muscles. *Maybe I should've had a little wine.*

As they came around the bend in the main road, her heart skipped a beat. It was a stupid reaction to seeing a police car when she'd only drunk lemon squash. In an instant, her eyes took a snapshot of the scene captured in the pool of light that spilled from the general store's porch. There was a police car with a Harley Davidson behind it, two men standing on the footpath.

Hang on a minute. Cops always parked behind someone when they pulled them over and flashed their blue rooftop lights. So it was unlikely he'd pulled the biker over for an offence. Maybe they knew each other.

Her left wheel dipped into a pothole, and the headlights bounced off the men's faces. Micah gasped at the same time she did.

"You recognise him?" she asked.

He was rigid. His head turned as they passed, studying the men carefully.

But that didn't make sense. She'd been the one to see the skinny mechanic when she crept around the Mutts' shed this afternoon. Micah was around the back at the time. He couldn't know what the mechanic looked like.

Micah turned towards her. Now that they were between streetlights, the whites of his eyes were bright in the dark car.

"Pull over," he said.

Tony and Jack cut off midchorus.

Neve steered into a driveway next to the bakery, and they all turned to stare up the road. The two men were no more than a hundred metres away. Their faces and street side were in shadow, but the porch lighting was enough to make out a few details. One was thin with a leather jacket, ragged jeans, and black leather boots. The other wore a police uniform and held a hat in his hand, making his short, blonde hair obvious.

The men gestured with their hands, more like an antagonistic debate than authoritative counsel.

"That's the officer who took my statement when the rental car was stolen," Micah said without taking his eyes off them.

Neve tilted her head to one side. "But why is he talking to one of the Mutts?"

"What?"

"I recognise the skinny biker. He's the mechanic I saw today."

"Are you sure?"

"Absolutely."

Jack leant between the front seats. "Are you both sure?"

"Yes," they answered simultaneously.

Neve's side of the car was the closest to the men, so she unwound her window but couldn't make out any words. The slightly more than comfortable distance between them suggested they weren't chatting about their favourite sport. The mechanic punctuated his side of the argument by stabbing a lit cigarette in the air. The cop flung a hand above his head and paced a few steps towards his car.

He turned and pointed a finger at the mechanic, then barked what sounded like a demand.

The mechanic nodded reluctantly and walked back to the cop. They talked more calmly, the thinner man shifting his weight from foot to foot and edging closer to his bike. A moment later, the mechanic tossed his cigarette into the gutter. They shook hands and moved to their respective vehicles.

Neve shifted in her seat. "What should we do?"

"What does this mean?" Micah asked.

"Get out of here," Jack told them.

"Maybe we should follow them?" Her stomach lurched at the idea.

"No, we should go home and talk this through." Jack twitched one shoulder at Tony, who nodded his agreement.

The boys seemed to have instantly sobered. Neve waited until the cop did a U-turn and disappeared up the hill and the mechanic roared past and turned up Potter Road. She reversed out of the driveway and headed home. There was no way they could trust involving the cops now. It was all up to them.

Chapter 30

Micah braced a hand on the bedroom wall to steady the thrum of agitation coursing through his veins. All the way home from the pub, Tony insisted they had to do a snatch and grab, but it wasn't his wife and child in danger. Besides, involving the police wasn't the only course of action. There were people who specialised in difficult extractions. For a price.

Neve hadn't said a word, and still didn't as she turned back her bed.

He couldn't stand the silence a moment longer. "I don't want any of you in danger. It's time to get professional help."

She shrugged.

"You're going to tell me I'm doing the wrong thing too?"

Neve shook her head. "No. It might not be the same choice I'd make, but I've had enough taken away from me to know that you can't live life with regrets. If you say we need more information, then we'll get closer tomorrow. And afterwards, if you want to trust someone else to go get your family, then it's your call."

His chest expanded. *When all of this is over, I'm going to make sure you never want for anything, Neve Botticelli. Whether you want to see me again or not, someone needs to repay the kindness you send out into the world.*

"I can't wait to put my feet up. That was some hike today." She rolled her shoulders and sighed.

"It doesn't even seem like today." The soles of his feet still burned from the kilometres walked across hot soil. "You know,

I'm surprised Tony was the one who suggested going to the pub. Has he done that before?"

"Not in a *long* time."

"He's different when he's enjoying himself. Almost human." He jabbed her in the ribs to punctuate the joke.

She smiled. "It sure was nice. Maybe pushing his boundaries a little has been good for him."

"Hey, my mind's doing somersaults right now. I don't think I can go to sleep, so I might check on the business world."

"Sure. I might read for a while in bed."

She stood on tiptoes to brush her soft lips across his cheek. The gesture was casual and all the more special for it. A man could get used to living with Neve. Then her cheeks pinked, and she stepped back.

"Umm, good night," she said.

There were a dozen messages on his phone awaiting attention, but it was too late to return them, so he flicked through the e-mails and flagged a few urgent ones. The business world would have to wait another day, maybe longer if things didn't go well tomorrow. He did, however, need to make sure that his accountant made the money transfer by the deadline, no matter what. If something happened to him, the money could be the difference between life and death for Rowan and Chelsea.

He glanced at the time—9:30 p.m. in Sydney—late, but not too late. He dialled, and the pickup didn't take long.

"Hi, Mum."

"Darling, is everything all right?"

"Yes, I'm fine," he lied. "Hope you weren't in bed."

"No dear, I was just watching "Downton Abbey." Do you have any good news about Rowan?"

"I'm hoping to see him tomorrow, but don't get your hopes up. If it doesn't go to plan ..." There wasn't any way to prepare her for the worst. "I'd better let you go, Mum. I just wanted to tell you I love you and it'll all be over soon." He pinched the bridge of his nose between two fingers.

"You mean you'll be home soon?"

"Sure thing. Good night, Mum."

"Stay safe, Micah."

He put the mobile down and sat in the dark with his eyes closed. Talking to his mother had reminded him of the family that still cherished him.

Reflexively he spun the gold band on his ring finger. All this time he'd worn it to protect Chelsea, okay, maybe hoping life would go back to the way it was when he thought he had it all, but he'd been doing the *right* thing for long enough. Chelsea was his past, not his future.

Whatever was developing between Neve and him, it was compelling but would never have a chance to flourish unless he adjusted his inflexible standpoint on what made an ideal family. It wasn't like his own father had set a good precedent, so it was up to Micah to swim against the tide.

The wedding band slid easily from his finger, as though it had never settled into place. He dropped it into the front pocket of his laptop bag and rubbed the bridge of his nose.

A lamp flicking on followed soft shuffling from behind, and Neve folded herself into the armchair beside him, her feet tucked under her.

"Still working?" She entwined her fingers through her hair and sectioned it into three parts.

"Would you like some help?" Micah moved to stand behind her. "I used to do this for my little sister."

"Sarah?"

"You remembered. Mum used to work long shifts, so I would help Sarah and Matt get ready for school. Her hair was so long that if it wasn't plaited, it would be like a clump of tumbleweed by the end of the day."

He smiled at the memory and placed his hands over Neve's to take her crimped hair between his fingers. Efficiently he interwove the three thick bands, twisted a hair tie back and forth at the end of the plait, and kissed the top of her head.

"Big day tomorrow." That was an understatement.

"Do you think everything will turn out all right?" he said, even though he knew it could go either way. It was the eleventh hour. A time for blind belief that the good guy always won.

"I think we're making good headway, and I can feel it in my bones that we're going to bring them home safe. Once we know where they are, we can get them out." She reached a hand behind and touched his arm, slid down it, and entwined their fingers.

It was a show of solidarity when the reality wasn't as certain.

· · ·

Every time Micah closed his eyes, he could see the terrified faces of Chelsea and Rowan, pleading for him to help them. He'd woken covered in sweat several times before giving up and sneaking into the library.

There were plenty of business e-mails screaming for his attention anyway. Of course, he'd been side tracked by Facebook and today's news. A bold heading caught his eye: "Kuitpo Forest Murder Linked to Bikie Gang." It was accompanied by a photograph of crime scene investigators standing by a white tarpaulin that was stretched between two thick pine trees.

A woman's body was found at Kuitpo Forest in the southern Mount Lofty Ranges last night. A camper discovered it in a shallow grave at around 8:00 p.m.

The deceased is said to be Caucasian and aged in her thirties, with blonde hair, 155 cm tall. Although SA Police have not yet released her identity, Senior Sergeant Stratton confirmed that she has been linked to the notorious outlaw motorcycle gang, the Mutts.

The coroner has indicated that the woman was not killed at the gravesite, but suffered significant trauma injuries, and there were signs that she struggled with her attacker.

Police are awaiting forensic results and following several promising leads.

A shiver quivered from his head to his toes. Neve had mentioned Kuitpo Forest as they'd driven to the hand over. It wasn't that far away.

What if something had gone horribly wrong? Maybe Boiler got sick of Chelsea's brand of haughty condescension and killed her.

Chelsea was already dead.

The god-awful scene wouldn't stop playing out in his head. Chelsea struggling against a huge, tattooed biker, begging for her life. She would have been so afraid, and he wasn't there to protect her. No matter the mistakes she may have made, she didn't deserve to die like that. And to add insult to injury, after the last breath had left her fragile body, they'd shovelled damp soil over it.

Please don't let anything happen to Rowan. He's just a little boy.

What if Rowan's body was out there too, and the police just hadn't found it yet? A sharp stab of terror shot through him.

No, that couldn't be true. It would be more than he could bear.

I'm going to tear those animals limb from limb. The bastards had gone too far, and it was time for him to put a stop to it. There wasn't any way Neve needed to be in harm's way again. No, it was his wife and his money that got him into this mess, and he was going to be the one to resolve it.

Micah snuck back into the dark bedroom and dragged out the clothes he could find by feel. As luck would have it, a black ensemble that would work for the clandestine activities he had planned.

• • •

Every crunch of stones beneath the slow-turning tires grated on Micah's nerves. Despite clouds of vapour pouring from his mouth at each breath, beads of sweat trickled down his temple from the exertion of pushing a quarter-tonne Bentley.

He tripped on a rock that he couldn't see in the dark and lost his grip on the steering wheel. The Bentley ground to a halt.

The Botticellis' shack was barely visible through the trees now. This would have to do. Hopefully, they wouldn't hear the engine start, and if he got out of there quickly, he might get enough of a head start to do this thing alone.

It would have to be enough.

Chapter 31

Neve sat bolt upright and clawed at the dark, her heart racing. She'd woken every hour on the hour all night, but at last the slight glow of dawn slithered through the gap at the edge of the bedroom curtain.

Finally, the stealth she'd learnt while sneaking around the bush with Tony came in handy as she fossicked for clothing and stole from the room without waking Micah.

The sly smile dropped from her lips when she realised that the glow wasn't daylight. Micah's laptop was on in the library, but he was nowhere to be seen. She pulled the bedroom curtain back and turned on the light. The bedroll was rumpled and empty. The clock read 4:52 a.m.

Clothes still in hand, she tiptoed into the lounge room, the wintry cement floor biting the soles of her feet like shards of ice. No light in the bathroom or kitchen. Where the hell was he?

Back in the study, she pulled on her clothes and read the news report that was open on the laptop screen.

Crap! It had to be Chelsea. It was just too much of a coincidence not to be. *Oh hell, Micah's gone after them alone. What the hell is he thinking? In the dark too.*

Within ten minutes, she was geared up and standing in front of the shed with keys in hand. Tony was going to hit the roof when he found out they'd gone without him, but the fewer people involved, the fewer people who could be hurt.

It was still dark, which meant the birds weren't chirping yet. No noise to distract a sleeping Tony from the raucous scrape of the shed door being dragged open. She glanced at her station wagon. There was no way she could push that far on her own.

Inch by inch, she edged the corrugated iron door along its runner, clenching her teeth at each squeal and grate, until there was just enough room to push one of the motorbikes out. It was still a long walk to the gate, but if she started the two stroke anywhere near the house, Tony would wake for sure. As it was, his natural body clock would rouse him within the hour.

It wouldn't take him long to figure out where she'd gone and follow, and the last thing she needed was two gung-ho old blokes traipsing about the Mutts' property. The idea caught in her throat. They might be trained killers, but she refused to have Tony or Jack in danger. They were all the family she had left.

It was better if she went with Micah anyway. It wasn't like they even knew where Chelsea and Rowan were yet. The property might be another dead end.

On the way past Tony's Jeep, she stopped to cut the fuel line and plunged her knife into the sidewall of two tires for good measure.

"Sorry, Dad."

By the time she'd pushed the bike all the way to the front gate, her first layer of clothing stuck to her skin and sweat dampened her hair, but she still pulled on the heavy jacket. The cold she felt on the ground would be nothing compared to the wind chill as she raced along the dark country roads.

Riding along unlit, winding roads at night was harrowing. A single headlight just didn't cut it for seeing around corners, and her knuckles about cracked from being frozen in a death grip for half an hour. If Micah had been paying attention during their planning discussions, he should have entered from the opposite side of the Mutts' property to where they'd first come.

And there it was, Micah's car tucked under a stand of wattle trees, right beside the driveway they'd spotted on the map. It was private property, but from the satellite view it looked like a hard-packed dirt road that went all the way through to the main Cherry Gardens road. A shortcut they might be thankful for if they had to make a speedy exit.

She kicked the side stand down and pushed the motorbike under the trees too.

Please let Micah be hiding somewhere. Don't let him do anything stupid.

She ducked between the strands of a wire fence and headed down the hillside, stumbling on tree roots, rocks, and grass tufts.

Bloody hell, I'll be lucky if he hasn't broken his neck on the way down.

The darkness was too dense this far from a township to consider using a torch because it would stand out a mile off. A twist of her ankle and Neve went down hard on her left knee. She whimpered but bit her lip to stop from crying out. The denim wasn't torn, but it sure felt like her skin was.

It would be another forty or so minutes before the first rays of dawn would illuminate the landscape, so she pressed on, feeling her way more slowly. It wouldn't pay to get too close before there was some light, so she headed for a rock outcrop halfway down the hill. By the time she leant against the rough stone, the cold seeping through her clothes was a welcome relief to her flushed skin. She needed to calm down and keep her head if they were going to do this and get out alive.

A shadow to her right detached from the rock too fast for her to bring her elbow up to block it. Large hands wrapped firmly around her wrists.

"Neve, it's just me. What the hell are you doing here?"

With one hand across her racing heart and the other on her hip, she said, "I could ask you the same thing, but I already know. It was a dumb idea to come on your own."

"I don't want you here. Go home."

The comment stung. At least he was prepared to do the dirty work himself to protect his family. When Rowan had first been ransomed, she'd been sure that Micah would just pay someone to clean up the mess, but here he was watching a gang clubhouse in the dark. Well, his protective instinct might be strong, but so was hers.

"We need two of us if we're going to stay safe." It sounded logical. Didn't mean they would be safe though. "Besides, I'm the one with the training, remember?"

The shadow beside her huffed.

"How could I forget when I've been living the rudimentary life with you? I suppose you've brought your knife."

"Damn Skippy I have. These are gang members we're talking about."

"A gun?"

Was he checking that she *wasn't* that crazy or hoping that she was? "No gun."

"So what are we going to do?" he asked. "I need to get a look inside that house to see if Rowan is in there."

They sure as hell had to do something before Rowan met the same fate as Chelsea. The little trooper shouldn't have to face this all alone.

"We could walk into a trap, or a guard dog, or anything in the dark. Besides, there's no point peeking into dark rooms or at closed curtains. It'll be light soon, and then we can sneak up to the back of the shed again under the cover of the scrub, and go around the side to the front of the house. With the driveway on this side, they won't be expecting anyone to come from there."

"Looks like there's a light on near the shed."

"Could be a security light." She eyed the faint glow but couldn't tell if it was coming from within or the other side.

"What's in the knapsack?" he said.

"Water, first aid kit, binoculars, capsicum spray." Still a prohibited weapon, but not a deadly one.

"Is there anything I need to know before we go in? I mean, Tony's trained you for this sort of thing, right?"

Neve glared at him, but it was pointless in the dark. "Not exactly this sort of thing, although I do have some tricks up my sleeve. I guess we should keep our mouths shut and eyes narrowed until dawn, which is around seven, because our teeth and eyes will draw the most attention if they catch any light, but most importantly, we need to stay calm and move slowly. Can you do that?"

She felt him shrug beside her. His whole body jiggled with pent-up energy, like a bomb waiting to explode. Yeah, like he was going to stay calm.

"How long has it been?" he asked.

She pressed the button for the tiny light on her watch. "Twenty minutes."

The faintest hint of purple bruised the horizon. Not long now. Reflexively, she stooped to touch her leg. The Fox combat knife was comforting, but it was still better to use speed and cunning to outmanoeuvre them.

"Now?" Micah tugged on her hand.

"Not until we can count all the vehicles and get an idea of how many are onsite." From this elevation, they should have a good view of the property.

The constriction of her chest reached unpleasant strength as the tops of the hills on the other side of the valley were backlit by an amber glow that gradually cast long ribbons of light across the treetops.

"There's a sedan and a four-wheel drive in the car park." Micah pointed to the right. "That twin cab looks a lot like Dave's again, and seven motorcycles over there." He indicated left.

"Could be as few as nine or as many as twenty-four if they're two-up on the bikes. That's a *lot* of muscle."

"No, the Mutts wouldn't go two-up, unless they have women in there," Micah said. "Let's do this before they wake up."

She nodded. "Okay, let's take a look around the shed. Stick with me and watch where you put your feet."

As they crept through the bush, she rolled her tongue around her parched mouth and scouted for movement. The last hundred metres to the back of the shed were steep.

"Wait!" Neve whispered.

She ducked down and held her breath. Micah did the same beside her.

The sound of deep voices carried from the back of the house, followed by a door banging, but she couldn't see anything over the bushes. She sought out Micah's hand as the voices got louder. Only to comfort him, of course. This was what she'd trained for, and she was looking forward to a bit of payback on Dave. She was going to find Rowan and get him out safely, and kick arse if it came to it.

Heavy boots clomped along a dolomite path. And then they came into view. Two weedy blokes wearing oil-covered jeans and checked flannelette shirts, followed by four big bastards covered in tattoos, black denim, and leather, with bandanas slung around their necks.

This was one time she would have preferred not to be right. Especially seeing as there were bulges in the back pockets of two. Guns against knives. She'd better execute Tony's lessons without hesitation this time.

Chapter 32

The mechanic and his scrawny mate headed for the shed, and there was a clatter of doors opening. Light flooded through the small windows, and a radio went on. Micah's nerves knotted together.

The rumble of Harley Davidsons shattered the crisp morning. *Please let them leave. Please let them leave.*

He counted as the chromed beasts glided past: one, two, three, four. Neve's white-knuckled grip on his hand didn't relax until the engine sounds were distant. Four down, umpteen to go.

The rest of the bikers were probably in the house, so peering in windows wasn't appealing. There were still too many unknowns. He shook out his stiff hands and focused on what he had to do. It wasn't easy to think rationally with every muscle poised to flee, but leaving wasn't an option. Not now that they'd come this far. Rowan could be inside the house, all alone and waiting for them to come to his aid.

The queasy feeling he had woken with turned into full-blown nausea. The usually peaceful sounds and scents of nature were amplified to an intolerable cacophony that bombarded his senses: the sharp tang of eucalyptus leaves, the fresh dampness of the residual dew on the ground, the hum of bees hovering around a hollow in the tree they were using for cover, and its rough bark scraping his arm. Air whistled in and out of his lungs as loudly as a gale.

If he had to be still much longer, he would scream.

Neve suddenly tapped his arm and moved in a semicrouch towards the shed. He hurried after her. Every footstep seemed as loud as a dozen men traipsing through the tinder, and by the time they were pressed against the long, green rear wall, his pulse was frantic. Neve looked tense but in control as she headed for the other end of the shed.

In and out before they even know we're here, he reminded himself.

At least it was easy to hear where the two mechanics were. Micah was poised to run towards the house, but when Neve paused to glance in the back window of the shed, she gasped and pulled her head back.

The fearful whites of her eyes flashed at him. There was something that hadn't been there last time. He moved around her and turned his body so that one eye could see through the window and scan the narrow room, past a packet of cigarettes and a lighter on a small round table to a hulking guy dressed in black, slouched on a kitchen chair. Unable to drag his gaze away, Micah watched the hulk pick at a spot on his forearm and then rest his hand on the barrel of a sawed-off shotgun across his lap.

Micah crouched and Cossack-walked under the window. From this angle, he could see the internal door, a pedestal fan oscillating in one corner, and right under the window, curled up on a folding bed, was a small figure with a mop of brown hair. The lead in his stomach dropped to his feet. He didn't need to see the child's face to know it was Rowan. Reflexively, his fingers reached to soothe his son's terror.

And then rage ran hot and strong through his veins. How dare they subject an innocent four-year-old to this. How dare they kill Chelsea. He was wild enough to tear the window out of the wall with his bare hands.

He lurched at a light tap on his arm and turned to glare at Neve. She cupped a hand to her ear and nodded in the direction they'd come. The mechanics were still chatting, radio blaring, and a bird called from the hillside. Then the dry grass fifty metres away rustled, and a beige-clad figure moved towards them. Damned if it wasn't Tony. The khaki and tan blended perfectly with the dry terrain, unlike the dark colours Micah had thrown on in the wee hours. Tony barely made a sound and was soon standing beside them with an incensed scowl.

Despite trying to sneak away this morning, Micah was glad to see the old man. His special skill set would mean a better chance at getting Rowan out and less chance of Neve being hurt.

Neve pointed to the small room and made a gun shape with one hand. She jerked it up and down to indicate a pump-action. Tony nodded. He grabbed his own throat and held a hand to the side of his hip, as though patting a child's head. Neve nodded.

Enough with the chitchat. He lifted his chin to indicate they should move. They gathered a few metres away from the window.

"You'll be changing my tires later," Tony growled at Neve.

"How did you get here?" she whispered.

"Same as you."

"I forgot about the other motorbike." She glanced up the hill. "Jack?"

Tony shook his head. "It's bad enough that you're here."

This was all very touching, but there wasn't time. "Rowan is in that room," Micah reminded them.

"The mother?" Tony asked.

Micah shook his head. He explained about the armed hulk, then listened as Tony and Neve made an extraction plan that didn't include him.

"I should be the one to get him out," Micah said.

Neve placed a hand on his shoulder. "You know that Tony has the best chance of dealing with the mechanics quickly and quietly, and don't forget that Rowan knows me ..."

That stung. His own son might not want to come with him.

Neve continued. "Rowan is likely to be traumatised by these men, so a female presence is going to be more pacifying."

She didn't need to convince him further. Whatever would keep Rowan safe was what he'd do, and right now that meant Neve facing the guard.

"I'll stick with Tony, in case he needs help," he said, "and meet you around the back for a fast getaway."

She wrapped her arms around him and squeezed tightly for a brief moment and then hugged Tony too. "See you on the other side."

Tony mimed turning a pretend key on his lips and throwing it away.

Micah took a deep breath and held it. *This is it. Either we come home with Rowan or none of us will.*

Chapter 33

Micah wiped slick palms against his jeans, his gaze following Neve as she crept along to the back window again, crawled under it, and waited at the corner of the shed. A sick feeling that this could be the last time he would see her, made him unwilling to follow Tony, but Rowan needed each of them to play their parts.

After a last thirst-quenching draught of her slim figure and determined stance, he hurried after Tony. The old Italian barely came up to Micah's shoulder, but there was ferocity in the way he moved that would make most people steer clear. His beige camouflage outfit was loose on his small frame, but there didn't appear to be any weapons bulging under it.

When he arrived at the front corner of the shed, Tony held his arm in a right angle, fist clenched. Micah stopped. Local radio station Triple J was clearer here, drowned out every few minutes by the whir of an electric grinder. His heart thundering, he waited for Tony's signal.

Tony held a flat palm towards Micah and then disappeared around the corner.

Be damned if I'm going to stay here.

The house was hidden from view by thick bushes and a rainwater tank, and it was easy to duck under the surveillance camera. Micah sidestepped to the open roller door. The iron was warm under his hand as the sun climbed higher, and he leant forwards until he could see the two mechanics. The car they were working on was unrecognisable in its bare form, and they were engrossed in their tasks. Tony squatted behind a forty-four-gallon drum only metres away from the first biker.

Hairs on the back of Micah's neck rose, and his fingers tingled as his gaze roved from the direction of the house to Tony. What was he waiting for?

The mechanic on the farthest side of the car shell picked up a grinder and pressed it against the metal. Tony rushed in, clamped one hand over the mouth of the closest mechanic, and used the other to pinch his trapezium muscle. The guy crumpled to the floor, the clatter of the screwdriver he'd been holding lost in the screech and sparks from the grinder.

Micah stepped into view, prepared to make a run for the other mechanic. The movement must have caught the man's eye, because he looked up, straight at Micah. Tony jabbed a pressure point on his wrist and then forearm. A swift karate chop below the ear, and the guy blacked out.

Tony lurched and caught the grinder with one hand. He carefully laid it on the ground, then used the electrical cord to bind the mechanic's arms and legs. Micah snagged a couple of cable ties from a workbench and knelt to secure the first mechanic. When they were both bound, he helped drag them out of sight. Neve probably wouldn't be happy with Tony stuffing oil-infused rags in their mouths, but Micah wouldn't tell if Tony didn't.

Two men down without a sound. They might just have a chance of success.

Tony cupped a hand around his mouth and made a birdcall—the go signal for Neve. Micah was already headed out and around to the back of the shed. Nothing was going to stop him being there for Rowan.

• • •

Neve's shaky breaths matched the pulse quaking through her veins. *You can do this. Tony and Micah have your back.*

She peered through the window again. Rowan was awake now—who could sleep with the noise those mechanics were making?—and sat cross-legged on the foldout bed, playing with plastic soldiers. Of course, there was no Chelsea. The poor woman.

At least the hulk and his malevolent shotgun were well clear. What kind of idiot thought a four-year-old was enough of a threat that he sat in front of the door with a shotgun? Well, he was about to learn that the real threat was outside, and she was pissed.

The weight of the blade against her calf was comforting, but there was no point in using it right now. Better to have her hands free. There was no doubt in her mind that she could take him out before he raised the weapon or used his superior body weight, but the other men on the property worried her. If this one made a sound, it would raise the alarm and all hell would break loose.

An internal chill raised goose bumps up her arms.

It was difficult to hear over the thunder in her head, so it took a moment to notice when the grinder ceased. She cocked her ear. Tony's well-practised birdcall sounded, and she took a deep breath, closed her eyes, and then blew it out, focusing on what she had to do. Picturing the narrow room. Rowan on the bed.

She stepped slowly and deliberately along the sidewall. There were no more voices, just Smashing Pumpkins yelling an angry tune that masked her footsteps. She took a quick glance around the front corner. All clear. It took only three steps to reach the door and wrap her trembling hand around the cold metal handle, and then turn it slowly.

One. Two. Three.

Neve shoved the door as hard as she could with the weight of her shoulder against it. The unprepared guard sprawled on the floor, the chair tipped over him, and the shotgun landed a foot away. Rowan squealed. A thick, tattooed arm reached for the weapon as Neve's boot connected with the hulk's ribs. He grunted. The internal door slammed open, and Tony lunged. His lightning-fast strike caught the biker's temple, rendering him limp.

"Thanks, Dad."

"Get the kid and let's get out of here in case someone heard something." Tony flipped the biker onto his stomach and used cable ties to secure his hands.

"It's okay," Neve said, approaching a cowering Rowan with palms raised. "It's Neve. I'm here to help you."

It broke her heart to see the little boy's wide eyes, a toy soldier clutched in one hand. Micah appeared at the window, a desperate look in his eyes, and Rowan jumped.

There was no telling what lies Chelsea might have told the boy to make him afraid of Micah. "Do you know who that is, Ro?"

He turned his attention back to her and nodded.

"It's your daddy, and he's going to take you away from the bad men. Okay?"

He nodded again.

Tony checked the window. "Locked." He started searching the small room.

"Mummy?" Rowan asked.

Neve reached a hand towards him. "We'll find her, too, but we have to go *right now*."

"I can't find a key for the window," Tony said. "We'll have to go out the front."

"We could break it," Neve whispered.

"Too much noise. I'll have eyes on you." He sounded so sure; the kind of surety a person could have only after being in a situation where co-reliance was the only option for survival.

She didn't feel the same way.

Rowan was collecting handfuls of toy soldiers.

Neve grasped one small hand. "Leave the toys. Daddy will buy you new ones." She tugged the reluctant child towards the door.

"Carry him!" Tony said urgently.

She scooped Rowan's hot little body into her arms and held him close as they dashed outside. Something caught her eye as she turned sideways, and she stopped dead. Tony was so close behind; his breath was hot on the back of her neck, an arm held out to one side in a protective gesture.

"Mummy!" Rowan called.

Beside the rainwater tank, a woman struggled in the grip of an immense, denim-clad bloke sporting a wild black beard, and stars tattooed up his neck and jaw.

Chelsea!

Neve swallowed. The biker looked solid enough to repel a bullet. Next to him, Chelsea appeared juvenile. Her blonde bob swung beside her horror-stricken face.

Rowan wriggled in Neve's arms.

Her gaze locked on to the pistol by the biker's side. It seemed to take a long time for him to raise it and even longer for her to turn her back and run, Rowan cradled in the protective wrap of her arms.

Please let the bullet stop at me.

The report from the pistol sounded. Neve gasped and ducked her head. Metal pinged the shed wall and the sound reverberated from the hillside, but she was around the side now. Micah caught her in his arms as she staggered forward.

"Was that you screaming?" he asked.

"Chelsea." She gasped for air.

"She's here?" He grimaced.

"Yes, and Tony needs help."

Micah's expression was torn as he stared at his son. Another shot rang out.

"I'll get Rowan out of here," she assured him.

This would not be the last glimpse he would have of his son. She'd take care of him. Her own life depended on it.

Chapter 34

Micah kissed Rowan's head and made for the front of the shed, shaking a can of capsicum spray furiously to charge it. The palpitations in his chest reached a crescendo as he took a deep breath and stuck his head around the corner.

The scene smouldered in his retinas. Tony slid along the ground feet first towards an enormous wall of a man. Spittle sprayed from Chelsea's mouth as she screamed and struggled.

She's alive!

Tony's feet made contact with the rock holding Chelsea and swept his legs from under him. She screamed again and broke free from her captor, staggering towards Micah's open arms, but the big guy rolled on the ground and grabbed her ankle. She went down hard.

Tony sprang to his feet and dropped an elbow onto the guy's belly.

"Get her out of here," he yelled to Micah. "We're going to have company after all that noise."

A bloke with a taut beer belly overhanging tatty denim ran around the bushes from the direction of the motorbikes. He had a greasy rag in his hand, his mouth agape as he stood there.

Micah judged the distance between this new threat and Chelsea, who still panted and sobbed on the ground. The bloke's interest moved towards her.

"No!" Micah fumbled with the capsicum spray, pressed the nozzle, but the biker was out of range.

The bloke reached to the back of his pants and Micah waited for the gun that would end it all. He threw the aerosol can, and the big man automatically raised both hands to fend it off. Too late to avoid Micah's shin kick, followed by a punch to the nose. The guy stumbled back from the force, bright blood dripping over his lips and down his chin. Just like he'd seen Tony do, Micah bent the guy's arm backwards and secured his wrists with cable ties.

Chelsea scrambled to her feet, still sobbing.

Boiler appeared beside the rainwater tank. The thug looked just as mean as his mug shots and rap sheet suggested. Tony was busy, so it was up to Micah to save Chelsea. Thank goodness Neve had gotten Rowan safely away.

He took a step.

"I wouldn't do that, mate." Boiler was still a couple of metres away, but his sawn-off shotgun was aimed steadily at Chelsea's head.

That kind of firepower wouldn't miss.

Micah swallowed. "Don't hurt her."

A menacing grin stretched Boiler's lips, and his attention turned to Tony. "You, old man. Over there." He motioned with a wave of the gun barrel.

Tony was crouched beside an unconscious biker whose pistol was a metre away on the ground.

"Don't even think about it," Boiler growled.

Tony hesitated a moment, then raised his hands in surrender. He stepped close enough to bump Micah's shoulder, causing him to sidestep. Then repeated the move. What was he trying to do?

The malice that spread across Boiler's face made Micah's stomach flip. This wasn't a man you could reason with or who would back down under pressure.

Tony shouldered Micah again and they both shuffled to Boiler's unarmed side.

"That'll do." Boiler's shotgun barrel pointed at Micah.

Chelsea either didn't realise she was free or was too terrified to make a move. Her shoulders and hands visibly shook. Tears leaked from her eyes and collided with the arc of her pink lips. Violent, hiccupping sobs rent from her.

"Shut the fuck up." Boiler cuffed the back of her head, and she fell to her knees again.

How dare the bastard! Micah calculated how close he would get to the biker before he could get a shot off, but Tony's restraining hand gripped his forearm.

Boiler pumped the shotgun to chamber a bullet, and Micah's already thundering heart took flight.

This was it. Everything he'd achieved in his life was going to be blown away by this money-hungry thug. All he'd ever wanted was to protect his family, and he'd thought his wealth had given him the means to do it. Now it was the reason they were all going to die.

Boiler aimed a malicious stare and his weapon at Micah. "So you thought you'd come and take them without paying, did you?"

Micah's mouth popped open. He would give this greasy bastard every penny in each one of his bank accounts in exchange for his son and Chelsea's safety.

I don't want the damned money without my family.

"Just let Chelsea go. The money is being transferred tomorrow morning. You'll see it in your bank by the afternoon. It's already organised." He needed to keep Boiler busy long enough to give Tony an opportunity to do something.

For crying out loud, what is the man waiting for?

"I think we're a bit past promises now, don't you?" Boiler sneered. "In fact, my feelings are hurt that you didn't take my offer seriously. I would've thought ten mil for your kid would've been a no-brainer, but I guess you like having money more than you like having a brat, eh?"

"No! That's not what this is about." Micah moved another step to the right, turning Boiler farther away from Chelsea. *How much more does Tony need to take him out?* "All I want is to keep my family safe. I read about the woman buried in the forest and thought you'd already killed Chelsea. Why don't you lower the gun, and we can figure this out. I can see I've underestimated you. You've taken good care of them, so you deserve your money."

"Damn straight. It's only fair for the shit this bitch has put me through." He nudged Chelsea's back with his boot, and she sprawled on her stomach.

Micah leapt towards her.

"Hey! You don't wanna be doing anything stupid," Boiler told him, realigning the barrel of the gun.

From the edge of his vision, Micah watched Tony step closer to the biker.

Boiler's eyes widened and he turned his body, but the gun took longer to follow. Tony rolled under the first shot and used momentum to slam his head into Boiler's stomach. Arms wrapped around the man's waist, his tackle toppled them both.

Another shot resounded in the clearing, and Micah ducked.

Tony and Boiler hit the ground together with a grunt, scattering gravel and dust. The biker rolled free and sprang to his feet, heading for the house with Tony in pursuit.

Micah turned towards a wet gurgling sound. Chelsea was prone, a small patch of crimson spreading across the back of her cream blouse.

An animalistic sound bubbled from his throat as he ran to her.

"Chels!" He knelt, rolled her over to assess the extent of the injury.

She winced. "You came."

A heart-shaped stain seeped from a jagged wound on her chest. "Of course I came. You needed my help. I *told* you I'd always be here for you." With Chelsea's head cradled in his lap, he applied pressure to each side of the wound. "I'm going to call an ambulance. Everything will be all right."

"Make sure our baby is safe."

"Neve already has him. Everything is going to be all right," he repeated like a mantra.

He dialled 000, turned the mobile phone to loudspeaker, and put it on the ground so he could continue to apply pressure to the sticky wounds. An operator picked up the call.

"What is your emergency?"

"A woman's been shot and there's a lot of blood." Micah relayed as much information as he could to the soothing female voice and then the call was transferred to another operator.

Chelsea whispered, "Don't waste your time."

A pressure at the back of his eyes built as he stroked her blonde hair. Her clammy face blurred. "Don't ever say that, Chels. You're part of my family, and I'll always fight for you."

She sobbed. "I wish ..."

"Shh, you don't need to say anything. The ambulance will be here soon." *How long will it take to reach this isolated property?* Chelsea's skin looked grey.

The second operator fired questions at him. "Please state the address where the emergency is, sir."

"I just told the other operator. Will you please get an ambulance here? She doesn't look good."

"An ambulance has been dispatched, sir, but I need to relay as much information as I can to make sure they get to you as quickly as possible."

The operator took his call-back number and name.

"Okay, Micah, now tell me how many people are hurt."

"There are four men down but not dead, and my wife has been shot."

"Did you check the men's pulses or injuries?"

"No, but they're not moving. I don't care about them; I just want someone to help my wife."

"I understand, Micah. Help is on the way. Did you shoot your wife?"

"No! There are gang members with guns."

"Are you still in danger?"

"Yes. Maybe. I can't see anyone else at the moment. My wife has lost a lot of blood."

"What is your wife's name and age?"

"Chelsea, and she's thirty-three years old."

"Is she conscious?"

"Yes, she's talking to me, but she's very weak."

"Can you put pressure on the wound, Micah?"

"Yes, I'm pushing on the entry and exit wounds, but my hands are covered in blood. I don't think it's helping."

"What part of her body has been injured?"

"She was shot in the back."

"Keep applying pressure. The ambulance is about ten minutes from you. Don't hang up. I should warn you that the property you are at has been flagged as a potential high risk, so the police will be the first ones on the scene."

He yanked his T-shirt over his head, balled it up, and pressed it against the wound on Chelsea's chest. "Keep your eyes open, Chels. You keep your eyes on my face, all right?"

She smiled. "You're a good man. That's why I wanted to be with you, you know."

"I'm not going to leave you. Not now, not ever."

"I know that now. I'm sorry, Micah, for running away with Dave and keeping Rowan from you, for everything."

"You were afraid."

She frowned. "Yes, but it wasn't an excuse to hurt you. I shouldn't have let Dave make that deal with you."

"I don't care about the money, Chels. Only about you and Rowan."

"But I need you to understand. It wasn't always about money."

She coughed, and blood spattered his chest.

Shit!

"Chels! Don't talk anymore." He cocked his head. "I can hear the sirens."

She stared into his eyes and blinked. It was an exaggerated movement, as though it took a huge effort.

"Help is nearly here, Chels. Just hold on."

"I did love you in the beginning, Mikey." Her lips stretched to reveal red-stained teeth. "It wasn't your fault I didn't fit."

"Shh. You don't need to tell me this now. Wait until you're feeling better."

"Just couldn't s-stay in your world."

Her eyes rolled back, her head rested heavily against his stomach.

"Chels?" He shook her shoulder gently. There was so much blood now. The delicate silk blouse was tie-dyed red.

All the money in the world wasn't worth this. Everything he'd done was for his family, and without them none of it mattered.

Chapter 35

A bee hovered lazily in front of Neve's face, but she daren't swat at it. Rowan was pressed against her belly as they crouched under a bushy protea. One finger rested lightly across his lips to remind him to be silent. Soundless tremors vibrated through him and into her.

Dusty, leather boots had been waiting in the nearby grass for several minutes. They were an arm's length away and joined to denim-clad legs and muscular thighs. The hunter sighed and turned, as though to walk away.

A lick of wind rustled leaves, and Rowan whimpered.

"Gotcha." The boots spun and rushed towards them.

Bent over like this, Neve couldn't defend herself, so she settled for protecting Rowan. She pushed him behind a tree and braced for impact as steel-capped leather connected with her ribs. Every molecule of air was expelled from her body in a loud huff. Using the momentum, she rolled backwards, ribs screaming in protest.

Not good. Need to take this bastard down and get Rowan out of here.

The pain in her side prevented her drawing breath, but she gasped through it and pushed onto her hands and knees—a vulnerable position. A searing pain ripped across her scalp, and she was jerked to her feet, by her hair ... where she looked straight into Dave Wilks's eyes.

"You just don't know when to give up, do you?" He bared slightly yellow teeth.

When he released her hair, her first instinct was to rub her scalp, but she wasn't going to pass up an opportunity. Her knuckles connected with his exposed trapezium muscle, right where it joined the front of his shoulder.

"Shit!" He clamped his arm to his side and rubbed the injury.

This wasn't a fair fight while he was still on his feet though, so Neve spun and kicked the back of his knee. Dave wasn't as solid as some of the other gang members, but he obviously wasn't a lightweight. The move should've dropped him, but he just stumbled. Worse still, now he looked really pissed off.

Damn. I need to bring him down to a manageable size.

She somersaulted across the twigs and leaf litter, coming into a crouch and swinging her own booted foot into his ankle. This time he toppled sideways. It was the break she needed to gain the upper hand. Pushing off a tree stump, she launched.

A familiar click turned her tensed muscles limp mid-air. Impetus carried her into Dave's shoulder, and they ended up flat on the ground in a tangle of limbs. It was close enough to gouge his eyes or something ... if he didn't have a Smith and Wesson pointed at Rowan's head.

"Baby, I didn't know you felt that way." The pig thrust his pelvis into her. "Normally I'd be happy to oblige, but how about you get off me now? You wouldn't want this gun to accidentally go off, eh?"

She glanced from Rowan to the silver pistol. *All I need is a moment.*

"I wouldn't if I were you," Dave growled.

Rowan's eyes were wide and dark from fear. The fight went out of her in an instant.

"Don't hurt him," she begged.

"Then how about you stand up and put your wrists together?"

She complied. How could she release the blade on her calf without him getting suspicious? Damn it, she couldn't.

Surely, Tony had incapacitated Boiler by now and would be headed this way with Micah and Chelsea. There had been several shots from the vicinity of the shed. Perhaps there was no one left to come to her aid. Rowan might have a better chance if he ran away. No, Dave wouldn't hesitate to shoot.

It was too late to make a decision as Dave ripped the leather belt from his waist and wrapped the thick binding tightly around her wrists. At least he hadn't been to Tony's school of "always bind hands *behind* the back." Although it didn't seem like it just now, every mistake Dave made could be to her advantage.

"Right, now we're going to walk back to the house and see what Boiler wants to do with you. This little bloke"—Dave ruffled Rowan's hair, and Neve wanted to punch his nose—"is worth a whole lot of dough."

At least that meant he didn't intend to kill them right away.

Dave grabbed the belt around Neve's wrists and dragged her forward. He turned to
Rowan. "Come on, kid, let's go see your mum, eh?"

Neve stumbled as she was pulled along.

Hell, this sucks. It should've been easy to get Rowan out with Tony and Micah occupying the other men. Bloody Dave. "You don't have to do this, Dave. You know there isn't any way you're going to get away with this. Micah's accountant isn't going to transfer the money if anything happens to him. Your cover is blown."

"Shut up."

"You could just let us go. You don't need to tell Boiler you saw us." *God, I hope Tony and Micah have the situation at the house under control, or I'm walking into a shit fight.*

With any luck, Tony would overpower Dave before he knew what hit him.

Rowan fell behind, so Dave scooped him up and tucked him under his arm like a football. The little boy squealed.

Neve ground her teeth. "Please don't do this," she said.

"It doesn't matter what I want to do. If I go back there without the kid, Boiler will shoot me without a second thought." He shoved her ahead of him.

"Not if you don't go back to him. Micah has contacts. He'll give you the whole ten million dollars if you let Rowan go. I know he will, and then you can retire anywhere you want."

"You're ignorant if you think the Mutts won't track me down. Now shut up and get moving."

"With that much money, he will never find you."

He cuffed her across the back of the head. "Shut the hell up!"

She trudged forwards, sneaking a glance back to see Rowan's little legs dangling from under Dave's arm, his head bobbing in time with the man's gait.

He was just a child. Who knew what kind of long-term scars he would have after this?

As she rounded the corner of the shed—the very place she'd started from and had hoped never to see again—Neve's stomach lurched into her throat. She staggered forward, but Dave tugged her T-shirt to stop her.

Micah raised his head, and his blank eyes were a stark contrast to his flushed cheeks. He stared as though he wasn't really seeing her, or Dave, or Rowan. He was hunched over Chelsea, shirtless, and they were both covered in blood. Neve choked on a scream, her eyes searching for Micah's injury.

"Mummy!" Rowan squirmed and sobbed.

"Boiler?" Dave's deep voice rumbled through the air as he called to his mate. It didn't sound like just a question though. He was worried about what had happened in his absence.

"Down here, mate." Boiler's call came from near the house.

Dave dragged Neve away from Micah. Her desperate gaze held his empty one until bushes came between them. She didn't cry out for him, though. There wasn't any point. Obviously something had gone very wrong with their plan.

None of them would be going home today. Or any day.

They rounded the rainwater tank and stepped onto a patch of sparse lawn by the house. Boiler stood over a limp body. It was slim with withered arms and a full head of dark hair.

"Tony!" This time Neve broke from Dave's restraint and flung herself over her father. "Daddy." Her vision blurred as tears squeezed out.

Dave was relaying the story of finding her to Boiler, but she tuned them out. With her face pressed onto her father's chest, she felt warmth and heard his strong heartbeat. *Oh, Dad, thank goodness you're alive.* "I love you," she whispered in his ear.

"Yeah, yeah, touching." Boiler grabbed Neve's arm and yanked her to her feet. "You're coming with me. Stick the kid in the ute, Dave, and get him to the city clubhouse."

This was bad. They were going to separate them. She glanced around for a makeshift weapon. Rowan was still limp under Dave's arm, tears streaming down his screwed-up face. The poor little guy had probably been so traumatised that he had no fight left.

The men were both armed and bigger than her. She wasn't afraid of their size, but she wasn't foolish enough to think she could successfully take them down before one got a shot off. Her best bet was to wait until she was alone with Boiler and then try to incapacitate him. Once she was free, she could help Rowan.

There wasn't any point hoping that Micah would come to her aid. He appeared to be bleeding out beside Chelsea. And Tony was down for the count. It was all up to her now.

Boiler didn't bother dragging her; he pushed her ahead of him with the barrel of his shotgun. At least he couldn't see her working on the belt around her wrists. They moved towards the parked cars, her gaze following Rowan to Dave's twin-cab ute.

Boiler held the passenger door of a black sedan open for Neve. After a moment's hesitation, she slid into the seat.

"Don't get any stupid ideas," he growled. "This gun would make a hell of a mess of your pretty little skull."

She shivered. The layers of leather around her wrists were unaligned now, and it made them loose enough for her to wriggle her wrists. There was the wail of sirens in the distance. Help would be here soon.

Boiler moved around to the driver's door. "I'll see you there, Dave," he called.

This was her opportunity to leap from the car. The scrub was only metres away, and she could be lost from view in seconds ... but now was no time for running and hiding. Instead, she turned so her now free hands gripped the car seat, and struck out with one foot to hit the side of Boiler's leg as it entered the car. He yelped and fell backwards, butt first onto the ground. A car door slammed. The engine of Dave's ute started, and Rowan was inside.

Boiler was struggling to his feet.

Under the power of an almighty adrenaline surge, Neve launched herself the rest of the way out of the driver's door, latching both hands onto the gun barrel and aiming the crown of her head at Boiler's gut.

They hit the dust in a tangle of limbs and curses. With her legs wrapped around his, she kept him off balance. Briefly she had the advantage, and landed a blow to his face with her elbow. The big man cried out, and she snatched the gun away from him.

This was no thug catching her by surprise in a dark carpark. This time she was going to get the upper hand and keep it. For Rowan's sake.

Chapter 36

The sound of a struggle brought Micah back to his senses. He ought to stay with Chelsea, but there was nothing he could do for her and the sirens were close now. There was another scream from near the house.

Neve needed him.

With a last glance at his wife's ashen face, he swallowed all of the emotions that threatened to overwhelm him, and got to his feet. His chest and arms were slick with blood, but forcing the thought from his mind, he wiped his hands on his jeans and moved towards the sound of a scuffle in the car park.

Neve was wrestling a biker twice her size.

Boiler.

But if Neve was here, where was Rowan?

Micah sprinted towards the fray and leapt at Boiler, his foot connecting with the biker's ribs, followed by a satisfying yelp. Boiler broke away from Neve, and Micah took the opportunity to reach for her. They clasped hands, but Boiler grabbed his ankle and whipped him onto his back. The long, dark barrels of a shotgun came towards him, but he kicked it away with his free foot.

The boom resounded through his body and left his ears ringing. Everyone held their breaths for a moment, waiting for the blooming pain of the pellets.

No pain.

But then Neve's brows crumpled, her eyes focused somewhere far away.

No! Not Neve too.

A desperate shriek flew from her open mouth.

Micah scrambled to his feet to help her, but he couldn't see the wound. His gaze followed hers to Dave's ute, where a spider web of cracked glass in the back window was mirrored by blood splatter on the inside of the windscreen. Dave slumped forward onto the wheel. The engine revved, and the vehicle started to move.

Rowan's pale face pressed against the passenger window, eyes wide.

He lurched towards his son, and something solid struck the side of his head.

Micah collapsed to his knees, gaze still on Rowan's terrified face as the ute disappeared over the lip of the car park, headed for the dam.

No, he wasn't going to let this happen. He brought his arm up to deflect Boiler's next blow, and latched onto the cold metal barrel of the shotgun. Boiler's finger reached for the trigger.

If he had to swap his life for his son's, he'd do it.

In a heartbeat.

• • •

Neve heard the men wrestling beside her, but she didn't spare them a glance. Micah was strong enough and motivated enough to handle Boiler. It was Rowan who had to be saved. She left behind the man she loved, maybe for the last time.

Her feet soared across the car park, arms pumping, heart in her throat, eyes on the wheel ruts in the soft soil at the edge. Without pausing, she leapt after the out-of-control vehicle, her feet sliding and tripping on the rough terrain of the steep descent.

A gunshot echoed around the valley, and she lost her footing.

Micah must have lost his battle too.

Stones bit into her flesh as she tumbled over tufts of grass and stopped in the bristles of a low shrub. The ute's left tire rolled over a sturdy bush and veered right. It narrowly missed a gum tree and then nose-dived into the murky water of the dam.

"No!"

Spray washed over the bonnet and it slowed, floated momentarily, and then the engine spluttered and died. Neve scrambled to untangle herself from the bush as the weight of the ute's engine took it down nose first.

Rowan's high-pitched scream ripped through her soul. His contorted face appeared at the back window, red with anguish as he climbed to the top of the cab to avoid the rush of cold, silted water.

"Open the window, Rowan!" she screamed.

He reached for the door, but snatched his hand back from the rising water. The ute was sinking fast.

Neve reached for an old fence post, but it was soft with termite damage. Then she saw a chunk of slate bigger than her fist. It would have to do. She tumbled the last few metres and launched into the murky water. Thick mud sucked at her legs and claimed one shoe, but she forced her way through the water, using her arms to propel her.

The water level in the ute's cab was halfway up the windows now. Endless, terrified screams came from within.

No one will die in my place again. I won't let it happen. "I'm coming, Carlos."

She reached the cab and smashed the rock against the back window. The existing crack from the bullet barely widened, but the rock shattered. *Give me a break!*

Fighting wet fabric and a slippery handle, she unsheathed the knife from its leg scabbard. The handle was solid. She raised her arm and brought it down with force against the window. A web of fractures formed. One more time and the shattered glass bowed inward.

"Move away from the window, Rowan."

Brown rivulets leaked in faster now around the windows. Neve didn't wait for Rowan to move; there wasn't time. Kneeling in the sloshing tray, she raised her arm again and hit the glass as hard as she could. Splintered glass sliced her hand as the window gave way. She had punched a hole through it, but the damned sheet of glass held together.

Water rushed through the opening, and Rowan thrashed at the deluge with his tiny fists. Neve pulled the glass from the frame, cast it aside, and lunged through the opening, but Rowan had backed to the far side. She couldn't reach him.

As the cab fully submerged, she took a breath and plunged inside, her arms extended. Razorlike fragments scoured her stomach as she wriggled forward, clasping in desperation, but unable to see anything through the silt. The filthy water rushed up her nose and pressed against her clenched lips like gritty earthworms trying to get in.

It's been too long!

The air in her lungs faded; Carlos was drowning centimetres away from her all over again. But this time no one was going to pull her to safety. She was all alone, and she *wouldn't* fail him.

• • •

Micah and Boiler lay in the dirt, panting. Apparently, they were evenly matched when it came to wrestling. Every time Micah made a try to follow the ute and Neve, Boiler dragged him back for another hiding. But he'd given as good as he got, and this was no time to give up. Even now, Boiler's gaze shifted to the shotgun a few metres away.

He could only trust that Neve was strong enough to save Rowan.

Sirens screamed nearby. If he could last just a few more minutes, help would come.

They both scrambled for the weapon, but it was too far. Instead, Micah latched on to Boiler's leg. A boot connected with his jaw, but he didn't let go. And then the sirens were upon them. Boiler twisted and rolled. As two police cars skidded to a halt, he crouched low and ran into the scrub.

Micah stood to greet the officers, hands on his head, like he'd seen in the movies.

An officer with a blonde ponytail leapt from the car, pistol drawn. "Get face down on the ground and put your hands behind your back," she said.

"I need to find my son. He was in a car that went over the edge there." He pointed.

"Get down on the ground now!" A male officer pointed his weapon over the bonnet of the car.

Micah obeyed. Dirt clung to his lips and scraped his cheek as he lay face down with an officer's foot pressed into the small of his back. He could barely raise his head high enough to spit blood beside him. The male officer patted him down, and then cold handcuffs snapped around his wrists. Red and blue lights flashed across the landscape and, through the eye that wasn't pressed against the ground, he watched the female snap a plastic glove on and carry the gun to the boot of the patrol car.

"You can sit up now."

Micah rolled onto his side and sat. "These aren't necessary." He wriggled his wrists but stopped as the metal bit into them. "I'm the one who called for an ambulance."

"Whose weapon is that?" his guard queried.

"Boiler's. Look, he might still be here. We're in danger."

"I'm well aware that the Mutts own this property, but the area is being secured by other officers. If Steven Boil is here, we'll find him."

"None of this matters. I just need to make sure Rowan is safe." Micah struggled to his feet.

"Sit. Down. You will remain in custody until I figure out what's going on here. Now what's your name?"

"Micah Kincaid. Has anyone been down the hill? Rowan is down there in a car."

"Another officer is attending to that vehicle, so you don't need to worry about it."

"Don't need to worry?" Rage swept through his veins, pounding in his ears so that it dulled the sounds around him. "I'm not answering any more questions until I see my son."

The officer pursed his lips. "I suggest you cooperate or I'll put you in the back of the car and you can explain your story to the magistrate in the morning. Do you understand?"

"Look, I know you're just doing your job, but I need to find Neve and Rowan. Can you please just go and check? I promise I'll stay here." Dust stung his eyes and they watered. His fists clenched.

"Another officer is attending to the vehicle in the dam, but as soon as you answer a few questions, I'll get more information for you, okay? Now, can you tell me what has gone on here today?"

Micah wasn't listening anymore. He was focused on the paramedic who disappeared towards the dam, carrying a first aid kit. Towards Rowan and Neve. It was as though he was listening to his own body through a stethoscope: blood rushing, heart thumping furiously against protesting ribs, air rasping in and out of his lungs.

"Mr. Kincaid, did you hear me? I need to know how many people are on the property and why you're here."

"No! Look, my son was in a car that went over the edge and crashed. I *need* to know what happened to him."

He jumped to his feet and made a run for it. To hell with playing by the rules.

Chapter 37

Neve's diaphragm spasmed as it fought to draw breath. She would have to pull out of the ute to breathe, and Rowan would drown.

Not again. I can't survive this again.

At last her hand closed around a thin, slippery limb, and she pulled it towards her. She struggled to back out of the cab and push towards the surface, her chest convulsing in protest by the time she broke through. Oh, glorious air.

Rowan sputtered beside her. It was the most fabulous sound she'd ever heard, but he wasn't out of danger yet. Water poured from his tiny mouth, and then his face screwed up and he burst into tears.

Using just her legs to propel them, she floated on her back, holding Rowan on her chest, his head safely above the surface. Carlos's face had been blue and unresponsive, but Rowan's was flushed, his eyes blinking. He would live.

Her foot hit the bottom and she turned onto her side, gouging sludge with one hand to haul them onto the bank. Still half submerged, she lay in the putrid mud, clutching Rowan like the treasure he was. Sediment from the dam was up her nose and in her mouth. It was all she could smell and taste, and no amount of spitting freed her from it.

"It's all right, Ro," she whispered in his ear. "You're okay now."

A murmur of voices from above made them both look up to see a tall blue-clad figure at the top of the hill. Rowan trembled in her arms, and she instinctively pushed him behind her, but the figure coalesced into a uniformed man picking his way down the slope.

"It's okay, the police are here," she told Rowan.

The officer's hand was on his holstered pistol. "Ma'am," he called, "I need you to put the child down and put your hands on your head."

"He nearly drowned and he's frightened. I can't let him go," she implored.

The officer stopped a few metres away. "Step away from the child and raise your hands now. An ambulance officer will attend to the boy."

It wasn't a question, because Neve didn't have a choice. Everyone needed to play their part, so she kissed Rowan's head and lifted him to his feet. He whimpered and shook his head against her chest.

A woman wearing green overalls and carrying a red kit appeared at the top of the hill.

"Rowan, the ambulance lady needs to make sure you're not hurt. Remember that you swallowed a lot of water, and I'm going to be worried until I'm sure you're okay."

The paramedic stopped a safe distance behind the cop and said, "Your mummy needs to talk to the policeman." She smiled and held a hand out to Rowan.

He looked between the paramedic and Neve.

"I'll be right here where you can see me," Neve promised.

The woman placed the red kit on the ground and opened it. "Rowan, is it? Would you like to come and look inside my special medicine box?"

Curiosity won, and Rowan stumbled up the hill.

All Neve wanted to do was run after him, but she stayed ankle-deep in the dam, covered in sticky mud, her hands on her head.

The officer approached. "Do you have any weapons on you?"

"No."

"Turn around."

She complied and received a pat down.

"Is there anyone else in the vehicle?" The officer nodded towards the roof of the ute, which was all that was left protruding above the surface.

"Yes, a man called Dave, but he's dead."

The officer kept his eyes on her but relayed the information through his radio.

"How do you know he's dead?"

She gave him a very brief rundown of the events, pleading for information about Tony, Micah, and Chelsea.

"It seems we have a lot to discuss, Miss Botticelli. How about we head up to the ambulance and get you both checked out. Then you're going to need to accompany me to the station to give a full statement."

The officer held an arm to one side to indicate she should go ahead of him. His gaze still roamed cautiously, but he hadn't cuffed her.

She scooped Rowan's tiny body into her arms on her way past.

"I want Mummy"—tears crowded his eyes again—"and Daddy," he said like an afterthought.

Neve looked at the paramedic, who shrugged, as did the cop. Her stomach flipped as an ache began to spread to her heart. Chelsea's bloody body ... Micah covered in blood and then wrestling Boiler. And Tony, where was Tony? Bile burned its way up her throat as she followed the trail of broken vegetation the ute had made on its way down.

She paused near the top and pressed Rowan's head to her shoulder.

"I'll take him if you like," the paramedic said.

Neve was about to look over the edge and see the end of life as she knew it. After a deep breath, she took the final step.

Boiler's car was still there, with the door open. Cop cars were everywhere, bathing the landscape in flashes of red and blue. Two-way radios crackled, and four bikers were sitting along one wall of the shed, their hands secured behind them. Boiler gave her a death stare as she hurried across the car park, searching.

Her boots stopped before her brain registered the blood-soaked sheets covering two bodies.

"No!"

If one of them was Chelsea, the other had to be Tony or Micah.

Pain ripped through her, so strong that it doubled her over and the meagre contents of her stomach spilt onto the ground.

• • •

"Please hold still." The frustrated paramedic brandished a blood-soaked wipe at the graze on Micah's bicep.

He leapt from his seat in the back of the ambulance, and Officer Wagner stepped forward.

"You need to get that looked at, Mr. Kincaid."

"It barely scratched the surface. For God's sake, will you just tell me how Neve and Rowan are?"

"You are going to be detained for questioning, but I can put the handcuffs back on and arrest you if you don't cooperate."

"That won't be necessary. I just want to know if they're safe." Micah pushed his way around the ambulance doors and stopped dead.

Neve was bent over in the middle of the car park. Alive, but she must be hurt, and here the paramedics were wasting time trying to bandage his scratches. Her dark hair was matted, clothes caked in mud, and ...

No Rowan. She'd tried, but was too late. Rowan was gone.

Air came in gasps, but it wasn't enough. He dropped to his knees.

He had done this. Chelsea would still be alive if he hadn't acted impulsively this morning. Rowan would still be alive if he'd just followed Boiler's orders. And where was Tony?

Neve looked up, and their eyes met. The corners of her eyes were pinched with anguish, but it was the most beautiful sight he'd ever seen. His vision blurred. Her unsteady legs propelled her towards him, and he opened his arms to receive her.

"Your arm." Her hand hovered over the wound.

"I'm all right." He took her face between his hands. "Are *you* hurt?" It was difficult to tell through all the grime.

She shook her head, but tears flowed down her cheeks.

"I know," he said, and pulled her to him. "I can't believe he's gone."

"No." She whimpered against him. "Not Tony ..."

He pulled back. "They have to get him out of there."

Neve cocked her head. "What are you talking about?"

"They can't leave Ro—" His voice caught. "Can't leave him in the water."

Her eyes widened in horror, and she grabbed his hand, tugging him towards a second ambulance. He was reluctant—not yet ready to see Rowan's body—but Neve was as persistent as ever. When he stepped around the open double doors at the back, there was Rowan, sitting on a bed, swinging his muddy legs back and forth as a paramedic pressed a stethoscope against his back. Filthy and bewildered, but smiling.

"Rowan! Thank God." Micah bear-hugged them both, until Rowan wriggled to get free.

"Daaad, you're squishing me."

They all laughed.

"I can see the celebrations have started without me."

It was a voice Neve would know anywhere. One she cherished and trusted. She held her breath and turned slowly. "Dad!"

Chapter 38

Neve swiped at the grit that clung to her skin. The cops had allowed Bronwyn to deliver a change of clothes to the station, but you could only clean so much silt off with paper towels in a public bathroom sink.

A rogue yawn forced its way past her pressed lips and out her nose.

For crying out loud. How much longer are they going to keep me in this room?

She'd been staring at the same scuffed, white walls in the interrogation room for hours, and if it had felt small in the beginning, now it felt like a closet. The recording device they'd used during several interviews had been pushed up out of the way, but the intrusive, glossy black security dome still clung to the ceiling in one corner.

Was Officer Wagner watching her now? Waiting for her to lose it and confess to multiple murders? He'd circled around a lot of questions during the last few hours, leaving the room and coming back several times. Asking the same questions in different ways, but none more frequently than, "Why did you help Micah when you had no prior relationship and the child isn't yours?" He'd been very interested in how Chelsea got shot, too.

As if I'd shoot her so I could have Micah all to myself. What kind of person did a thing like that?

Her poor dad. He must be beside himself being inside a police station, let alone being questioned and sampled. Hopefully, he wouldn't do anything stupid enough to get him locked up.

She folded her arms on the table and rested her head on them; let her eyelids close ...

• • •

Neve woke with a start at the sound of footsteps.

"I'm sorry to have kept you waiting, Miss Botticelli. As I've already explained, you've been charged with aggravated trespass, because you went onto the property without lawful intent. It will be up to a judge to decide if you entered the property with the intent to inflict grievous bodily harm.

"However, I'm sure the judge will take the extenuating circumstances into consideration, and the fact that you helped us break up the Mutts' southern operations. For now you are free to leave with your father, but I'd appreciate it if you would make yourself available to answer further questions that may assist our investigations."

She was on her feet and out the door without another word, but halfway down the corridor, she paused.

"What about Micah?"

"He has been cooperating with police and will be released shortly. I believe he wants to spend the night at the hospital."

"What? I didn't think he was hurt badly."

"He's not. Mr. Kincaid's son is being held overnight at Flinders Medical Centre so that an officer can question him in the morning, when someone from child services will be available to sit in on the interview. Mr. Kincaid won't be allowed to see him until after the interview, but he insists on staying close."

Micah had nearly lost it when he wasn't allowed to go with Rowan in the ambulance. He must be beside himself not being allowed to go to him now. What if child services decided he wasn't a fit father anymore? Hell, it didn't even pay to think about Micah losing Rowan over this.

Micah will want to take Rowan home now. His home, not mine. Far away in Sydney.

"Honey, are you all right?"

The reassuring voice immediately relaxed the knot of angst in her gut.

"Dad." She flung her arms around him, breathing in his comforting scent.

He squeezed her back.

"I love you," she said against his shoulder. "I'm so glad you taught me to defend myself."

It was only as she stepped back and studied him under the harsh fluorescent lights that the shadows under his eyes stood out and the texture of his skin looked papery, as though this ordeal had aged him decades.

"Are you all right, Dad?"

He draped an arm around her shoulders. "Let's go home."

Walking ahead of the officers must've given Tony the same uneasy feeling she felt—as if the cops might change their minds at any moment and march them back into the interrogation room—because they both quickened the pace and practically burst through the door at the end of the corridor. Neve fell straight into Bronwyn's arms.

"Thank goodness Micah organised lawyers for you," Bronwyn said, wrapping Neve in a bear hug. "I thought the next time I saw you, you'd be wearing an orange jumpsuit."

"We've organised for you to leave through the rear door," Officer Wagner said, "because there's quite a media contingent out front."

Of course Micah's involvement would hit headlines. Not good for any of them, but especially not for Tony. Officer Wagner opened the rear door, scanned the car park, and closed it again.

"There are a couple of reporters out there, but you'll be away before they realise who you are. Call me if you have any trouble or think of anything else." He passed a business card to Neve.

"My car is right by the door." Bronwyn squeezed Neve's hand reassuringly.

• • •

No one spoke during the drive home. No doubt Bronwyn had a million questions, but Neve ignored her worried glances. She didn't have an ounce of energy left.

It seemed like an eternity since Micah had strode into the kindy, demanding to see Rowan. In a single week, he'd ingrained himself in her life, in her home; even Tony and Jack seemed to accept him now. Beneath the Louis Vuitton, there was a determined, practical man who cared deeply and would fight for what he believed in. And despite his barbed comments about Neve giving up her life for Tony, she believed he respected her life choices.

Micah was someone who understood the importance of keeping family close. The loss he'd suffered as a child hadn't been death, like hers, but his father's abandonment had been just as permanent and had caused just as much upheaval in his life. How ironic that, because he valued his family, she was going to lose him now.

He didn't have a choice though; his mother relied on him and Rowan would need stability more than anything after losing Chelsea. Micah would be Rowan's rock. She had no doubt he'd put his son's needs first, and he could offer financial security and extended family. Far more than Neve had to offer.

A warm hand patted her shoulder, and she turned to smile at Tony in the back seat.

He reached up to wipe away her tears, his mouth turned down in sympathy. "We're going to be okay, honey."

"I know," she said. Physically they were all okay. It was emotionally that frightened her. Right now her heart felt like a porcelain trinket that had been shattered and fitted back together again without glue. It wouldn't take much force for it to fragment irrevocably.

Chapter 39

Micah pushed a coil of sleek brown hair from Rowan's forehead and watched his son's chest rise and fall with the slow rhythm of slumber. The child had cried for a long time, asking intermittently for his mother. It wasn't possible to adequately explain the finality of death to a four-year-old.

I'm never letting him out of my sight again.

Micah had spent the whole of the previous night pacing hospital corridors, unable to tear himself away. Many times he'd thought of calling Neve, but she would be nursing her own wounds. They were all criminals now, at least until his lawyer worked his magic. Worse still, they would all be subjected to an intense media spotlight. Neve and Tony didn't deserve to have their peaceful life cracked open like a walnut shell; each piece delivered as public fodder and chewed over by the masses.

No, it was better if he steered clear of them until the worst of it had blown over.

This morning, an endless compilation of doctors, social services workers, and police detectives had gone in and out of Rowan's room, and it took his lawyer's intervention before Micah was allowed to take Rowan back to the Travaglias' bed-and-breakfast.

There was a gentle knock on the cabin door. He got up but hesitated at the bedroom door, unwilling to leave Rowan. Finally, he left the bedroom door ajar so he could still see his precious son.

Taking a deep breath, he checked that the door chain was in place. Although the media was camped at the end of the Travaglias' driveway, you never knew how bold they would be. He opened the front door a fraction.

"Sorry, I hope you weren't asleep." Bronwyn Travaglia proffered a glass bowl lined with a chequered tea towel. "I didn't think you'd want to leave Rowan, so here is some lunch."

He sighed and rolled his shoulders, then slid the chain aside and fully opened the door. The bowl was warm, and the steamy aroma of scones made his mouth water in an instant.

"Thanks, Bronwyn, you've been very good to us. I appreciate how difficult having me here must be with the media camped out, but we'll be out of your hair tomorrow."

"Don't worry about it. Mum and I have got the *no comment* thing down pat, and we let the answering machine get the phone calls. I'll bring some roast pork and vegetables by around six, if you like."

"That would be lovely. Rowan's asleep at the moment, the poor little tyke is exhausted, but I'm sure he'll be ravenous when he wakes."

"If you need anything at all, just let me know. You're part of the family now."

It was a nice notion, but he couldn't be sure about where things stood between Neve and him. Not yet. "How is Neve?"

"Not great. She misses you and Rowan ... but she'll be fine. She has Tony and me to look out for her."

He smiled. Neve certainly had a protective extended family. "I'll call her," he promised.

Bronwyn seemed to relax a little. "Great, see you later."

As he pushed the door shut and relatched the chain, a faint pinking of the skin across his knuckles caught his eye. It was fading faster than the impression Neve had made on him on his first day in Turners Gully.

Neve's stoic resolve had so frustrated him then, and yet even through his haze of desperation, the fire in her eyes had caught his attention. Their potent attraction had taken him completely by surprise, and no matter how much she denied it, he knew she felt it too. It was a magnetism that set his skin on fire and clouded his mind, but it had developed into so much more for him. She was everything he had never known he wanted: independent and fragile, stunning without the least bit of effort to flaunt it, she fought for her fundamental beliefs, and would challenge him on every level, but most importantly, she loved Rowan.

In just one week, he'd fallen for her—harder than he'd ever fallen before. He desperately wanted to be sure her feelings were as strong ... but couldn't ask, not until he was sure he wouldn't put her at risk anymore.

He slumped into the armchair beside Rowan's bed and let his eyelids close for just a moment ...

The sight of blood oozing into creamy silk fabric made Micah gasp. He clawed at the air to stop the sensation of falling into an abyss ... and then opened his eyes.

He couldn't breathe until he turned his head and saw that Rowan was sleeping safely beside him. Even though Micah was awake now, the images of Chelsea lying on the ground, her blood oozing between his fingers, wouldn't fade.

"It wasn't your fault I didn't fit. Just couldn't s-stay in your world," she'd said. What if all of this god-awful mess could have been avoided if he'd done something differently? Chelsea shouldn't have felt like she didn't belong in his world. But Neve would see a life with him exactly the same way: as though she would have to forfeit her own career and beliefs and be uprooted from her father.

I won't do that to you, he promised.

Chapter 40

A Barnevelder hen ruffled the double-laced pattern of its black-and-brown feathers and pecked the fluff at the top of Neve's Ugg boot. She flinched and the hen gave a shocked squawk before fleeing across the yard. She must have been sitting still for so long that it forgot she was there.

A chill from the slab of granite under her, cut through her jeans. The peace and quiet of her home had never before felt lonely, but she couldn't stand it any longer. Tony was a man of few words, and she didn't even have Bron and Jack to visit because the media was still camped at the end of each driveway. Then a reporter got her mobile number, so she turned that off too.

Even Kookapie didn't bother with his infectious cackle as he perched on the low bough of a nearby gum tree and puffed his feathers out against the bitter wind.

At first she'd put the emptiness inside down to the shock of the near-death experience, and then the grief of losing two people she wanted in her life, even though she'd known they couldn't stay. The truth was, she would never again be whole without them.

Her nightmares had been replaced by new ones, where murky water swallowed Rowan whole. She rubbed her nose to banish the stench of mud that just wouldn't leave her. Her whole body ached with the need to see Rowan and Micah, to wrap her arms around them and feel them safe and vital.

And to think, all of this trauma had been caused by the pursuit of the almighty dollar. Well, she couldn't be entirely ungrateful, because it also brought Micah to Turner's Gully, and he'd be back soon.

There was one thing that clarified in her mind during that first long, bleak night without him. Only the absence of someone she loved could hurt her that much. She just had to last a few days.

A single, large raindrop hit the middle of her nose, and she looked up at the dark sky. She had no idea how long she'd been sitting in the garden. The weak sun had moved across the sky— that much she knew. The thrum of a helicopter passed overhead as one of the news crews made its regular pass.

It was difficult to believe that a few days ago, she had been hiding on a dark hillside with Micah, weighing up the best course of action to save Rowan. It seemed like an eternity. It was important for everyone to get their lives back on track though: Rowan needed to be around family, Micah needed the distraction of work, and she needed ... She needed ... no, she *deserved* to make some changes in her life too, so she wouldn't remain stagnant.

Something touched her shoulder, and she leapt to her feet, hand on heart.

"Sorry, I didn't mean to startle you." Bron looked as elegant as always, proffering two mugs of tea. "Can I share your seat?"

Neve shrugged at the granite boulder and sat back down. "Sure."

Bron settled beside her and nestled the mugs between them. The hot ceramic was the only sliver of warmth on Neve's body.

"Are the reporters all gone?" she asked.

"No. They're difficult to extract, like ticks," Bron said bitterly, "but I kept the car windows up and didn't look at them."

"You shouldn't have bothered coming. I'm not much company."

Neve picked up her tea and let the warm steam waft across her face. Plump yellow-and-black-striped bees buzzed sluggishly through the chaos of flowers interspersed amongst the herbs and vegetables. The strong scent of jasmine carried on the breeze, from the back of the chicken coop. This had been a place where she used to sit with Bron and solve the world's problems through their teenage and university years, and here they were as adults.

Bron bumped her shoulder against Neve's. "Well, at least you're out of bed."

"I plan on returning to work next Tuesday."

"That could be good. We'll get through this together."

"Yeah, I'll be okay. Eventually."

"I'm sorry he left, Neve. I really thought you two suited one another."

"He's coming back!"

"Oh, of course."

Neve turned to look Bron in the eye. "We might be from different worlds, but there's something special between us. That will be enough for us to find a way to make it work, won't it?"

It had taken Neve far too long to realise that, despite all the money and trimmings, Micah was just a man, who needed love and acceptance like anyone else. Something she'd denied herself.

Bron sighed. "I only hope he realises how special he is to be trusted with your heart."

"Yeah, I think he does."

No matter how well Neve had tried to keep the walls of caution up, Micah's chivalry and quiet strength had wormed their way under her defences. He'd seen the way she lived, understood that her values were different to his, and yet still he loved her. Would it be enough?

You didn't get any say about who you loved or were related to. This was her life, in Turners Gully, taking care of Tony. It didn't seem too much to ask for someone to share her secrets with, and even her own children one day. But the trouble with loving someone was that it left her vulnerable.

Micah wasn't suited to the life she'd built here, nor she to his. *Who am I kidding? No man is suited to this.* He had enough of his own problems without buying into her complicated life.

"I've never felt like this before," she said, "and I don't want to lose it, but I'm not sure what to do about Tony."

Bron patted her knee. "What exactly is it you think he needs help with?"

For the first time in days, a smile crept across Neve's lips. "I guess he *is* trained to survive in the wilderness ... but the only way I can see this working is if I move to Sydney, and he'll get lonely."

"He has Jack, and flights are cheap."

"*I'll* get lonely."

"If it's meant to be, it'll all work out in the end."

"Thanks, Bron." She picked a stalk of English lavender and crushed it between her fingers to release the perfume. "So did you come over for a reason or just to chat?"

"Actually, Tony was worried about you seeing the newspaper."

The blood thundered through her veins as Bron passed a folded paper over.

What the hell kind of bad news do they have that needs them both to be here? Oh, please don't tell me something has happened to Rowan after everything he's been through.

On the front page was a huge colour photo of a solemn-faced Micah surrounded by black-clad supporters, but it was the sight of Rowan perched on his lap, tears trickling down pale cheeks, that crushed her. There was nothing she wanted in the world more right now than to comfort them, but she hadn't been invited.

"Other woman at wife's funeral" would probably cause a scandal. Not good for a business magnate's reputation.

No, that wasn't fair. Micah had never been a snob. She might never have realised it if they hadn't been thrown together in such odd circumstances, because she wouldn't have given a man like him a chance. And yet he was now integral to her happiness.

Her gaze skimmed the columns of news text, and it blurred. "I want to give them time to grieve, to be with family, but I don't know how much longer I can wait before I go after them Bron." It sounded like a plea. Bron handed her a tissue, so she swiped her watery eyes and got to her feet.

"They need me." It didn't matter that she wouldn't fit into the lifestyle of the rich and famous. They were meant to be together. If Micah was in too much pain to think about her right now, then she would be the one to make it happen. Tomorrow she'd be on a flight to her future.

Chapter 41

Micah stood in front of the little shack he'd called home for a week, and breathed in the crisp eucalyptus scent in the morning air. He pulled a motorbike helmet on and cinched the strap.

"If she went for a walk, she could be anywhere," he said. And if she didn't want to be found, he was shit out of luck. "Do you have any ideas about where I should start looking?"

Tony rubbed the back of his neck. "Well, she does have a favourite gum tree that she does her thinking under."

"I know the one." He swung a leg over the 250cc trail bike and nodded at Tony.

The lightweight bike bounced over rocks and ruts as Micah made his way down into the valley, over the creek, and back up the other side. He scouted every bush and rock overhang to no avail. It had crossed his mind—about a million times—that she might not let him explain. He had no intention of forcing her into a situation she wasn't ready for, but neither did he want to live without her. The past few days had been long enough. Now it was time to put his multipart plan into action.

At the crest of the trail, he had to go bush to get around a fallen tree, but as soon as he was clear of the greenery, he spotted the enormous gnarled gum tree at the back of the property, and there she was, hugging her knees, back against the trunk.

Her forehead was resting on her knees, but as he got close, her head snapped up and their gazes met. She jumped to her feet and took a tense stance.

Micah skidded to a halt and kicked down the bike stand. He pulled the helmet off quickly and then slowed his movements so as not to startle her. With her eyes wide and muscles taut, she reminded him of a skittish horse, ready to take flight. He placed the helmet on the ground and took unhurried steps towards his destiny.

• • •

When the familiar blue-and-white motorbike lurched from between the trees, Neve had just been thinking about Micah—who was she kidding, she hadn't stopped thinking about him since the day he stormed into the kindy—but this couldn't really be him.

Great, he's in my dreams and every thought, and now I'm imagining him here while I'm awake.

Her hungry gaze raked up and down his lean body and scrutinised his round, boyish face. He was far more handsome than her carefully preserved memories recalled. The helmet had flattened his gel-spiked hair to one side and a couple of day's growth darkened his jaw, but it only added a slightly untamed edge to his image. His skin looked soft enough to stroke, but it was the intensity of his burnt-sugar eyes that held her captive.

"You aren't real," she told the apparition. In her dreams—the really good ones—he didn't just stand there; he took her in his arms and kissed her until she couldn't remember her own name.

He smiled, and his eyes lit up in the sun. "Well that's one I haven't been accused of before. I can assure you I am real, and we need to talk."

The sound of his voice was a balm to her raw soul. The breeze ruffled his shirt, and the scent of the exotic aftershave that was his unique blend, curled up her nostrils and infused her brain. Emotion swamped her like an equatorial tide.

"I tried to call, but your mobile was switched off," he said. "I'm sorry we didn't get to talk before I went back to Sydney, but Rowan needed me. Tony says you haven't left the property."

"The media has been camped out, and ... How's Rowan?"

"He's doing all right. I can never repay you for saving him."

"Anyone would have."

"You're selling yourself short. He would have died if it weren't you there."

He stepped closer and held her hand in his long, warm fingers. He really was here.

"You know, you're lucky you caught me at home," she said. "If you'd come tomorrow, I would have been gone."

"Oh?" The pucker between his brows squeezed tighter.

Life was too short for regrets. It was all in time. "I didn't tell Dad, but I have a red-eye flight booked. To Sydney."

"To see *me*?" His mouth curled into an uncertain smile, and the lines at the corners of his eyes softened.

She gave a measured nod, tucked her hands under her armpits and stared at a higgledy-piggledy line of ants on the ground.

Dry grass and leaves crunched, and his boots came into view. Heat radiated from his body; drawing her towards it and making her head spin. His hand rose slowly until one finger touched her chin and lifted her face to his. Her pulse accelerated.

"We belong together, and you know it, too, don't you?" he said.

If a single look could convey emotion, his would be pleading her to believe him.

She held her breath as waves of passion and grief and confusion rolled through her. A tremble started in her knees, and she swayed.

"The last three days have been the longest in my life," she whispered. "I couldn't wait another day to see you."

His large, hot palm rested at the nape of her neck, and the weight urged her to lean into him. Just her forehead touched his broad chest, but it was enough for her to soak in his scent and feel the power of his body. God she'd missed it.

"I didn't want to subject you to all the media hype," he said, "but it's part and parcel of my life. I realise I come with a lot of baggage."

"The newspapers said stuff … about the kindergarten teacher you left behind."

"That's the very reason I didn't want you exposed to this shit. They insinuate when they don't have facts and twist innocent situations into scandals. I've developed a thick skin over the years, but you are going to have to look inside your heart and *feel* the truth, Neve."

She lifted her head and looked him square in the eyes. "I do feel it. Sydney is your home, and my home is with—"

"Home is where the heart is," he said. "I have a proposition that might work for us."

She looked up, and there was nothing but sincerity in his eyes.

"Most of my work can be done from anywhere with Internet access and it's no big deal for me to travel regularly, but I would need someone around whom I trusted, to take care of Rowan if I was going to commute to Sydney."

What the—? "Are you asking me to be an au pair?"

"Of course not. You'll be more like Rowan's step mum if you're living with us."

Her mouth popped open and closed again. She shook her head. "But your whole life is in Sydney."

"Neve, I've achieved everything I ever wanted in the business world. I have more than enough money to take care of my family, and that's all I ever wanted. Without them, there's no purpose in my life. But there's one dream I haven't realised, and I can't do it alone. It's being with a woman who loves me just as fiercely as I love her."

There was a flutter of hope deep in her belly. He stroked a palm down the side of her face, and she couldn't help but lean into the comfort of it.

"Neve, *you* are that woman. I want to be with you, always."

She took several deep breaths, and was ready to voice the question she didn't want to hear the answer to. "What if things don't work out between us?"

"If you make that decision, then I'll abide by it. I won't make a nuisance of myself, but I hope it won't be too weird for you if I stay in Turners Gully. It's a nice place to raise a child."

"What?" Neve's brows pulled together. "You'd stay here, even if we weren't together?"

"I can't keep uprooting Rowan, and I hear there's a great kindergarten in the area." He chuckled.

Could he really *want* to live in Turners Gully? Could he value her choices so much that he'd be willing to sacrifice to be with her? Then she remembered the other important people in his life.

"What about your mum?"

"Oh, don't worry, she's already planning on staying every other week, and I think Matt and Sarah are looking forward to a holiday destination. Come to think of it, it might get kind of crowded."

"What do you mean your mum's *already* making plans?"

"Rowan and I moved into a rental place yesterday. It's a bit ostentatious, but the view of Adelaide city is amazing. You might know the place, it's on Sugarloaf Road." He grinned.

"You rented Chelsea's house?"

He shrugged. "I heard it was available, and I figured I'd need room for all the visitors. Not to mention Rowan is already comfortable there. I thought it would be one less change for him to deal with."

"Wow." She rubbed a kink in the back of her neck. "Wow. I don't know what to say."

"Neve Botticelli, kindergarten teacher extraordinaire, combat expert, and self-appointed martyr is lost for words? Well, I can tell you that I've never been surer of what I want."

He took her face between his hands and gazed into her eyes with wonder. "I'm a flawed individual in so many ways, but I would walk across hot coals for you. I'm so in love that I can't breathe when you're not in my sight."

Her lower lip trembled. He was offering her all of her dreams on a silver platter. "I was ready to move to Sydney. It's too much for you to give up."

Micah stroked her hair as he continued. "Your life is no less important than mine, and I'm not saying that anyone has to give their life up. This is important enough to find a way to make it work. I want you as you are right now, with everything and everyone that comes with you."

"Tony?" Her voice was a soft squeak.

"You're kind of a package deal," he said. "Anyway, it's your choice. I know I'm not your ideal man, but I'm hoping you'll give me a chance to work on that."

Neve pulled back so she could look at his face. Surely he didn't believe that, but the uncertainty was plain in his eyes. For the first time since he'd come into view, her chest relaxed and she took a deep breath. He felt her pain. Her arms wriggled up, and she touched a fresh cut on his lower lip.

"I had a chat with Tony before I came to find you," he explained.

This time she grinned and laced her fingers behind his neck. "You're wrong, you know. You are my ideal man. I trust you and want you with everything that comes with you," she quoted him back.

There was no more thinking as the energy between them swelled to engulf them in a scorching current. Neve pulled his face down and brushed her lips across his. Her heart thumped a hopeful rhythm as Micah melded to her. Joined heart and soul, as family should be.

Acknowledgments

The art of imagining a story and turning it into a saleable manuscript is a process that not only involves the creator but a collection of support people. It is these people who generously impart life wisdom, inspire me, provide moral and technical support, participate in brainstorming sessions over cups of tea, and encourage me to never give up that I wish to thank here.

First and foremost, I have to thank my family for their unwavering belief in me. My beautiful sons keep me on my toes by sharing their spirit of inquiry and discovery, and my husband does his best to play it cool when I'm researching the best way to poison someone or testing fight moves on him. Most of all I appreciate his firm confidence in my success and acceptance of the peculiarities that come with living with an author. It sustains me when I reach the inevitable point of self-doubt.

I rely on multiple technical guides, with the most prominent being the esteemed Senior Sergeant Steve Hammond. He generously explains police procedures in layman's terms and helps bring into focus the indistinct line between realism and artistic licence. You can be sure this story is fictional, and where I have strayed from the path of accuracy, the culpability lies with me alone.

A special mention to Rowena Holloway, my partner in crime. We have shared book tours, soul searching, and presented workshops together. I couldn't do it without her. Also Lynn Wallace, who is subjected to my *very* rough drafts and is responsible for the delicious lamb shank recipe that gets a mention.

The remaining members of my support network are so numerous, I must mention them in general terms, but they are no less a precious resource. Anyone who has ever listened to me ramble about my latest character, helped unravel a plot twist, or generously reviewed by books has kept me motivated.

And I love my merry band of newsletter subscribers, who had a great time helping me come up with a name for this book. I'd like to say a special thanks to Wendy Leslie and Sue Guest for their suggestions.

Finally, I must thank Tara at Crimson Romance for taking a chance on this Aussie author, Julie for digging deep to see my vision and making my rough manuscript shine, and all of the other hard-working folks involved in the production process.

Happy reading to all.

About the Author

Thanks for taking the time to read this book. If you enjoyed it, I'd really appreciate you leaving a review on Amazon.

You can also connect with me via my website: www.sandyvaile. com, on Facebook, www.facebook.com/SandyVaile, or Twitter @ Sandy_Vaile (www.twitter.com/Sandy_Vaile).

My motto in life: I'll try anything once. By taking every opportunity that presents itself, I have amassed a wealth of life experiences to draw from when writing, including jumping out of a plane, swimming with a shark, riding a motorbike, and carrying the Olympic flame.

I was captivated by creative writing from a young age, with a career in journalism mapped out. Unfortunately, I received some early lessons in the unexpected nature of life and was diverted from my true calling. It wasn't until I was forty years old that I rediscovered the joy of reading and writing.

Home is the picturesque McLaren Vale wine region, on the Fleurieu Peninsula in South Australia. It is one of the most beautiful places on earth, which is why I set most of my stories here.

As well as writing for fun, I run the Novelist's Circle critiquing group, judge competitions for the Romance Writers of Australia and the Romance Writers of America, run workshops about literary craft, and write procedures for high-risk industrial activities. (Yes, I'm a word nerd through and through.)

My goal when writing is always for readers to connect with my characters and their hardships as closely as I do. If you'd like to stay in touch, subscribe to my newsletter at www.sandyvaile.com/ contact-me.

More from This Author

Inheriting Fear
Sandy Vaile

Her brown combat boots pounded the bike track as her eyes searched the shadows on either side. Mya had made the same short journey five days a week for eleven years, but at night it still made the back of her neck prickle. She could buy a car and live in fear. Not a chance. Fear could go to hell.

Intermittent puddles of lamplight dripped onto the tarmac. Laughter and evening TV programs carried through the open windows of weatherboard houses along the railway track, and she inhaled a waft of grilled chops with the rail grease. She pushed her chef's skull-cap into the back pocket of her jeans and wrapped an elastic band around her long hair. On the other side of the tracks, the Croydon Hotel emitted a bass beat that vibrated in the viscous humidity.

She glanced at her watch and picked up the pace. It was supposed to be her night off work, but the sous-chef wanted to leave early for a party, and it was Mya's responsibility to make sure the kitchen ran smoothly. It wasn't like she had a social life anyway.

An androgynous shadow ambled from the bushes ahead, hands shoved deep into the pockets of a hooded jacket. She moved to the opposite side of the track. As the shadow solidified it looked taller, broader, with a hairy chin protruding from the obscurity of the hood. A flickering fluorescent streetlight alternated the image of a man and an ominous silhouette.

They passed one another and he looked up. Red, glassy eyes devoured her from head to toe. A shiver ran up the back of Mya's legs to her scalp. One side of his mouth lifted in a half-smile, so she nodded a greeting but kept walking.

With her eyes ahead and ears trained on his retreating footsteps, she breathed easier as each second passed. Walking the bike track at night certainly had its hazards, but it just wasn't worth getting the motorbike out of the shed and donning all the gear to go a few hundred metres. Besides, she had as much right as anyone to be there, and she'd made herself a promise a long time ago to never let anything or anyone stop her from doing what she wanted. Fear was just an emotion and she could overcome those with steely resolve.

The footsteps behind her ceased and her heart flip-flopped into her throat.

Mya turned around slowly. The hood guy had turned around too, and his left hand held a beer stubby, but not at the base like he was about to take a swig. His long fingers were wrapped around the neck of the bottle, making it look more like a weapon.

A lump of panic stuck in her throat. Best to get the hell out of there, but it went against her training to leave her back unprotected. Her kick-boxing mentor, Ned, would clip her around the ear if she let anyone get the upper hand on her. When the thug finally took a long draught from the stubby, she hurried in the direction of the Croydon Hotel again.

"Whocha doin' out 'ere in the dark, Mya?" he slurred.

She spun around and narrowed her eyes at the blackness beneath his hood. "Do I know you?"

He swayed closer. "Nah, but I know you."

"Look, I'm going to work. I don't want any trouble."

"Oh, you're in a lotta trouble, love."

Something glinted in the faltering light; his other hand strangled the hilt of a long blade. Her pulse thundered in her ears, drowning out the crickets in the grass. The hood slid back as they sized each other up. He looked a bit older than her, maybe mid-thirties, half a foot taller and beefy—although height and weight didn't always mean much in a fight.

After a deep, calming breath, she drew on the long hours spent in the gym facing her demons. She wasn't the angry teenager Ned had taken under his wing all those years ago. Learning how to kickbox had given her courage. No longer a victim, but in control. Another deep breath. Her pulse slowed fractionally. She *was* in control.

The thug leered with a mouthful of mangled teeth. She'd seen that look before, and it meant trouble. Whether it was trouble for him or her remained to be seen.

"I've gotta deliver a message." He tapped the corner of a white envelope that protruded from his pocket, sloshing beer down the side of his jeans. "She says it doesn't matter if I mess you up a bit, s'long as you're alive enough to read it."

"What? Who says?" Maybe he was hallucinating from drugs. Unpredictable, but she'd been taught to deal with that. A long time ago she decided no man was going to beat her the way she'd watched her mother get beaten. She summoned an inner calm, relaxed her stance, and held his gaze. "You know, alcohol slows your reflexes. Be careful with that knife."

A crease formed between his brows, but any doubts he had appeared to pass because he clenched the knife tighter and took a step toward her. She took a step backward and waited with feet shoulder-width apart, knees soft. The rumble of a train built in the distance.

Hood-man lunged, but his depth perception must have been distorted, because the blade was half a metre shy. He looked at it with a confused expression.

It was probably a waste of breath, but… "You *could* just give me the letter."

"And leave a fine piece of tail like you alone?" He lunged again.

This time she lifted onto her toes, raised a knee, and snapped the ball of her foot into his gut. He grunted and dropped the stubby in preference of clutching his stomach. Brown glass shattered and latte-looking foam pooled on the tarmac, circulating a yeasty smell. She was relieved to see the knife had slumped downward with his shoulders.

"I told you it was hard to concentrate when you're under the influence." With one finger she hooked her undie elastic out of her arse. Jeans weren't ideal for kickboxing, but her boots were solid. Old faithfuls, with years of stains slopped over them and frayed stitching.

"You're gonna be sorry for that, bitch."

"I doubt it," she muttered.

She'd spent too many years living in fear as a child. Now she was in charge of her own destiny, and no man was going to dictate to her. His eyes were wider now, and the whites were yellow with red capillaries tangled like a mess of string around the irises. Definitely drugs. Dark hair flopped across his face, and he pushed it back with a twitch. His weight shifted left and he feinted right.

Mya stood her ground.

"Why don't you give me the letter and we can call it a night?"

The sounds of crickets and a baby crying were swallowed by the rumble of the passing train. As he thrust the knife again, she pinned his wrist in her armpit, and elbowed him in the gut. He hunched over, and she snapped her arm back. Knuckles connected with his nose. *Crunch*.

He yowled and stumbled back, dropped the blade to better clutch his bleeding nose. Quickly, she snatched up the knife— cheap army disposals crap—and tucked it through a belt loop.

"Message delivered," she told him as she grabbed the envelope from his pocket.

He remained bent over, nursing his nose, as she jogged along a strip of moonlit track to the footpath. The envelope felt like a hot coal in her hand. She glanced over her shoulder. No hood-man, so she slid the blade up her sleeve, cupping the hilt in her palm, and crossed the railway track.

It looked like local band Shamrock had pulled a big Saturday-night crowd. Windows vibrated in time with the thud of the bass. Party-goers leaned against the faded blue pub front, and she held her breath to pass through the haze of smoke drifting in the warm air. She stepped through the back door of the pub and ... breathed. It felt safe here, almost like home. She'd worked her way from apprentice to head chef at the Croydon and was practically part of the furniture.

At the back of the store room, she stashed the knife behind a sack of rice, then wiggled a finger into the back of the envelope and split it open. Inside there was a lined page with a jagged edge, like it had been torn from a spiral-bound pad. The handwriting had a backward slant, but the note wasn't signed.

She could just throw the letter in the bin and pretend she'd never seen it, but whoever this woman was, she had gone to the trouble of paying off a druggie to deliver it, maybe hoping Mya would get roughed up some. The guy had said "she," and he didn't look in any position to improvise, so the author must be a woman.

More worrying, the woman knew her by name. That took motivation, and Mya needed to know what kind of person would go to those lengths. Sure, she'd pissed off a few people over the years—especially in the boxing ring—but an enemy? She couldn't think of anyone who hated her enough to bother.

After a fortifying breath, she read the letter.

You're good at running and hiding, aren't you, Mya? But I know who you are. I bet you thought I'd forgotten about you and your retarded mother. Thought you could hide from me, but I'm coming for you, bitch.

I'll be watching ... sleep well.

Something slimy slid down her throat and into her gut: familiarity. There was no way it could be who she thought it was, but the note gave her a sense of panic from a long time ago. It felt like when she was eighteen, standing in front of her government-appointed housing with a thirty-something redhead yelling at her.

The conversation had started civilly. The woman wanted to know about Jack Roach, but Mya's father had been dead a year by then, and good riddance to him. But carrot-top wouldn't leave her alone, insisting Jack had another family, and wanting to know things about Mya. Things she wasn't ready to share.

Bloody Jack had been the one who tore apart everything she knew and devastated the only person she cared about, her mum. There were only tatters of her life left, but they were hers and no sham relative was going to turn up for a hand-out and stop her from taking care of her mum.

It couldn't be possible for Rhonda to have tracked her down. Mya had changed her name and moved. It wasn't feasible. She forced short breaths out of her tight lungs. A shudder started at the crown of her head and made its way down her spine. She glanced at the darkness beyond the hotel's back door and then hurried to the bright kitchen. Service was in full swing and the din of the exhaust fan, crockery, and sizzling food soothed her raw nerves.

She'd left Jack behind, but the prick was still tormenting her a decade after he died.

"Hey, Mya, you look like you saw a ghost." Jilly tucked a pen behind her ear and dropped an order pad into the pocket on the front of her apron.

"You okay?" Marion, the sous-chef, stepped away from the grill.

Even the dish pig had stopped feeding greasy plates into the commercial dishwasher to stare.

"I-I'm fine. Just had a run in with a punk on the bike track, that's all."

Marion nodded knowingly. "Why you insist on walking along there in the dark is beyond me. It's not safe for a woman."

"I'm not scared of any man," Mya snapped a little too forcefully to be convincing.

Marion shrugged. "Well, thanks for covering for me tonight. I just put a medium-well rump on the grill and a salmon in the oven."

"Sure. You're still okay to work tomorrow?"

"Don't worry, I won't get smashed at the party. I'll be here at ten a.m. Enjoy your day off." Marion tossed her tea towel at Mya and circled her hand at the kitchen. "Have fun, peeps."

"Enjoy the party," everyone called.

With a shake to clear her head, Mya tucked the tea towel into the front pocket of her jeans, slid the white skull-cap onto her head, and familiarised herself with the dockets clipped beside the grill.

Worrying about the letter would have to wait until after service. God knew she'd lived through enough bad news to last a life time, but she wasn't the same girl now. Whoever sent the threat would have to wait their turn and, when the time came, she'd face them head on.

Praise for *Inheriting Fear*:

"The chemistry between these two was off the charts."
—4 stars, Pure Jonel

In the mood for more Crimson Romance?
Check out *Ready or Dead by P.M. Kavanaugh* at
CrimsonRomance.com.

Printed in the United States
By Bookmasters